For Tony,
   With every good wish,
      Carol

GRAMMAR OF DISSENT

poetry and prose by
CLAIRE HARRIS
M. NOURBESE PHILIP
DIONNE BRAND

edited by
CAROL MORRELL

Tony Boxill

GOOSE LANE

© Carol Morrell, Claire Harris, M. Nourbese Philip, Dionne Brand, 1994.

All rights reserved. No part of this publication may be reproduced, stored in a retrieval system or transmitted, in any form or by any means, without the prior written permission of the publisher or, in case of photocopying or other reprographic copying, a licence from the Canadian Copyright Licensing Agency.

Published by Goose Lane Editions with the assistance of the Canada Council and Multiculturalism and Citizenship Canada, 1994.

Cover photographs by Joanna Eldredge Morrissey (M. Nourbese Philip); Véro Boncompagni, courtesy National Film Board of Canada (Dionne Brand); and Reg Balch (background).
Book design by Julie Scriver.
Edited by Laurel Boone.
Printed and bound in Canada by Imprimerie Gagné, Louiseville.

10 9 8 7 6 5 4 3 2

Canadian Cataloguing in Publication Data

Grammar of dissent
   ISBN 0-86492-141-1

1. Canadian literature (English) – Black-Canadian authors. * 2. Canadian literature (English) – Women authors. * 3. Canadian literature (English) – 20th century. *
I. Harris, Claire, 1937- . II. Philip, Marlene Nourbese, 1947-
III. Brand, Dionne, 1953- .IV. Morrell, Carol, 1944- . V. Title.

PS8235.W6G73 1994   C810.8'09287   C94-950195-6
PR9194.5.W6G73 1994.

Goose Lane Editions
469 King Street
Fredericton, New Brunswick
CANADA E3B 1E5

CONTENTS

ACKNOWLEDGEMENTS 7

INTRODUCTION 9

CLAIRE HARRIS 25

from *Fables from the Womens' Quarters* (1984)

from *Translation Into Fiction* (1984)

from *Travelling to Find a Remedy* (1986)

from *The Conception of Winter* (1989)

from *Drawing Down A Daughter* (1992)

Why Do I Write? 26
Nude on a Pale Staircase 34
Where the Sky Is a Pitiful Tent 40
This Was the Child I Dreamt 47
Policeman Cleared In Jaywalking Case 48
By thy senses sent forth 51
Translation into Fiction 55
A Black Reading 56
August 60
Fleshed with Fire 61
Travelling to Find a Remedy 62
Framed 65
And So . . . Home 66
Mysteries 67
from *Towards the Color of Summer* 69
A Dream of Valor and Rebirth 70
Death in Summer 74
Conception of Winter 75
No God Waits on Incense 76
[Gazing at piles of newspapers she is wondering] 77
[Daughter to live is to dream the self] 80
[It is a matter of fact] 83

M. NOURBESE PHILIP 97
from *She Tries Her Tongue, Her Silence Softly Breaks* (1989)
from *Thorns* (1980)

from *Salmon Courage* (1983)

The Absence of Writing or How I Almost Became a Spy 98
Oliver Twist 105
Fluttering Lives 106
Jongwe 107
Blackman Dead 109
Three Times Deny 111
E. Pulcherrima 112
Anonymous 117
Sprung Rhythm 117
A Habit of Angels 118
Salmon Courage 120
July Again 122

from *She Tries Her Tongue,*
Her Silence Softly Breaks (1989)

What's in A Name? 123
You Can't Push Now 123
Planned Obsolescence 127
And Over Every Land and Sea 128
Discourse on the Logic of Language 136
The Question of Language Is the Answer to
    Power 139
She Tries Her Tongue; Her Silence Softly
    Breaks 143

from *Looking for Livingstone*
(1991)

Whose Idea Was It Anyway? 150
The First and Last Day of the Month . . . 160
The Hundredth Day of the Hundredth
    Month . . . 161

DIONNE BRAND 169

from *'Fore Day Morning* (1978)

Bread Out of Stone 171
Since You 181
Old I. 182
Old II. 182
Afro West Indian Immigrant 183
Shanty Town 183

from *Primitive Offensive* (1982)

Canto I 184
Canto II 185
Canto VI 188
Canto VII 192

from *Winter Epigrams and*
Epigrams to Ernesto Cardenal in
Defense of Claudia (1983)
from *Chronicles of the Hostile Sun*
(1984)

Winter Epigrams 197
Epigrams to Ernesto Cardenal 203

Amelia 209
Diary – The Grenada Crisis 211
October 19th, 1983 214
October 25th, 1983 216
On American Numeracy and Literacy in the
    War Against Grenada 218
P.P.S. Grenada 219
[untitled] 226

from *Sans Souci* (1988)
from *No Language is Neutral*
(1990)

Blossom 228
Jackie 237
from No Language Is Neutral 237
from Hard Against the Soul 239

Out There 242

BIBLIOGRAPHY 245

INDEX TO FIRST LINES AND TITLES 253

ACKNOWLEDGEMENTS

I wish to acknowledge gratefully the University of Saskatchewan for granting me the sabbatical leave in 1991-92 that enabled me to accomplish the primary work for this book. To colleagues near and far who provided factual information and moral support, my thanks: John C. Ball, Anthony Boxill, Susan Gingell, Barbara Godard, Lynette Hunter, Kathleen of *Fuse Magazine*, Gail Osachoff, Robin C. Pacific, Leslie Sanders, Diane Relke, Camille Slights, and the staff of the Inter-Library Loans Section of the University of Saskatchewan Library. Finishing the book has been made pleasurable by the ever-patient, efficient help of the editor at Goose Lane Editions, Laurel Boone, whose belief in this project was heartening. My departmental research assistant, Jesse Stothers, is much appreciated for his diligence and promptness. My most profound feelings of gratitude go out to Claire Harris, M. Nourbese Philip, and Dionne Brand, not only for assisting me to locate less-accessible publications, but for their writing itself.

CLAIRE HARRIS "Why Do I Write" (1994), © Claire Harris; used by permission of Claire Harris. "Nude on a Pale Staircase," "Where the Sky is a Pitiful Tent," "This was the child I dreamt," "Policeman Cleared in Jaywalking Case": *Fables from the Women's Quarters* (Williams-Wallace, 1984), © Claire Harris; used by permission of Claire Harris. "By thy senses sent forth," "Translation Into Fiction," "A Black Reading," "August," "Fleshed With Fire": *Translation Into Fiction* (Goose Lane Editions, 1984), © Claire Harris; used by permission of Goose Lane Editions. "Travelling to Find a Remedy," "Framed," "And So . . . Home," "Mysteries": *Travelling to Find a Remedy* (Goose Lane Editions, 1986), © Claire Harris; used by permission of Goose Lane Editions. "Three bells calm . . . ," "A Dream of Valor and Rebirth," "Death in Summer," "Conception of Winter," "No God Waits on Incense": *The Conception of Winter* (Williams-Wallace, 1989), © Claire Harris; used by permission of Claire Harris. "Gazing at piles of newspapers . . . ," "Daughter to live is to dream . . . ," "It is a matter of fact . . .": *Drawing Down a Daughter* (Goose Lane Editions, 1992), © Claire Harris; used by permission of Goose Lane Editions.

M. NOURBESE PHILIP "Oliver Twist," "Fluttering Lives," "Jongwe," "Blackman Dead," "Three Times Deny," "E. Pulcherrima": *Thorns* (Williams-Wallace, 1980), © M. Nourbese Philip; used by permission of M. Nourbese Philip. "Anonymous," "Sprung Rhythm," "A Habit of Angels," "Salmon Courage," "July Again," "What's in a Name?," "You Can't Push Now," "Planned Obsolescence": *Salmon Courage* (Williams-Wallace, 1983), © M. Nourbese Philip; used by permission of M. Nourbese Philip. "The Absence of Writing or How I Almost Became a Spy," "And Over Every Land and Sea," "Discourse on the Logic of Language," "The Question of Language is the Answer to Power," "She Tries Her Tongue; Her Silence Softly Breaks": *She Tries Her Tongue, Her Silence Softly Breaks* (Ragweed, 1989), © M. Nourbese Philip; used by permission of Ragweed Press and M. Nourbese Philip. "Whose Idea Was It Anyway?": *Tessera* 7 (Fall 1989), © M. Nourbese Philip; used by permission of M. Nourbese Philip. "The First and Last Day of the Month of New Moons . . . ," "The Hundredth Day of the Hundredth Month . . . ": *Looking for Livingstone* (Mercury, 1991), © M. Nourbese Philip; used by permission of M. Nourbese Philip.

DIONNE BRAND "Bread Out of Stone": *Language in Her Eye* (Coach House, 1990), © Dionne Brand; used by permission of Dionne Brand. "Since You," "Old I," "Old II," "Afro West Indian Immigrant," "Shanty Town": *'Fore Day Morning* (Khoisan Artists, 1978); used by permission of Dionne Brand. "Canto I," "Canto II," "Canto VI," "Canto VII": *Primitive Offensive* (Williams-Wallace, 1982), © Dionne Brand; used by permission of Dionne Brand. "Winter Epigrams" 4, 9, 11, 12, 15, 18, 22, 28, 34, 37, 41, 43, 45, 47, 50, 53, 54; "Epigrams to Ernesto Cardenal in Defense of Claudia" 2, 3, 12, 13, 14, 27, 30, 32, 33, 34, 35, 39, 40, 47, 54: *Winter Epigrams and Epigrams to Ernesto Cardenal in Defense of Claudia* (Williams-Wallace, 1983), © Dionne Brand; used by permission of Dionne Brand. "Amelia," "P.P.S. Grenada," "Diary – The Grenada Crisis," "October 19th, 1983," "October 25th, 1983," "On American Numeracy and Literacy in the War Against Grenada," "Four hours on a bus . . . ": *Chronicles of the Hostile Sun* (Williams-Wallace, 1984), © Dionne Brand; used by permission of Dionne Brand. "Blossom: Priestess of Oya": *Sans Souci and Other Stories* (Williams-Wallace, 1988), © Dionne Brand; used by permission of Dionne Brand. "Jackie," "I walk Bathurst Street . . . ," "But wait, this must come out then . . . ," "Hard Against the Soul": *No Language is Neutral* (Coach House, 1990), © Dionne Brand; used by permission of Coach House Press. "Out There": *The Malahat Review* 100 (September 1992), © Dionne Brand; used by permission of Dionne Brand.

INTRODUCTION

The "locality" of national culture is neither unified nor unitary in relation to itself, nor must it be seen simply as "other" in relation to what is outside or beyond it. The boundary is Janus-faced and the problem of outside/ inside must always itself be a process of hybridity, incorporating new "people" in relation to the body politic, generating other sites of meaning and, inevitably, in the political process, producing unmanned sites of political antagonism and unpredictable forces for political representation. (Bhabha, 4)

Claire Harris, M. Nourbese Philip, and Dionne Brand, born in Trinidad and Tobago, living in Canada, are a particular kind of exiled woman, each of whom has made a strength out of the experience of multiple displacements. Of African descent, their cultural and linguistic history has been foreshortened: much of Africa was lost when their ancestors were forcibly brought to the New World. Having themselves voluntarily emigrated to Canada, they have become distanced from their childhood experiences of family and community in Trinidad. In Canada, because of what they call subtle but systemic racism, these women do not readily fit in. To many Canadians, they "are" the colour of their skin. Each has had some of her writing rejected by Canadian publishers as not being "Canadian" enough. As Linda Hutcheon has put it, "Doubleness ... is the essence of the immigrant experience. Caught between two worlds, the immigrant negotiates a new social space; caught between two cultures and often languages, the writer negotiates a new literary space" (9).

Harris, Philip and Brand cannot credibly now be called immigrants, since each has lived and worked in Canada for over twenty years. Still, their differences from European-descended Canadians and European-descended Canadian writers persist, both in their daily lives and in their writing projects. As Henry Louis Gates, Jr., has written in *Black Literature & Literary Theory*:

> In the case of the writer of African descent, her or his texts occupy spaces in at least two traditions: a European or American literary tradition, and one of the several related but distinct black traditions. The "heritage" of each black text written in a Western

language is, then, a double heritage, two-toned, as it were. Its visual tones are white and black, and its aural tones are standard and vernacular. (4)

Or, as Diana Fuss puts it, "A critic involved in the interpretation of Afro-American [or Afro-Caribbean-Canadian] texts is engaged in a complicated process of 'bitranslation' – of translating in at least two directions at once" (83).

The essay that follows attempts, for the benefit of readers new to the work of Harris, Philip and Brand, to analyze their writings as important contributions to contemporary Canadian society and literature. The more extensive project of placing their work in its other proper context, the critical theory and creative practice of the black Americas and/or Africa, remains to be undertaken.

Harris, Philip, and Brand all employ three grand strategies in their otherwise highly individual writing projects: they take an essentialist subject-position, they use that subject-position for political intervention, and they startle the reader by interrogating standard English and substituting new usages, often in the Caribbean demotic, for old ones.

All three will assert that they speak "for" their history and "on behalf of" their people, especially the women, however distant in time or place. All "throw their voices," speaking through these other people with whom they identify. This strategy allows them both a community and a coherent sense of self – however fictive or imaginative – from which to act and write.

Asked whether it is a burden always to have to write about being black, Dionne Brand points to the difference between white writing practice and her own:

> There is never room, though there is always risk, but there is never the room that white writers have in never speaking for their whole race, yet speaking in the most secret and cowardly language of normalcy and affirmation, speaking for the whole race. There is only writing that is significant, honest, necessary – making bread out of stone – so that stone becomes pliant under the hands. ("Bread Out of Stone," 179)

Arun Mukherjee elaborates Brand's indictment of white writers' using the "language of normalcy and affirmation" in *Towards an Aesthetic of Opposition.* She writes there about her experience of being taught an Anglo-American canon of literature in India and in Canada. The texts chosen were ahistorical and apolitical, she says, and the responses required were the cultivation of certain emotions – "sentimental effusions over the beauty of nature, anguish over mutability – and a high-minded disdain for all rationality and abstract thought" (4). She was encouraged to look for universal themes in these texts: heroes and heroines on voyages of self-discovery, wilderness versus civilization, creativity versus madness, and "the celebration of complexity that perpetually wrings its hands in the face of the grandeur and terror of the universe" (4). "The universalist methodology, in its exaggerated focus on form and character, neglects referentiality and context, thereby failing to assign inventiveness to writers who structure their work on those principles" (13). In other words, "universalizing" on the part of writer and/or reader affirms a traditional cultural hegemony that actually erases the particular experiences of various less-powerful groups.

Something like Brand's comments about the necessity to speak honestly about significant matters on behalf of the black community were earlier made by Claire Harris in a note to her poem "Policeman Cleared in Jaywalking Case" (*Fables From the Women's Quarters*, 1984): "In the black community to signify indicates an act of acknowledgement, of sharing, of identifying with." And that poem begins and ends, "look you, child, I signify." The terms "to signify," "sign," and "signifier" may be variously interpreted. In Harris's work, and in the works of Philip and Brand, too, signifier and signified stand in a close relationship that stresses referentiality and context. Harris, Philip, and Brand also create new language usages, extraordinary modes of "signifying" realities obliterated by standard English.

There has been much debate in the past few years in Canadian literary circles about the ethics of white creative writers using, or telling, the stories of ethnic minorities, particularly of Native or Métis peoples. A new-found reticence on the part of white writers to speak *as* members of an oppressed or silenced minority group is based on consideration and tact, themselves based on a realization that for too long certain groups have in fact been denied the opportunity, through access to publishing outlets and the mass media, that would allow them to tell their own stories from their own points of view. "Appropriation" is now wisely regarded as unethical, and there is a growing movement to encourage publishing houses actively to seek out writers from identified minority groups. Even so, most white writers do not consciously attempt to speak on behalf of their whole racial group or, indeed, any particular sub-group. Some immigrant writers in Canada are exceptions, as are some women writers. Feminist writing also can "signify" in Harris's sense of the term.

The old feminist rallying cry "the personal is political" has recently been interpreted as inviting women to concentrate merely on their own personal lives, avoiding involvement with large social and political issues. Harris, Philip, and Brand, however, understand and apply the phrase in its original meaning. By understanding one's own experience, one is reaching out, finding that what is personal to oneself is *also* personal to many others, and thus that one's experience is not unique, to be suffered through in isolation, and that the large social patterns that underlie the similarities among the personal experiences of so many are in fact politically, materially, and economically based. The purpose of such understanding is exactly not to become mired in personal problems, but to participate in effecting social change. From these realizations it is just a step to not only writing about others but writing on behalf of them and their concerns. These three authors do just that, "throwing their voices" in order to represent a wide variety of women. Harris, Philip, and Brand's speaking for their community of women is "appropriate essentializing" in its bringing diversity together because doing so provides a position of strength. Diana Fuss, in *Essentially Speaking*, makes my point in her discussion of Spviak's "Subaltern Studies: Deconstructing Historiography":

> [W]hen put into practice by the dispossessed themselves, essentialism can be powerfully displacing and disruptive.... [T]he determining factor in deciding essentialism's political or strategic value is dependent upon who practices it: in the hands of a hegemonic group, essentialism can be employed as a powerful tool of ideological domination; in the hands of the subaltern, the use of humanism to mime... humanism can represent a powerful displacing repetition. The question of permissibility, if you will, of engaging in essentialism is therefore framed and determined by the subject-position from which one speaks. (32)

When these three authors take up the black, feminist, signifying subject-position, they create a new subject-position: they become teachers of the white Canadian literary and political communities.

Their second grand strategy is that they use that subject-position as a tool for political intervention. Their collective project, and their distinctive contribution to Canadian literature, is to insert their own and other voices into what has (following the European tradition) been considered the "high culture" of poetry. Poetry, and creative writing generally, is more politically engaged than the adherents of the "aesthetic response" school of criticism would suggest. As Linda Hutcheon points out, "literature depends on the whole of culture, of history and social traditions" (5); "History leaves its mark on our literature. It always has" (10). Our literature has always carried more than merely the mark of its historical context: it has always been, as has every national literature, either subtly or overtly political. Writers take up subject-positions. One might consider the social protest literature in the English-speaking world, first in the 1930s then in the 1960s, as an overt example. As Dionne Brand has said:

> I think that we are probably the new wave of Canadian writing. Twenty years ago there was a national wave of Canadian writing which set itself up against American writing and the deluge of American culture in Canada. We are the new wave of Canadian writing. We will write about the internal contradictions. (Hutcheon 77)

In their creative writing, essays, and interviews, Harris, Philip, and Brand accuse Canadian society as a whole of racism, sexism, and classism, and Canada's cultural institutions of zenophobia. In the context of discussing Canadian debates about appropriation, censorship, and free speech, Philip shifts the terms of the argument to the repressed issue of racism:

> The ideological framework of Western democracies has been erected upon and is supported as much by the ideology of freedom of the individual (and its offshoots) as by the ideology of racism. However, one discourse, censorship, becomes privileged; the other, racism, is silenced. To insist on its lesser status, to exclude it from the dominant forms and forums of discussion becomes one of the most effective ways of perpetuating racism. To do so is, in fact, profoundly racist.... To those who would argue that, in a democracy, everyone has the right to write from

any point of view, I would contend that for far too long certain groups have not had access to any of the resources necessary to enable *any* sort of writing to take place, let alone writing from a particular point of view. Education, financial resources, belief in the validity of one's experience and reality, whether working class, female or Black: these are all necessary to the production of writing. (*Language in Her Eye*, 210-11, 212-13)

Harris also takes up the topic of cultural institutions and the dispossessed:

Canadian culture is not an integrated culture. As a matter of fact, that we have is essentially Euro-British forms, Canadian content. Old skins, new wine. Painfully "High-Can." ... But we have a large and various new immigrant population, and a second chance. We could have a vibrant, original synthesis. ... We have twenty years, perhaps, to work things out. And one of the things we have to discover is that my images are not a sign of natural inferiority. That they belong here, just as much as the Franco-British image. ... One in three young people are of various Asian, and African, ancestry. And there are, of course, the Aboriginal peoples. More important, unless every Canadian woman of child bearing age has five children, or more, that number is going to increase. If we're going to share this land safely, we better get to know each other, fast. (*Language in Her Eye*, 133, 134, 138)

These comments show a very real, very material understanding of ideology, cultural institutions, and demographics. As Hutcheon says, racial discrimination has always existed in Canadian immigration policies and cultural attitudes (7-8). She also contends that "the single most significant factor in the response to multiculturalism in Canada today appears to be race. ... [W]ith increasing numbers of immigrants who, as Jacques Godbout puts it, are 'visibly different, have different religions, different attitudes toward women' and different political histories, racism is once again a concern that cannot be ignored" (7). Harris, Philip, and Brand position the writer as a central contributor to dissecting these "internal contradictions" and conflicts, particularly those of race; to effecting cultural and political awareness of inequality; and to avoiding a disastrous future of racial conflict. As Philip asserts in a recent interview, "I believe, as James Baldwin said, my job as a *writer* is to disturb the status quo" (Williamson, 244).

In order to enact their political interventions in poetry, Harris, Philip, and Brand engage the reader in a variety of consciousness-raising experiences through linguistic innovation. These poets must be innovative, because they are aware of always speaking *against* (the dominant white society) in order to speak *for* (the experience of blacks and women). In order to mark their different position, they also must write against dominant language use and "correct" poetic images and themes. This writing against is essential because language encodes the cultural and political facts of dominance and exclusion. Here again, these authors continue a long tradition of feminist writing. Angela Ingram, in *Women's Writing in Exile*, describes the problem and some solutions:

> Voluntary exile . . . constitutes for a number of writers an escape from the entrapping domain of the silenced mother-under-patriarchy, the manifestation of women's internalized exile/estrangement. . . . Such an escape into the world of the apparently liberating Word, the world of culture, of adulthood, though, often means entry into the confines of patriarchal languages and heterosexual and heterosexist imperatives. Enabled, on one hand, to write, to create new worlds and to recreate what should have been home, many writers find the other hand shackled by the expectations and rules of the world of works they have chosen to inhabit. . . . Such writing, even by white women, is often sharply perceptive of dissonances in the dominant culture. . . . [F]urther, it interrogates the gendered nature of those dissonances, building from them literary structures that conflate inside and outside, margin and center. (5)

Leslie Sanders quotes Claire Harris as saying that the English language is inimical to black people and women, and that in her poetry she works to reverse customary connotations and meanings (12). Sanders believes that most of the black women writers in the anthology *Daughters of the Sun, Women of the Moon* would agree: "[They] likewise write in order to create a language which illuminates the complexity, richness, and variety of people and worlds which English customarily negates or marginalizes" (12). And Nourbese Philip, in conversation with Janice Williamson, explains that in *She Tries Her Tongue, Her Silence Softly Breaks* she was:

[P]articularly engaged ... in subverting in a very conscious way all the traditions of poetry. Poetry came to us in the Caribbean as another form of colonization and oppression. So, for instance, in the poem "Discourse on the Logic of Language" I set out to subvert the poem itself. Usually a poem is centred on the page with the margins at both sides clearly demarcated. Also there is the prescription of certain traditions like Eliot's objective correlative: you remove the poem from its morass of history, so to speak, clean it of its personal clutter, and anyone anywhere ought to be able to identify with and understand it. I deliberately set out to put the poem, that particular poem, back in its historical context, which is what poetry is not supposed to do. ... [T]he centre piece of this poem is surrounded [on the page] with a short story ... with historical edicts about African slaves being prohibited from speaking their mother tongues and having their tongues removed for breach of this edict. On the pages facing the poem ... I have a physiological description of how speech takes place and a series of multiple-choice questions. ... What I was mainly concerned with in "Discourse" was the colonizing experience – how what we call a mother tongue, in this instance English, was, when you traced its lineage, really a father tongue, in that it was the White male colonizer bringing us language. (227-28)

■

From the beginning of her writing career, Claire Harris has worked in the long-poem form. Three of the poems chosen for this book from *Fables from the Women's Quarters* (1984) display her habitual topics and formal devices. "Nude on a Pale Staircase" anatomizes the perceptions and memories, the regrets and final separation from self of an East Indian woman, married to an Italian man and living with him in Calgary, who hears a radio report of "massacres in Assam." Parenthetical phrases signal the woman's inward, unuttered thoughts; prose poetry, for her more factual, day-to-day experiences, alternates with poetry for her sexual and emotional responses. "Where the Sky is a Pitiful Tent" juxtaposes on each page Harris's poetic rendering of events as experienced by a woman whose husband is a guerrilla fighter with italicized prose passages quoting Rigoberta Manchu's description of the horrors of the Guatemalan struggle. The famous poem "Policeman Cleared in Jaywalking Case" begins with an account of the incident, a black girl's arrest, strip-search, and imprisonment for jaywalking in Edmonton, which was reported in the *Edmonton Journal*. The rest, in prose poetry, introduces the poet herself – "look you, child, I signify" – and her memories of a similar incident in Trinidad in order to express her outrage, her condemnation, and her refusal to fit quietly into a society capable of such viciousness. This was the first poem Harris wrote consciously intending to respond to examples of Canadian racism no matter how uncomfortable that response might make her readers. All three poems – "Nude on a Pale Staircase," "Where the Sky is a Pitiful Tent," and "Policeman Cleared in Jaywalking Case" – focus on women who have been displaced and traumatized, and all demonstrate the tension, maintained throughout Harris's work, between the large narrative impulse and the impulse to detail, in a more traditional lyrical sense, the inner life of emotion and sensory response. "By thy senses sent forth," from *Translation into Fiction* (1984) is exactly analogous to "Nude on a Pale Staircase," "Where the Sky is a Pitiful Tent," and "Policeman Cleared in Jaywalking Case," both in subject and in its contrapuntal form.

Harris's poetry is never straightforwardly life-writing. Even her shorter lyrical pieces using "I" begin with an arresting image or incident around which Harris constructs the responses of a female psyche other than her own. Consider the shorter poems "This Was the Child I Dreamt," from *Fables*, and "August" and "Fleshed with Fire," from *Translation*. Here we may glimpse the childless woman, the expatriated woman, the woman who remembers.

Both "Framed" and "And So . . . Home," from *Travelling to Find a Remedy* (1986), vividly picture loss of home and family, while "Mysteries" and "Untitled," from the same volume, contemplate what has been gained: that mysterious poetic vision in which every thing, scent, and sound is significant, a part of the unified whole of female experience. Such musings reveal a religious, mystical turn of mind. The long poem "Travelling to Find a Remedy" (*Travelling*) is a narrative of a love relationship between an African man and a West Indian woman. Harris has commented that the man can stand for Africa itself and concretizes the difficulties of re-transplantation for a woman raised in a Westernized context. This poem, too, ends with loss – for refusal can also mean loss – with the woman concluding: "I had thought to jeer at history/ that here knowing what it meant I could throw/ my heart across alien centuries/ and slavery   to follow safely/ but I cannot dream in another tongue/ I cannot." The poet's mind matures, comes to terms with the certain facts of expatriation and loss. Yet, in these and other pieces, she balances the equation with gratitude for the poetic gift and with a generous resolve to use it to speak out on behalf of others and for a saner, more equitable society.

The narrative basis of the poems in *The Conception of Winter* (1989) is the journey to Spain of three women friends. The superficialities of tourism are set against the news of a friend's death, and, in "A Dream of Valor and Rebirth," against the historical knowledge that slave ships set out from Barcelona. In this poem, dream, racial memory, identification of the narrating "i" with a woman taken in slavery, and street images merge into a perpetual but fruitless search for "the hand of god."

Harris's work with the long poem reaches a high point in the book-length *Drawing Down a Daughter* (1992). It is the story of a pregnant woman addressing her unborn daughter, telling her her racial and family history, advising her how to thrive in the world she will enter. One of the selections reprinted here, "Daughter to live is to dream the self," is fashioned around the recitation of a family recipe for bakes. Harris chose to include part of this piece in her anthology *Kitchen Talk* (1992) as "Child This is the Gospel on Bakes." The significance of the recipe is that with it the child will also keep her mother's memory of learning it in a particular kitchen in a particular place, a memory of her grandmother, and a memory of the class and gender relationships in which her mother's life was embedded. The history of food is social history.

"A Matter of Fact" is one of the longer prose pieces included in *Drawing Down a Daughter*. Written partly in Trinidadian dialect, the story recounts a man's supposed encounter with La Diablesse and the narrator's attempts to ascertain the facts of the case. These cannot ever be pinned down, and so the tale, with its non-sequential time scheme and its contradictory yet confirming testimonies, remains in the mind as an impossible truth. The daughter in *Drawing Down a Daughter* will inherit an entire history: of slavery, of West Indian cookery, social relations, and mythology, and of the relationship of her parents and the story of their sojourn in Canada. This volume brings together all of Harris's concerns and beliefs. Here especially she establishes her belief in memory and the telling of memories as essential to both preserving the past and reshaping the future.

In a passage from "The Absence of writing, or How I Almost Became a Spy" not included in *Grammar of Dissent*, Nourbese Philip says, "[T]here was a profound eruption of the body into the text of *She Tries Her Tongue*" (1989). In fact, one of Philip's most constant concerns was already the female body – seen usually as the site of struggle. "Three Times Deny" and "E. Pulcherrima," from *Thorns* (1980), and "You Can't Push Now" and "Planned Obsolescence," from *Salmon Courage* (1983), establish the connections among giving birth in a hostile world; the bleeding poinsettia as woman and Christ and the denial of both; the alliance of the goddesses Isis and Ta-urt with the birthing woman, and their collective resistance to the white-robed doctors who try to prevent the natural process; and, finally, tubal ligation as violent "inner mutilation for outward freedom/ that bodily balance of terror." While the poems against racism and the poems of reminiscence and expatriation, in these two early volumes and later, echo topics addressed by Harris and Brand, Philip's emphatic insistence on the suffering, bleeding yet triumphant female body as the focal point of experience and meaning for women is unique to her work.

"And Over Every Land and Sea," from *She Tries Her Tongue, Her Silence Softly Breaks* (1989), rewrites the Proserpine and Ceres story: the West Indian mother and daughter, parted by emigration, search endlessly but fruitlessly to find one another again. In the section titled "Dream Skins," the bodily relation between the two women erupts in the suckling breasts, the swelling of pregnancy, the blood-cloths and menstruation, and the recognition of the other's smell. "Discourse on the Logic of Language," also from *She Tries Her Tongue*, juxtaposes a mythic vision – the mother tonguing the newborn child clean, then blowing her woman's words into her daughter's mouth – with a notation of the historical fact that West Indian colonialists not only separated slave families but could cut out the tongue of any slave caught speaking his or her native language. This powerful poem is central to Philip's work: it brings together her concerns with the West Indian loss of language and culture through slavery with the submerged power of women and with the "science" (which can be the racist discourse) of the Western world.

Looking for Livingstone (1991) reverses the lament for loss of language expressed in *She Tries Her Tongue*. Here, silence, like the subsumed woman, is chosen as a positive value and potential strength. Africa, traditionally labelled "the dark continent" by Europeans, is explored as an area of timelessness and silence. The "NEECLIS" episode in *Looking for Livingstone* takes the narrator into a love relationship with the weaver/needlewoman Arwhal. This is a departure from the heterosexual relations of Philip's women, but it is also a continuation of the spiritual and physical bond between mother and daughter in "And Over Every Land and Sea." Arwhal tells a symbolic story and forces the narrator into confronting her own silence, advising her to weave "word and silence" into her own tapestry of meaning.

The short story "Whose Idea Was It Anyway?" (1989), if less affirmative than *Looking for Livingstone*, is, on the other hand, a bold analysis of the premises of European exploration and colonization: pride, greed, Christianity, and racism. Underlying these, however, is the desire and disgust felt by the supposed architect of the large-scale plan of slavery for his wife's black maid. Sexual enslavement to her produces his need to dominate her and her people. At the core of this historical fiction is – again – the black female body, here defined as different from, and more natural, beautiful, and powerful than that of the European wife. Quotations from historical sources counterpoint the fictive musings, and lend weight to this story's condemnation of the institution of slavery. Such a technique is not new in Philip's work, dating back at least as far as "Blackman Dead" (*Thorns*, 1980). Quotations from religious as well as historical sources culminate in *She Tries Her Tongue* (1989), which indicts all of Western culture, past and present, for the silencing and dehumanizing of an entire race.

Particularly in her more recent work, Philip makes a conscious attempt on the life of the English language as it is usually employed. Like Philip, Harris and Brand also use dialect, or demotic speech; all three call into question habitual usages, substituting new perceptions and alternative namings of reality. But Philip, especially in *She Tries Her Tongue*, writes "language poetry," poetry that focuses on the construction and connotations of words and phrases themselves. Consider these excerpts from "Discourse on the Logic of Language": "I must therefore be tongue/ dumb/ dumb-tongued/ dub/ tongued/ damn dumb tongue" and "and english is/ my mother tongue/ is/ my father tongue/ is a foreign lan lan lang/ language/ l/anguish/ anguish/ a foreign anguish/ is english – ... english/ is a foreign anguish." The stuttering of syllables into words and then into unusual part-rhymes is a brilliant rhetorical device that encapsulates the meaning of the whole poem and, indeed, of much of Philip's work.

"The Question of Language is the Answer to Power," also from *She Tries Her Tongue*, is more humourous in its delivery but equally serious in its intent. It begins by giving non-traditional examples for the pronunciation of vowel sounds: "oo as in 'look' at the spook, OH as in the slaves came by 'boat,' AW as in they were valued for their 'brawn,'" for instance. These meanings are repeated later in the poem, serving as a chorus to the speaker's consideration of how to "make new" words like "nigger slave coolie/ the wog of taint," and again when the speaker lists the unacceptable varieties of English. Philip's contribution to the literature of dissent, both black and feminist, is her probing analysis of the relations among body, speech, and racial and gender identity.

■

While one of Harris's recurring topics is death of friends or family members, or one's own death, Dionne Brand occasionally focusses on old age, valuing women at that time of life for their potential insouciance, experience, and wisdom. The theme occurs early in "Old Age I" and "Old Age II" in *'Fore Day Morning* (1978), and again in "I Am Not that Strong Woman" in *Chronicles of the Hostile Sun* (1984). She elaborates it in her essays "Black Women and Work" (*Fireweed*, 1987 and 1988), in her film *Older Stronger Wiser* (1989), in the autobiographical essay "Bread Out of Stone" (*Language in Her Eye*, 1990), and in *No Burden to Carry* (1991). The examination of old black women's lives and voices is, like every other topic in Brand's work, a conscious and overt political challenge. By recording their voices, she frees them into speech long-denied and also provides younger black women with a new source of their own history of oppression and strength.

Primitive Offensive (1982) and *Winter Epigrams and Epigrams to Ernesto Cardenal in Defense of Claudia* (1983) are three long poems. Each is comprised of numerous sections of varying lengths, structured as cantos or epigrams. *Primitive Offensive* was written as a response to hearing African peoples called "primitive"; in this volume, Brand often addresses others directly as "you" in an "offensive offensive" against the brutalities of racism perpetuated, in past and present, by the white "civilized" world. Here, the ancestors, African and West Indian religious terms, West Indian heroes and place names, and the suffering resiliant female body counter the weight of Rockefellers, colonialists, and South

African apartheid. "Canto VI" of *Primitive Offensive* addresses others of African descent met in Germany and France as brothers and sisters of the African diaspora, still lost, still "trying to pass," still frightened and insulted. "Canto VII" visits Cuba, where the narrator finds recognition from other African Caribbeans and revisits the history of black revolution in Haiti around the turn of the nineteenth century. In this poem, Toussaint and Dessalines, the black Haitian leaders, are invoked as heroes, while De Las Casas, Napoleon, and the Christianizing mission itself are excoriated.

Winter Epigrams (1983), as Roger McTair says in his Introduction to that book, are "sarcastic, lyrical, and keen epigrams ... [that] confront that most insistent season – winter – in all its moods. They are a reaction to that most deterministic reality by a writer nurtured in sunshine and transplanted to the cold North." The selections printed here from *Epigrams to Ernesto Cardenal in Defense of Claudia* (1983) were chosen to exhibit Brand's meditations on the making and meaning of poetry. For instance, the limited linguistic resources available to women poets is posited (30: "since you've covetously hoarded all the words/ ... since you've massacred every intimate phrase/ in a bloodletting of paternal epithets/ like 'fuck' and 'rape', 'cock' and 'cunt',/ I cannot write you this epigram"). But this limitation is countered by Brand's own social and political lexicon.

The wit and constrained form of *Winter Epigrams* explodes into larger, looser, more passionate separate poems, principally about the American invasion of Grenada, in *Chronicles of the Hostile Sun* (1984). "October 19th, 1983" sounds the dirge-like repetition of the names of the dead, questions whether words can convey the tragedy of the invasion, and keens the death of the dream of socialism in the Antilles.

No Language is Neutral (1990) continues the prose poetry begun in *Chronicles* and shows the work of a poet rapidly maturing both in vision and in craft. The title series, "No Language is Neutral," explores the contrasting sensations and experiences of Trinidad and Toronto, nostalgia and longing to return home balanced by the realization that now no place is home. The immigrant is stranded, with only her belief in the power of her words to sustain her: "What I say in any language is told in faultless/ knowledge of skin, in drunkenness and weeping,/ told as a woman without matches and tinder, not in/ words and in words and in words learned by heart,/ told in secret and not in secret, and listen, does not/ burn out or waste and is plenty and pitiless and loves." "Hard

Against the Soul" is another sequence of prose poems, this time affirming the importance and validity of loving another woman. The old woman from "'Fore Day Morning" is recalled, her significance reinterpreted: "that was the look I fell in love with, the piece/ of you that you kept, the piece of you left, the lesbian,/ the inviolable, sitting on a breach in a time that did not/ hear your name or else it would have thrown you into/ the sea."

"Blossom," from *Sans Souci and Other Stories* (1988), introduces, in an approximation of her own speech patterns, a Trinidadian woman who overcomes the harsh unreality of life in Toronto by becoming an obeah woman who is entered by the powerful Yuroba goddess Oya. Black people come to consult her, and to dance the "Oya freeness dance" in Blossom's speakeasy. Like Harris's story "A Matter of Fact," "Blossom" records and validates the West Indian folk belief in spiritual forces. Brand, however, moves community participation in obeah rituals from Trinidad to Toronto, suggesting both that psychic health may lie in keeping alive old beliefs and also that communities of immigrants subtly but surely alter the social landscape they enter.

Dionne Brand's work is direct political challenge. Her outspoken poems use repetition, direct address, slang and street idiom, and a vocabulary drawn from her own political reading and involvement. *No Language is Neutral* consolidates and complicates Brand's earlier topics and techniques. It is a moving testimony on behalf of all outsiders – black, immigrants, women, and lesbians.

To read the writings of Claire Harris, M. Nourbese Philip, and Dionne Brand can be to feel oneself entering a new universe of meaning. Their eloquent contribution to literature in Canada is their making their universe visible, persuasive, acceptable. They have proven that oppositional literature, literature that is formed from a context, that speaks directly and passionately about the contradictions in our society and its oppression of certain groups, can be also excellent, stunning not only thematically but technically.

Saskatoon, December 1993

SECONDARY SOURCES CITED

Bhabha, Homi K. "Introduction: Narrating the Nation," *Nation and Narration*. London: Routledge, 1990.

Fuss, Diana. *Essentially Speaking: Feminism, Nature and Difference*. New York: Routledge, 1989.

Gates, Henry Louis, Jr. *Black Literature & Literary Theory*. New York and London: Methuen, 1984.

Hutcheon, Linda and Marion Richmond, eds. *Other Solitudes: Canadian Multicultural Fictions*. Toronto: Oxford University Press, 1990.

Ingram, Angela, ed. *Women's Writing in Exile*. Chapel Hill and London: University of North Carolina Press, 1989.

Mukherjee, Arun. *Towards and Aesthetic of Opposition: Essays on Literature, Criticism and Cultural Imperialism*. Stratford: Williams-Wallace, 1988.

Sanders, Leslie, "Introduction," in Ann Wallace, ed., *Daughters of the Sun, Women of the Moon*. Trenton: Africa World Press, 1991.

Williamson, Janice. *Sounding Differences: Conversations with Seventeen Canadian Women Writers*. Toronto: University of Toronto Press, 1993.

CLAIRE HARRIS

Claire Harris was born in Port of Spain, Trinidad, in 1937. Educated at home until she was seven, she then attended St. Rose Girls' Intermediate School and St. Joseph's Convent. She subsequently took a BA Honours degree, with a major in English and a minor in Spanish, at University College, Dublin, and a Post-Graduate Diploma in Education at the University of the West Indies, Jamaica. In 1966, she emigrated to Canada to teach English and drama, secondary level, in Calgary's Catholic school system. In 1974-75, Harris read mass media and communications at the University of Nigeria, Lagos, and in 1975 she began to write for publication.

On her return to Canada, shocked at Canadians' lack of knowledge of Canadian poets, Harris published a series of works by major poets on posters under the trade name *Poetry Goes Public* (1977). She was a poetry editor at the literary magazine *Dandelion* from 1981 to 1989. In 1982, she proposed an all-Alberta literary magazine: *blue buffalo* was the result, and she was its managing editor from 1984 until 1987. A member of the Writers' Guild of Alberta since its inception, she has done a variety of odd jobs for the organization.

Harris's poetry has appeared in numerous literary magazines and several dozen anthologies, including *The Penguin Book of Caribbean Verse in English* (Penguin, 1986), *Imagining Women* (Women's Press, 1988), *Displaced Persons* (Dangaroo Press, Denmark/Australia, 1988), *Poetry by Canadian Women* (Oxford, 1989), *Celebrating Canadian Women* (Fitzhenry & Whiteside, 1989), and *Kanada* (Konigshausen & Neumann, 1991). Some of her work has also appeared on the CBC.

Harris has written a dozen articles. With Edna Alford, she edited an anthology of Canadian women's writing, *Kitchen Talk* (Red Deer College Press, 1992). In addition, she has published six books of poetry. For her first book, *Fables from the Women's Quarters* (Williams-Wallace, 1984), she won the Commonwealth Award, Americas Region, in 1985. *Translation into Fiction* (Goose Lane, 1984) was followed by *Travelling to Find a Remedy* (Goose Lane, 1986), which won the Writers' Guild of Alberta Award for poetry in 1987 and the first Alberta Culture poetry prize. *The Conception of Winter* (Williams-Wallace, 1988) won an Alberta Culture Special Award in 1990. *Drawing Down a Daughter* (Goose

Lane, 1992), her most recent book, was nominated for a Governor General's Award, and *My Sister's Child* is forthcoming from Goose Lane Editions.

Harris lists the influences on her work as Fanon, Sartre, and Césaire; bell hooks and Doris Lessing; "the great European surrealists and prose poem writers ... among the French, Baudelaire, Rimbaud, and Claudel; among the Spaniards, Lorca, Alexandre, and Machado ... I *studied* Rexroth's translation of a hundred Chinese poems – the fruits of which are to be found in everything I write. Ideas that exhilarate me – the new physics, which influenced *Travelling to Find a Remedy*. *Translation into Fiction* comes out of the French and Spanish and Rexroth. Shakespeare, the romantics, plainchant, the New Testament, West Indian folk tales, and calypso – all seeped into the soul before I was sixteen."

Harris has retired from teaching. She lives in Calgary and travels widely in Africa, Europe, Latin America, what used to be the USSR, the far East, and the subcontinent.

■ ■ ■

WHY DO I WRITE?

> *To write ... is to have recourse to the consciousness of others in order to make oneself be recognised as essential to the totality of being. (Jean-Paul Sartre, "Why Write?," What is Literature?).*

In 1939, when I was two years old, George Orwell wrote in an essay on Marrakech, "All people who work with their hands are partly invisible, and the more important the work they do, the less visible they are. . . . In a tropical landscape one's eye takes in everything except the human beings. . . . [They are] the same colour as the earth, and a great deal less interesting to look at. . . . It is only because of this that the starved countries of Asia and Africa are accepted as tourists' resorts. . . . No one would think of running cheap trips to the Distressed Areas (of Europe)." ("Why I Write," *Such, Such Were the Joys*). In 1974, a well-intentioned, well-travelled high school teacher of Social Science, with a Master's Degree in her subject, asked me, "What do people like the Bedouin, peasants in Egypt, people like that, what do they think about? I know they think about the animal things like warmth, food . . . but what goes on in their minds?" Around the staff lunch tables, people munched on home-made sandwiches; at another table the hockey argument continued, at mine people waited for a reply to an obviously puzzling question to which I might have the answer.

Not really a thunderclap. Simply a quiet confirmation that in the last quarter of the twentieth century, we of the "South" were still perceived as irredeemably other. The last four hundred years of Western history had not been, as I had thought, merely a matter of economic barbarism. Everything I had observed about the Western World, most specifically the vast gulf between its moral and social philosophies on the one hand, and, on the other, its unrestrained violence both in the South and in the "south" of its own reserves, its ghettos, its slums, slotted quietly into place. I have always known that I was a writer. Finally, I had my subject.

Surveying our absence, or the caricature that was our presence in the post-renaissance world, it was clear that, first, my work had to take part in the reinscription of Africa on the Western consciousness; secondly, it seemed necessary to examine what it means to be human in the context of the social and economic, the historical and environmental fractures we have constructed over the last five hundred years. Thirdly, since women remain doubly subjected, I would try to reveal what happens when a woman must deal with the realities of racial as well as gender subjugation. Because the favorite portrayal of Africans, Asians, Latin Americans, and women is the portrayal of the victim/fool/the earth/the tool, my characters would have to fight back. Somehow. I knew that only the ability to do this would make them *real* in the "North." More important, Western African that I am, it was the only thing that would make them real to me. Besides, I wanted to find out what happens when people violate their ethical principles. With what, when that was done, was one left?

I don't want to spend time on the effect of mass culture on such a project, or on the effect of technologies which turn everyone into a consumer. However, since they make the job all but impossible, that is the job of re-introducing the human scale, the cosmic/communal scale, the job of reality check that art should perform, I must mention the communication technologies, if only in passing. Suffice to say that to a civilization, a culture, a country organized in denial of what warring parties call the facts on the ground, I, like most artists of the South, face the caricatures conjured by the media with what reality can be seen in a mirror.

Needless to say (but I am going to say it), this is not a subject which either my adopted country, Canada, or the larger Western culture can accept with equanimity. Thus marginalization by literary category: Immigrant Literature/Writing by Women of Colour/Feminist Writing/Political Literature/Post Colonial Literature/New Literature in English. In fact, I write in a tradition, some enterprising critic will one day discover, that is in direct descent from European Literature though it clings to what is left of the ancestral cosmos not ripped from me, even as it elaborates Africa in the Americas.

Let's consider literature, the framing discourse of a society but also the school subject, the object of veneration. The study of novels, plays, poetry was first established in India in the early nineteenth century by colonial administrators in an attempt at ideological pacification. When it was seen to work it was then brought back to England for similar purposes in the British population. Thus we owe English literature studies, possibly all modern literary studies, to colonialism and the need to propagate the notion of effortless and *moral* Western superiority. (This gloss is owed to Guari Viswanathan's *The Masks of Conquest* as discussed by Edward Said in *Culture and Imperialism*.)

The North exists because of the South. It is impossible to define oneself in opposition to something unless there already exists an obvious and intimate relationship. We – that is, Africans in North America, and of course, Europe – have suffered a traumatic loss. The nations which inflicted and continue to inflict that loss have never acknowledged their crime, nor have they ever been contrite. (Consider that at the abolition of slavery, Britain secured all compensation both legal and financial to slave owners for the "wrong" done them.) Instead, the West has externalized guilt and self-loathing, projecting it onto us. As a result, Europeans, North Americans, and Africans of the diaspora still have a great festering boil to lance, one for which they carry unequal burdens of responsibility but which, nevertheless, they must lance together. There can, of course, be no healing while Europeans continue to see Africans as some version of failed humanity, even as Africans see them as deluded monsters. There still is little or no acceptance, on either side, of the world we have made together; no recognition of the scar tissue embroidering it. Thus there can be nothing to discuss, nothing to share. This becomes increasingly farcical when one considers the tremendous influence of Africans on every aspect of the contemporary culture of the US, thus of a world where "US" equals "modern."

It seems to me that the very refusal to acknowledge Africa (see *Black Athena* by Martin Bernal) makes its influence more potent. The first signs of this potency are beginning to appear in Canada, as it becomes obvious that the theory of satellite communities to the larger central community isn't going to work. Instead, the culture captured by capitalism and now seeing itself as host to that virulent virus, Africa and the South, must do everything to protect itself from infection. Thus the five-hundred-year marginalization of Africans in the diaspora, and of Africa itself.

To mirror the profound disharmony of such a world, collages would have to take form, languages would have to knock against each other, genres would have to dissolve. I would have to batter at closed doors, at accepted definitions of closure and harmony. But, *pace* Ghandi, holding my mirror to Western civilization would not only be a good thing; it was also too long delayed. I did not think I could change the world; I could no longer not write. This was all there suddenly, confusing, to be frank, terrifying. I set off for Africa. There, in Lagos in 1975, my career as a writer began.

Before I continue with this description of my voyage of discovery, I think we should pause here to consider the mythology surrounding the words North and South in the West. The North is up, like heaven/goodness/light/a preserving cool. The South is down, like hell/morally ambiguous/dark/a corrupting heat. On this more-or-less round planet the South is forever, naturally, under the North, the *true* north. Interesting then that this construct should be applied as a shorthand for naming those who control the world economy and its media, and those who don't. Especially as most of the poor people of the world inhabit nations that lie well above the equator, above the tropic of Cancer, in the northern hemisphere. As we say in Trinidad, it aint have nuttin' like de words what come out of people mouth. Do it?

I have said that I write to displace the notion that the South and its people are not integral to modern Western civilization. This continent after all is the true heart of darkness. Here capitalism, memorably described (by God knows whom) as capitalism with its clothes off, inscribed forever the African presence onto the frozen heart of Europe, using slavery, bound labour, and colonization as its chisel. Equally important, it introduced a quality of fantasy into the ways of perception. That is why I write poetry, poetic fiction, and not essays: for the fantasy at the centre of things, for the purity of the stripped-down hard-packed line, for the game at the heart of language. The world we have today is as much a result of these fantasies of God-like power, of wisdom and ease, as it is of greed. For what is harder in our world than a missile, purer than our love of death, more careless than our exercise of power?

Consider the horror of the new technological ways of slaughter.

During the Gulf War, I saw on a US television broadcast young blond men in navy whites sitting before computer screens in an atmosphere of white and glass, playing what seemed to be a video game. Naturally they cheered when they made a hit. Everything so clean, so sterile. After lunch and some shipboard R&R, they would do it again. Twenty, thirty, forty miles away, villages dissolved in dust, slabs of concrete, trailing guts, shattered bodies, blood. Of course we were never shown this, we and those young "fighters" so far from the smell of blood and terror, so far from any possibility of reprisal. "Savages" face their opponents, feel the hot blood spurt onto their hands, know when they have taken a life, understand what it means, risk themselves.

No human being can bear to see himself/herself in the terms I have just described. How then to escape responsibility for the last five hundred years? The reaction of Europe, both in the Americas and at home, was to set its heart/its body/its head to scramble at the margins of backyard sinks, while its mind entertained in the drawing room. (After that what could we expect but Freud?) To do that it reaffirmed Descartes. Africa became the body: here viewed as slow, stupid, seamy, sensual, strong, slobbish, of the soil; Europe became the mind: free, source of all genuine (i.e. scientific) creativity and knowledge, and – to distinguish it from clearly rich and dazzling native cultures – font of high (that is, real) culture. (Ever noticed how European cultures are never "native"? "Folk," perhaps, but "native" never. Apparently the whole shebang has been imported.) The profound marginalization of peoples of the South in North America and Europe, and of Africa in the world, springs from notions like these.

Unfortunately, it has always been easy as an African in the diaspora to pretend that one has no responsibility for any of this. After all, one is here against one's will; one has been largely refused admittance; one clearly and as a matter of public record is on the receiving end of the worst excesses of barbarism. How can one possibly be accountable? Well, we are now of the North. We think, we believe, we dream, we live in some version of the idioms of the North. Like most other northerners, we think we have no choice, no reason to do other than buy into the dream. The vast majority of us do so willingly. We happily pay taxes to build those death machines, sign up in record numbers for armies, very happily indeed use up more than sixty percent of the earth's resources. We are therefore responsible. That responsibility I hope to inscribe as well. But I live in Canada. Of course, the gatekeepers here are, on the whole, intent on preventing the revision and reinscription of North American culture bound to follow on recognizing Africa. It is on this recognition and the resulting destabilization and reorientation of philosophies that I and my work insist. As such it bears some resemblance, indeed is intrinsically and intimately bound, to the feminist enterprise – an enterprise not of displacement but of essential enlargement.

Post-modernism asks: whose body, whose gaze, whose history, whose personality, etc. etc. The response embedded in my work is not the disembodied "I," nor is it everyone's "I," both of which are rooted in faulty and debilitating versions of history, in notions of power and control over both persons and nature central to modern European culture, to its cult of individualism, and to the Americas. Nor is it the naive "I" of autobiography. Instead it is the "I" of specific body, the African body, the female African body, as well as the "I" of imagined, and selectively structured, narrative context. It is also offspring of the only "I" possible in the integrated, many-faceted culture grounded in the geography, environment, and history of the Americas. As such it seeks to reverse the continuing attempts to split minorities into further minorities and to provide a ground for community on which we can all stand, as it tries the stance, no doubt utopian, of claiming the centre.

The forms my work takes reflect this refusal to accept boundaries, even the boundaries of genre or of the page. As do the varieties of English I exploit in a text. One thing I've learnt: one can't bother about the critics who, whether they are black or white, have their own rows to hoe. Consider Fraser Sutherland, terrified of dispossession, who, in an article entitled "Poetry in Adverse Times" in which *Drawing Down a Daughter* was discussed (*Globe and Mail*, 13 Nov. 1993), writes first about what he considers the "lowered threshold" of Canadian poetry, and his "barely concealed yawns." Then he writes "the future of English poetry may belong to Africa, Asia and the West Indies, and to their visible, audible minorities in Europe and North America." One lovely thing about words is their deeply communicative function. One can so very seldom use them to conceal who one really is, or the specific ploy on which one is engaged. Let's see. Until the Second World War, poetry was the queen (that is, the apex) of the literary arts. We know from the histories of feminism that as soon as a significant number of women gain access to a field, the field begins to lose status, social significance, and naturally the financial rewards decrease. Obviously if women can do it well, it's been overvalued. Similarly, when people of the South demonstrate their ability in any area, then clearly it is time for those of European descent to abandon the field, to marginalize the project.

Finally, and because I'm always asked, of course I am a political writer. Like all other writers. One either supports the *status quo* or one doesn't. In any case is it really possible to write, to act publicly from a field other than the political/cultural? If so, what is the source of the form, the gesture? As Stanley Fish says in *There's No Such Thing as Free Speech, And It's a Good Thing Too*, "the political – the inescapability of partisan, angled seeing – is what always and already grasps us.... [W]ithout some unquestioned ideological vision, the act of speaking would make no sense."

In Canada it is possible to read twenty-five books for a national poetry competition without coming across two books which in any way reflect the varieties of people or the transitional cultural signs which enrich and complicate the lives of our great cities. This negation is considered "literary." It may even be considered "authentic." No surprise then that most people consider poetry irrelevant. It remains possible to read nineties novel after nineties novel in which Toronto remains trapped in the amber of the fifties, a more or less WASP city. This is called being sensitive to the issue of appropriation. However, in 1991 Vachel Lindsay's "Congo" was taught to school children of all races for the Calgary Music and Speech Arts Festival. This is called, aptly and accurately enough, "teaching the great traditional literature of the West."

Like most artists of the diaspora, I present what reality can be seen in a mirror: we are here; we have always been here; we have always been central. "Here," of course, stands in for the eternal present. You are what you are because we are. But in the final analysis that is all content. There is also poetry. My interests lie in the metaphysics of the pre-Western world and of the new physics: chaos/multiple worlds/time confounded with space/the notion of every gesture changing the universe/the forever "now"/the notion of unity and aloneness. The work is an attempt to transform, however tentatively, those interests into art, and so, in the words of the Sartre of 1945, "disclose the world and offer it as a task to the generosity of the reader" ("Why Write?"). In the end, I suppose, I'm an artist seeking questions in the last decade of the twentieth century. African in the West, one writes an individual vision of a splintered world to a splintered culture, and writes, one hopes, poetry.

Calgary 1994

[*A version of this essay appeared in* Jyan Aakaash ed Naganya Tamboo Chhe *(1991).*]

■ ■ ■

from *Fables from the Women's Quarters* (1984)

NUDE ON A PALE STAIRCASE

She awakes
and is
for the moment
herself
convinced by the hour
                      (that secret other incapable of
                      compromise inured to deceit)
As in the funnel dreams of the
near dead
she looks down on the woman drawn
stork like
tendrils of hair shifting in his
breathing
cloth loose-wrapped awry over bare
shoulders
Against a siren wind laden with
darkness
she waits for the pale erotic bells
signal
for midweek's ritual flirtation with passion
                      (this love nurtured as one nurtures
                      an invalid)
Still there
is a sound they have made together
a note
part anguish part estacy she
carries
unuttered under her heart to
utter
would be to dissolve

This is his village   its bells call the elderly black Italian women who
crunch their old faith   who trail their faint air of the women's quarters
past the small shops   bakery and upholsterers   past pasta in the wall
past sausages shoemakers and keys while u wait   past dusty chandeliers
and urns   past the Saigon restaurant to the early morning church
Once when she first arrived where nothing would bridge the space where
he stopped and she began   she followed them on this women's duty
watched them at their beads count off the days contract with God
Now she meets them   these other village women in the aisles of the
co-op together poring over the eggplant their noses wrinkling in the
sterile air they circle the old rituals of food   of caste   Their serious
hands give off a small light

    The bells
    echo in the pelvic
    bone cause
    a different peal
    across
    the pillows as across
    the width
    of a room she sees him
    closed
    on his back
    restless
    in the shallows
    of sleep
    impelled to intervene to
    enter
    her hand reaches out she
    hovers
    shadow
    mouth

Afterwards she floats clear waits for the first soft changes of January light to toll her to the strangling boredom of this solitary woman's life   she thinks idly of family compounds   susurrus of saries and barefeet   clanging of plots   charcoal fires   stringy dogs and curries   all the busy folk music of feuds and flies lit by passionate particular friendships   The sudden radio hauls her to alarm   *Massacres in Assam*   from her childhood a memory of blue bottles encrust swollen lips   the mad thunder of an ancient jeep ruts the dirt roads   small stones fly   the sludge in the ditch   the leaves quiver in a miasma of such fear that even today here   safe   her throat fills   The voice slides from disaster to music as soothing as a lollipop   while her secret self crashes against these cliffs   she clings nude rides this pale staircase the house collapsing around her   though it would have happened whether she had stayed to watch or not

    Once before she ran . . .
    but time
    this morning light nail her to
    the bed
    where these deaths demand
    a voice
    something more than the dry sigh
    of fact
    rustling in this room

                              (a chant bright with thick blood
                              a wail jagged and cruel)

    but words cannot absolve
    nor can
    distance shelter her who
    long ago
    invented her sacrament-
    a various
    grief chosen as once she
    chose fruit
    in the market place
    thumping
    melons then bargaining

Above the razor's whine he calls with a certain edged satisfaction *a hell of a mess   she retreats to the soft white pillows veils her mouth with the sheet   She herself has given him this right* who ignored the centuries' hollow voice in favor of youth's ache of the secret singleminded self opening   She begins to rise towards this wounded day where no one will ask anything of her (no mother-in-law bang at her door   no sister whisper   no child cling to her skirts) all that she has to give grown old and stale   grown rock hard   become a boulder that now thunders through her   splinters the rhododendrons   the deodars she waters with furtive care   She strips the bed   straightens the rocker   draws the blinds   remembering she chose   loving him   loving herself   immodestly   Sudden envy of those others huddled together in the scent of blood surprises searches her

    His hands once promised
    resurrection
    his self pouring over her
    like milk
    she risked the fundamental
    Eye and stones

                                            (from those musty sheets she thought
                                            to rise free to ease and gentler gods)

    While fireflies blinked
    on/off
    in the uncurtained night
    like passion
    like hope
    In their innocence the ancient
    flesh magic
    shocked
    arrested them
    now she counts on it for breath

Then she needed validation   and this inspite of the bittersweet pervasive ache of the women's quarters that should have been innoculation through the jammed phone-lines the operator repeating irritably *you can't get through* she clings dry eyed to the common rhythms of the voice stitched from the cries that run from courtyard to slums to flow unknotted through bazaars to these lines   She knows a ferocious fate hangs over those others   it is not just the dying   always the same jackals wait it is the life itself and yet... and yet...   Her forehead pressed to the cool glass she envisions a green rain soft on fields   on houses   ruffling streams   but unbidden the rain rises as brown rivers   storms banks (men tossed like refuse among swollen animals   cars   shacks uprooted trees) she flings her voice to the crackling distance   a hand reaching out to clutch at another and finding straw

    She knows
    he does not
    see her
    not as he used to
    naked
    in the eyes of
    others
    their rush of kindness
    bitter
    as herbs   Uprooted
    dry pressed
    between the pages of his
    culture
    the rough cut of her
    foreignness
    is faded to nuance
    he approves

Moving through the morning rooms   her hands full of dishes and mugs she avoids the eyes of the photograph on the wall   the slender school teacher poised in the village doorway her vibrant once-upon-a-time eastern self full of subtle calm and brilliance   Sudden anger wells in her as she waits for the toast   she cannot but think of cousins and aunts she takes bacon from the microwave empties the dishwasher struggles against the contradictions of grief/rage/pride rising in her like bile (one final act to free her from kinship to the formal contemptuous caricature the shorthand of gaunt eyes and CARE cupped pathos   those fly haunted dyings that this evening will spring from screen and newspaper confirming images of grotesque   otherness) she would be another walking past the lilac hedges to midweek Mass unnoticed and invisible

    Looking
    up at her from the shattered
    cups   he
    sees her suddenly
    riding
    a pale staircase her
    sari
    unwrapped and flailing
    the storm
    dazed searching for a word
    he can
    he says lamely as
    one might
    to the terminally ill
    some things
    get worse before they get
    better
    in the soft morning light
    she stoops
    picks up a fragment a
    handle
    curved and sure in her palm
    cool perfect
    and without feeling

WHERE THE SKY IS A PITIFUL TENT

Once I heard a Ladino[*] *say "I am poor but listen I am not an Indian"; but then again I know Ladinos who fight with us and who understand we're human beings just like them.*
                        Rigoberta Manchu (Guatemala)

All night the hibiscus tapped at our jalousies
dark bluster of its flower trying to ride in
on wind lacinated with the smell of yard fowl
Such sly knocking sprayed the quiet
your name in whispers
dry shuffle of thieving feet on verandah floors
My mouth filled with midnight and fog
like someone in hiding
to someone in hiding
I said *do not go*
you didn't answer
though you became beautiful and ferocious
There leached from you three hundred years of compliance
Now I sleep with my eyes propped open
lids nailed to the brow

After their marriage my parents went into the mountains to establish a small settlement . . . they waited years for the first harvest. Then a patron *arrived and claimed the land. My father devoted himself to travelling and looking for help in getting the rich landowners to leave us alone. But his complaints were not heard . . . they accused him of provoking disorder, of going against the sovereign order of Guatemala . . . they arrested him.*

---

* Ladino: a descendant of Spanish Jews who came to Guatemala during the Inquisition. Quotations in italics are taken from the testimony of Rigoberta Manchu, collected by Elizabeth Burgos, translated into Spanish by Sylvia Roubaud and into English by Patricia Goedicke, and published in the Mexican publication *Unomasuno* and in *American Poetry Review* (January/February 1983).

In the dream I labour toward something
glimpsed through fog   something of us exposed
on rock and mewling   as against the tug of water
I struggle under sharp slant eyes
death snap and rattle of hungry wings
                                      Awake I whisper
You have no right to act
you cannot return land from the grave
Braiding my hair the mirror propped on my knees
I gaze at your sleeping vulnerable head
Before the village we nod smile or don't smile
we must be as always
while the whole space of day aches with our nightmares
I trail in your footsteps through cracks you chisel
in this thin uncertain world
where as if it were meant for this mist hides
sad mountain villages   reluctant fields
still your son skips on the path laughing
he is a bird   he is a hare
under the skeletal trees

My mother had to leave us alone while she went to look for a lawyer who would take my father's case. And because of that she had to work as a servant. All her salary went to the lawyer. My father was tortured and condemned to eighteen years in prison. (Later he was released.) But they threatened to imprison him for life if he made any more trouble.

I watch in the market square
those who stop and those who do not
while my hands draw the wool over up down
knitting the bright caps on their own
my eyes look only at sandals
at feet chipped like stones at the quarry
There are noons when the square shimmers
we hold our breath while those others
tramp in the market place
Today the square ripples like a pond
three thrown   what is left of them
corded like wood   alive and brought to flame
How long the death smoke signals
on this clear day
We are less than the pebbles under their heels
the boy hides in my shawl

The army circulated an announcement ordering everyone to present themselves in one of the villages to witness the punishment the guerillas would receive ... There we could observe the terrible things our comrades had suffered, and see for ourselves that those they called guerillas were people from the neighboring villages ... among them the Catequistas and my little brother ... who was secretary to one of the village co-operatives. That was his only crime. He was fourteen years old ... They burnt them.

As if I have suffered resurrection I see
the way the grass is starred with thick fleshed
flowers at whose core a swirl of fine yellow
lines disappear into hollow stems
so we now into our vanished lives
Dust thickening trees we turn
to the knotted fist of mountains
clenched against mauve distance
Because I must   I look back
heartheld to where the mudbrick huts
their weathered windows daubed with useless crosses
their shattered doors   begin the slow descent
to earth   my earlier self turns in
darkening air   softly goes down with them
The boy only worms alive in his eyes
his face turned to the caves

When we returned to the house we were a little crazy, as if it had been a nightmare. My father marched ahead swiftly saying that he had much to do for his people; that he must go from village to village to tell them what had happened... A little later so did my mother in her turn... My brother left too... and my little sisters.

If in this poem you scream who will hear you
though you say *no one should cry out in vain*
your face dark and thin with rage
Now in this strange mountain place
stripped by knowledge
I wait for you
Someone drunk stumbles the night path
snatching at a song or someone not drunk
I am so porous with fear
even the rustle of ants in the grass flows through me
but you are set apart
The catechists say *in heaven there is no male
no female*   that is a far foolishness
why else seeing you smelling of danger
and death do I want you so
your mouth   your clear opening in me

We began to build camps in the mountains where we would spend the night to prevent the troops from killing us while we slept. In the daytime we had taught the children to keep watch over the road . . . We knew that the guerillas were up there in the distant mountains. At times they would come down in order to look for food, in the beginning we didn't trust them, but then we understood that they, at least, had weapons to fight the army with.

You will not stop what you have begun
though I asked in the way a woman can
Since you have broken thus into life
soon someone will make a pattern
of your bones   of your skull
as they have with others
and what will fly out
what will escape from you torn apart
the boy and I must carry
In your sleep I went to the cenote[*]
in the moonlight I filled my shawl with flowers
threw them to the dark water
the ancient words fluting in my head
your son pinched awake to know what must come

My mother was captured (some) months later ... when all she could wish for was to die ... they revived her, and when she had recovered her strength they began torturing her again ... they placed her in an open field ... filled her body with worms ... she struggled a long time then died under the sun ... The soldiers stayed until the buzzards and dogs had eaten her. Thus they hoped to terrorize us. She doesn't have a grave. We, her children, had to find another way of fighting.

* cenote: a well occasionally used in ritual sacrifice (precolumbian)

Oh love this is silence   this is the full
silence of completion   we have swum through
terror that seared us to bone
rage lifted a cold hand to save us
so we became this surreal country
We have been bullet-laden air   fields that sprout
skulls   night that screeches and hammers
we have been hunger   whip   wind that sobs
feast days and drunken laughter
a rare kindness and pleasure
We have come through to the other side
here everything is silence   our quiet breathing
in this empty hut   our clay jugs full of light
and water   we are our corn our salt
this quiet is the strength we didn't know we had
our humanity no longer alarms us
we have found who we are
my husband our silence is the silence of blue steel thrumming
and of love
Our deaths shall be clear

Our only way of commemorating the spilled blood of our parents was to go on fighting and following the path they had followed. I joined the organization of the Revolutionary Christians. I know perfectly well that in this fight one runs the greatest risk ... We have been suffering such a long time and waiting.

Your death is drenched in such light
that small things   the sky   branches
brushing against the cave mouth   the boy
stirring   make my skin crackle against damp blankets
As one gathers bullets carelessly spilled I gather your screams
all night I remember you   utterly lovely
the way you danced the wedding dance
rising dust clouding your sandals
your slow dark smile
You return to the predawn   leaving us
what remains when the flames die out of words
(small hard assertions
our beginnings
shards of the world you shattered
and ourselves)

Their death gave us hope, because it is not just that the blood of all those people be erased forever. It is our duty on this earth to revive it . . . I fight so they will recognise me . . . If I have taken advantage of this chance to tell the story of my life it is because I know that my people cannot tell their own stories. But they are no different from mine.

■ ■ ■

THIS WAS THE CHILD I DREAMT

soft as the dark and strong   strong
as her forefather's will fused in nightmare
and she was bright
as the splash of wings in the forest
yet she was delicate as spray
from mountain falls   and muted
as their distant water roar
she formed a space in me as deep
and calm as jungle halls   this child

                    who would inherit fable
              in her the genius of the ancestors
                         waited expectantly
                     to me she was entrusted
                        now the vault gutted
         I have become the charnel house of my own seed
                       the dead end of my line
               never again will their strength gleam
                      black in sunlight   never
                will a woman call and their eyes
                    look up in answer   nor ever
                will food be offered   or a candle
                        lit in their memory
                   moss grows over their names

■ ■ ■

POLICEMAN CLEARED IN JAYWALKING CASE

The city policeman who arrested a juvenile girl for jaywalking March 11, has been cleared of any wrongdoing by the Alberta law enforcement appeal board.

The case was taken to the law enforcement appeal board after the girl was arrested, strip-searched and jailed in the adult detention centre.

The police officer contended the girl had not co-operated during the first five minutes after she was stopped, had failed to produce identification with a photo of herself on it, and had failed to give the policeman her date of birth.
Edmonton Journal

In the black community to signify indicates an act of acknowledgement of sharing, of identifying with.

The girl was fifteen. An eyewitness to the street incident described her as "terrified."

The girl handed the officer her bus pass containing her name, address, phone number, her school, school address and phone number.

Look you, child, I signify   three hundred years in swarm around me this thing I must   this uneasy thing   myself the other   stripped down to skin and sex   to stand   to stand and say   to stand and say before you all   the child was black and female and therefore mine   listen you walk the edge of this cliff with me at your peril do not hope to set off safely to brush stray words off your face to flick an idea off with thumb and forefinger   to have a coffee and go home comfortably Recognize this edge   and this air carved with her silent invisible cries Observe now this harsh world   full of white works   or so you see us and it is white   white washed male and dangerous even to you full of white fire white heavens white words   and it swings in small circles around you   so you see it   and here I stand black and female bright black on the edge of this white world   and I will not blend in nor will I fade into the midget shades   peopling your dream

Once long ago   the loud tropic air   the morning rushing by in a whirl of wheels   I am fifteen drifting through hot streets shifting direction by instinct   tar heel soft under my shoes I see shade on the other side of the road   secure in my special dream I step off the curb   sudden cars crash and jangle of steel   the bump the heart stopping fall into silence then the distant driver crying "Oh Gawd! somebody's girl child she step off right in front of me, Gawd!"   Black faces anxious in a fainting world a policeman bends into my blank gaze   "where it hurting yuh?   tell me!"   his rough hand under my neck   then seeing me whole "stand up, let me help yuh!" shaking his head   the crowd straining on the sidewalk the grin of the small boy carrying my books   then the

POLICEMAN CLEARED IN JAYWALKING CASE   49

policeman   suddenly stern "what you name, girl?"   the noisy separation of cars   "eh, what you name?"   I   struck dumb   dumb "look child, you ever see a car in plaster of paris?"   dumb   "tell me what's your name? You ever see a car in a coffin!"   the small boy calling out my name into such shame   But I was released with a smile   with sympathy sent on in the warm green morning   Twenty years later to lift a newspaper and see my fifteen year old self   still dumb   now in a police car   still shivering as the morning roars past but here   sick in the face of such vicious intent

Now female I stand in this silence   where somebody's black girl child jaywalking to school is stripped   spread   searched   by a woman who finds that black names are not tattooed on the anus pale hands soiling the black flesh   through the open door the voices of men in corridors   and in spite of this   yea   in spite of this black and female to stand here and say   I am   she is   I say to stand here   knowing this is a poem black in its most secret self

Because I fear   I fear myself and I fear your skeletal skin the spider tracery of your veins   I fear your heavy fall of hair like sheets of rain and the clear cold water of your eyes   and I fear myself the rage alive in me consider the things you make even in the mystery of earth and the things you can   an acid rain that shrivels trees   your clinging fires that shrivel skin   This law that shrivels children and I fear your naked fear of all that's different   your dreams of power your foolish innocence but I fear myself and the smooth curve of guns   I fear   Look   your terrible Gods do not dance nor laugh nor punish men   do not eat or drink but stay a far distance   watch the antic play of creation and cannot blink or cheer   Even I fear the ease you make of living this stolen land   all its graceful seductions   but I fear most myself   how easy to drown in your world   dead believe myself living   who stands "other" and vulnerable to your soul's disease
Look you child, I signify

■ ■ ■

from Translation Into Fiction (1984)

> *By thy senses sent forth / go right to the rim of thy longing give Me garment*
>
> *(Rainer Maria Rilke, Gregor Sebba)*

Awakened
    by a touch
      or a rush of wind
spreadeagled
in the red light
flaring
through the corn
she lifted her head
to find herself
skewered
on the One Eye
of God
a quiet
    so intense
it was the absence
    of sound
eventually   Through the kitchen window
the color faded   she saw that the tropical sun
darkness   had begun to fade
seeped from   the children's hour was over
the western sky   "think" she said
And she ran   transfigured on the braided rug
    swiftly   in that hot wooden room
cautiously   the Bible closed in her hand
through the corn   "think of the cool benediction of snow"
home to hide   and seeing bright inquiry on their faces
a spatter of rain   "a down   a sort of icy down
dodging   billions of feathers"
her footsteps   and felt a fleeting pity

He worked alone   his green face tho' knotting into righteousness still smiled easily   he refused to acknowledge the heat the rains the wild tropical growing   even as he laughed about her open fear of giving birth alone (the baby and her entrails in a stream of blood   he taking her intestines in his curling fingers to put them back)   It had not happened except in dreams   and she still feared   He grew luxuriant   had won or almost won   his gardens bloomed flooded the sparse markets   still each night he searched the Bible and his conscience   joked at her   whittled his gifts and waited for Saturday while the years folded over him like scales on an armadillo   Fixed he supposed her always to be found   he grew careless of love   commanding her to a son she gave him seven daughters

In that land her fair skin burnt to a quick maturity   she learned early how to use suffering to weave the heart's invisible tales   to make out of that green boredom a home   content in her own unease she sometimes prayed   While he worked the wide fields endlessly

Years later
that sunset
dimmed by age
its metaphor drawn
by experience
gradually
she found herself
in a desolate place
without horizon
or color
hers was the sustained   In His name
noiseless terror   before night swooped down
of an abandoned child   over the pioneer farms
under the burden of furnishing   she would pick
the empty rituals   the purple berries for jam
she grew frivolous   and hasten home
longed to savor   before the unborn/undead
One day   left their caves of leaves
the dust began to settle   to call piteously in the twilight

possessed of craftsman's hands   before the plumed serpent
she furnished a Builder   soft as a dove from the trees
she adopted the Shadows   lest she answer
of Myth   the poetry of others   in spite of crosses
till possessed of metaphor   so become the fable
she found   told in the yellow light
The word was made flesh   of kerosene lamps

All that afternoon baskets on her arm she moves through sprung gates   moves over and over to walk outside secure fences often she drifts there her feet not touching ground   the gates swinging open at her glance click shut   she is beyond the perimeters of the farm and all its tame gardens where bell peppers hang free from wrath in Saskatchewan   she drives to school between fences a horse drawn sleigh bundling with straw and bricks section after section   till acres of open bush where berry plants cluster near a ditch   dense dark profusion   here every thing grows so easily   even death   and sees Naomi her first born weeding in the shimmering South American summer   beautiful hair clinging to her neck as she dreams of endless acres of cool white snow   hands swift and sure on the purple fruit the basket almost filled   she thinks suddenly *she is going home* sees prairie grass in the hot summer breeze   so never hears the warning rattle misses it again and again drawn towards the wild darkness of an open mouth its infinite allure   for that lethal second she stares then a strong body thrashes and coils in her hands   they struggle there together in bleak green silence   wide prairie summers her brothers hunt rattlers with a forked stick while she searches the hot rocks   calm she turns to out run the second strike its swift coil   gives vent   screams a wild abandoned trampling release   Homeward air dark with raven his wings his short scream as he dives into the fields   *prey*   sunflowers *pray*   snow   billions of tiny feathers black drifting over her melting in her hair   the young eastern teacher standing her before a mirror to frame her face in a new style   her father barring the doorway like Moses while the husband he chose weeps and returns the babies to her swelling belly one by one

from **Translation Into Fiction**   53

where she lies alone giving birth again & again in the awful
heat and viper darkness   From her wide open mouth
her past streams and flickers among shining leaves   her skirt
flaring   flaring   flaring
to catch flaming frangipani   purple berries   down that spill
from her womb   while her father watches darkly behind new
window panes

Her search
tempered to the summons
of his flesh
lost its sting
the frequent children
flat like the illustrations
in fairy tales
precipitous
towards the banal
she welcomed this
sleep
But soon enough
the air stretched and tucked
itself over an earth
stabled in some abandoned
corner of the galaxy   They laid her
and she wildfire   to rest
in her own storm flared   the ceremony
and shifted   like a thin sip
now guttering   of sacramental
now leaping to sear all   wine
their horizons   afterwards
She needed flight   rains came
she needed new spaces   dust settled
from which to search   hot vivid vines
she imagined herself walking   thrust tips
through some other tamed and foreign field   like spears
in the cool of the evening   through the
and in the ancient silence   small
touching Him   grave

54   CLAIRE HARRIS

TRANSLATION INTO FICTION

on the loss of culture/of the "God gone astray in the flesh."
(Paul Valery/Frantz Fanon)

I do not know your name   you came captive in folds of jute and I bargained for you   stuck my fingers between wooden teeth   caressed your elephant ears   examined the hollow back   then paid

Mask betrayed to snow and silence   hauled from woods and worshippers to hang shackled to my wall   Here where there are no drums   no chants   no dance you are empty a relic denied fear   Once the people called   their call conjured You out of nothing You came to dwell in jungle caves   in shrines   on mountain tops   They called and culled in the web of their need   You took shape in the sure subtle movements of their dance bound only by their dreaming

■

I have seen You on a road alive with lifting dust dancing the woman into small girls aquiver with the break of childhood they crouched before You milking the air of terror
Your whip sang:
    I am God
The drums barked:
    Others have danced with me
    fought with me
    Moremi fed me her child
And the whip cracked:
    Can you?
I watched You whirl away into the gloom of trees
borne on stamping feet and shouts   shuffling across the forests of their fear   rustling its leaves with Your hair of corn curls dried cream   God   calling them to the knife and to wisdom

■

In our dealings with You the knife and the whip in one form
or another have been a constant   One day we woke stretching
and shaking the sleep from our eyes to find ourselves
chattel   You did not erupt the elemental God

in Your silence
we were ravaged

The sky within us shifted and burned black   like leaves in whirl-
wind we were heaved and hiccoughed across the ocean   the
midwife's knife became a curse...
Now I stand outside your ease   now I wake wordless to your
mystery come empty to your altar   For Power denied even
disbelief has fled your black hulk of elephant ears   issued
out of the gashed mouth streamed through wooden teeth to
vanish in the air   stayed to dark drums and fire   You are
left a fiction carved from a tree trunk in Africa

■ ■ ■

A BLACK READING

>   *el nombre exacto de las cosas*
>   *(Juan Ramon Jiménz)*

Each day at firstlight
this anorexic ghost
thrusting out of my
mouth
as out of a womb
clouds the mirror

this bitter child
denied
as much by flailing hope

as by the knife
is and is not
a metaphor

■

In some lucid awful
instant
I chose
to ignore my momentous
murmuring woman's room

My child
is out there
stares blackly out of screens
in a pornography
of poverty
those who owned
the words
shaped this   this not merely
unsurprising but hallowed
the poor
that we have
always with us
whose poverty sears humanity
from the bones
flames in the hair
these babies pregnant
with need
simply
darkly
part of things
as they are
the word making substance

■

When I was
a girl
I turned away
from the sane and delicate
dreams of girls
wanting more
and less

∎

1983:
white kids
jostling among lockers

– hey watch
where the fuck
you're going –

– O.K. O.K.
so I'm black!
Forgive me! –

both white and safe
in the wide
white world
the words have made
the words/the translation

∎

This:
I did not close
myself in rooms
hurled
in my/your circles
I searched
the earth
from trains and buses
from carts

in films and books
to find myself
always here
stripped to skin and sex
the mythic
ballooning in the mud dragging at my feet
drawn curtains/flight
a luxury
history denies me

■

I dream of a new naming
new words   new lines
shaping a new world
I ride it
      as at a durbar
barelegged through wide fields
of baobab soaring in the wash
of midnight
I am real
      when my long
Arabian stride breaks through
daylight I cling to the black
truth   race
bareback towards the light
dream hooves churning
the yellow lies
I make anew the shape
of things

■

In the end
this life is shared
with the lidless eyes
of dreams   bones of fact
shells of words
and yet

this molten mask
these three hundred years
nightmares
straightjackets
slip a little
as I insist
on my small particular dance
dark
I move into the enormous dusk
my hands held out
to catch *the actual names of things*

■ ■ ■

AUGUST

Noon and the August haze veils gentle eastern hills the prim modest houses   along the Bow poplars grow yellow stranded on the deck of this ship perched on cliffs edge I watch the steel city flaring in high noon   so bright I must look away   here where no one walks the traffic strung out at the lights like coils of a python tightens around the city endlessly   in the median men on huge earth movers go busily about their work   cocooned in their own noise CP air drones through the pale blue   I imagine passengers settling back before long suspension   and home   So distant from my own rainforested mountains   mountains rounded like whales stranded against the dawn   light lapping their ridges tiny shacks like barnacles riding their flanks   palms burst into green spume against the sky   I remember dark faces streaming out of the valleys   black women flowing currents & waves   their feet solid on earth   their unreasoned unhurried grace   this forever and indelible on the inner eye   This summer shades into the sixteenth autumn   I grow yellow in exile

FLESHED WITH FIRE

there are days when no shout
in the streets can bring me back
from this place where faded dreams
their skin taut on bone intent on clear
cold air beckon me   I need their stark
skeletal definition of possibilities
here from blackened trees hang
the mumified issue of aborted
dreams their limbs sussurasant
when the day hedges me about   I am
called to this place of dusk and faint
distance   to these dwindling ghosts to
warm myself at their pale particular fire
to draw sustenance from what I could
have been   from what I slipped
casually into not being
in this pathless place where
the dried clusters of infinite
possibilities move me to a future
I walk as in a garden   and from this
place there are days when not even
a shout fleshed with fire
can bring me back

■ ■ ■

from *Travelling to Find a Remedy* (1986)

TRAVELLING TO FIND A REMEDY

I cannot be sure

    perhaps it was your stillness
perhaps the directness of your touch   I cannot
even remember whether we talked   only that it
seemed   common sense
the night dark and airless   the field wet
the hostel windows   blank yellow squares
still the next morning I came awake
thinking of you
how your shadow breached my wall   reached
for roof and stars   how the room was torn
but there were no stars   only globes
of light strung two by two across the campus

I cannot be sure
    I remember hovering

■

You offered me
a gift
wrapped in red
and hooped with gold
with reverence I
unfold the paper
boxes
ancient   inlaid
with bronze
each one
prisoned in the other
magic boxes
growing
smaller and smaller

■

We have loved when the moon washed our bodies of
darkness to glow in each secret place   we have loved

in sunlight sharp as a sword   the wheels of our
car sang like the wings of humming-birds feeding

we have loved in the late afternoon even in the market
place   though your eyes were red with the dust of

evening and the smell of rotten beef clogged my throat
why then did we unravel the snare of safety to slip

from glittering encounter to the moment of   contract
is it because we did not think to encounter ourselves

violent
unabashed

■

The car is blue   very cool in the heat   and sterile
burnished black you lean back against cushions
take my hand and say   "well..."
eyes straight ahead negotiating the contract   careful
there should be no misunderstanding
you say slowly
     "you must bear me a son"
sudden thunder   Orisa[*] three hundred years later
chuckling
I say nothing
drawn by my silence   "you have a choice
few women do"
Rain spilling over the hood   streaming down
the windshield   seen through sealed windows   Lagos
under water   distorted   a face

[*]   minor gods

TRAVELLING TO FIND A REMEDY   63

pressed against the window tapping   holding up
newspapers under tarpaulin
you shake your head   "remember it's different here"
rain searching its way   nosing a path down fine
blue upholstery
          "then I can take care of you"
a glance like mirror lenses on dark glasses
"we can be married quite quickly   but first..."
the grip on my hand tightens
I translate
lightning shocking the gloom   rain trickling
beneath my feet circles into a puddle
I ask   I say the unimaginable
"And if there is no child..."
Silence roars with the waves of the Middle
Passage crashing on African shores

∎

How can I taste the difference between you
what you are
and what I have invested you with
and this is not to deny
your particular brand
of beauty
but this burden of glory
I have laid on you
you must lay down
I know   inevitably the glow of party
light fades   in the harsh sunlight
waterlilies flower from
dark leaves in murky pools

There must be a parting

∎

    I cannot stand on the edge
of your life   giving way to club and custom
forever oyibo*
so I give you back   your heart   your piece of
mind   your safe ritualized living
I had thought to jeer at history
that here knowing what it meant I could throw
my heart across alien centuries
and slavery   to follow safely

but I dream in another tongue
I cannot

Still your absence thins the surface of things
when you said   "I love you"
I thought to infest your days
to swarm in your mind like bees in cloud
and you could rejoice in the colour of my murmuring

There are advantages
    to your ebon calm
your reason   but I was not born to it

■ ■ ■

FRAMED

She is in your painting   the one you bought when the taxi
snarled in market lines   you jumped out and grabbed
a picture of stilted wooden houses against the vivid island
even then there was recognition

She is the woman in a broken pair of men's shoes   her
flesh slipped down like old socks around her ankles   a tray
of laundry on her head   I am there too   but I would not

---

* foreigner (Yoruba)

be like her   at supper she set the one plate and the whole
cup at my place   for herself a mug a bowl my leavings
they said I resembled her   I spent hours before the mirror
training my mouth to different lines

At night while I read   she folded the blanket on her
narrow board   coalfire smooth on her face   she boiled
scrubbed   ironed   musk of soap and others' soil like
mist around her head   often she dreamed   I would have
a maid   like her   she laughed   I studied harder harder
she grieved   I was grown a woman   I was grown
without affinity

For the calling   her eroded hands   cupped like a chalice
she offered me the blasted world as if to say   this is our
sacrament   drink   I would not   this is all there is   I
could not   I left school   I left   she faded
the island faded   styles changed   you hid the dusty
painting in the attic   But I am still there   the one in
middle ground   my face bruising lines of soft white
sheets   my hand raised as if to push against the frame

■ ■ ■

AND SO . . . HOME

I walk the raw paths through winds that crowd me
now this autumn comes around before I'm ready
pulls at my slack time tautening
for a moment no existence at all

Behind the grave apartment towers clouds
pile up   rattle spare bones of rain   leaves
lift and twirl   among all that gold
the air is winged   crackling

Why now her song surprises me I'm not sure
memory spills from my lips   ribbons
crisp satin ribbons   grosgrain   so long ago

My mother   her fingers part my hair make
four neat plaits that dovetail on each side
become one that is crossed and pinned

She holds out a rainbow of ribbons says
choose one   ribbons hanging from her fingers
like paths   how can I choose when any choice
means a giving up   years later shucking the island

As painful as shucking skin   yet I left
weaving a new space to trap the voice
I thought I could   must return   my navel string

Buried where the rich fantasy   of peoples
stranded by empire jostled on those stunned hummocks
history's low road under the bruising sun

Now loving this chill autumn rain I know it has been too long
a memory of dark hands intelligent with a child's
ribbons   hands vulnerable among ruins
something to conjure with

■ ■ ■

MYSTERIES

and   at this moment   the accidental world
why   in the foreground   a framed
wire fence   cat's weathered step-ladder
in the dandelions   cat himself
rampant   considering intently this butterfly
its fluttering yellow statement at the grid

what does cat   butterfly
in mutual revelation

and I with them

beyond us poplars   dawn shadows wind-teased
in the middle ground
my feet released in wet grass   the fresh motion
of snails   earth-scent mingling
with the rising day that should be enough
on the valley floor trucks and cars fan out
sun-gleam whispering on hood/roof
an annunciation of other   of possible
unfathomable brightness

these and I   we absorb each other

a jogger labours past   an old man bends to frail
steps   a woman grey bleared
from the night shift   rungs
on which I bruise my feet towards
some curious perfection   no doubt as casual
as these hills
rounded   scorched green   mauve shadows
dark gashes of fir in cluster
the delicate tracery of pylon reaching above
a clutch of unfinished houses
to contain what/how   and these to bear
all unknowing on this one span

mine and not mine

the sky is russet   there is birdsong
far down the hillside a dog's bark opens
onto thunderless oceans   *all this*   in infinite
stretches of time   still rising
even as we stand still splitting
towards what   why

from *The Conception of Winter* (1989)

From TOWARDS THE COLOR OF SUMMER

Three bells calm the passing hour   a measured
clear-toned peace in Barcelona   I slip naked

from the narrow bed   slanted ceilings   I step
onto the night terrace   cool slate   stone pitted

rust red with the grit of ancient cities
to this landscape of roofs   dim wells   steep

slopes out-croppings chimneys   the weathered
expressions & dread hopes peeled to diseased heart

here and there shallow roof-rooms dim lit   wracked
stone heads square lives to cool realities

on this ruined dignity of terraces   of gargoyles
and grecian urns   I am stirred

would blend and flow with what is night
would become one with what moves in stone

all around like an exhalation the myriad ghostly
lives   ancient cities going down   then

rising again   generation after generation   ten
centuries jostle thinning air   convince

the future   what is human will rise again
and again   if only to sticks and stones

But this is not why we came here
three week exiles   we have chosen to lose

our place in the world   three women searching
a ledge for freedom   excitement   for self

(and I am here where the rivers   grief
and blood rose   think of it

where the lion's jaw crumbles   bearded by slime
its waters brackish   men with net and chain

and coffle may have drunk   kissed wives/babies
then slaved and died

their inheritors walk the streets   barefaced)
the night sky is assaulted by grids of antennae

west a crennellation of church towers   raised
above all a single red light   Four bells stir   fade

the silence is emphasized by caged birds   their sad
occasional night twittering   in the gorge below

a lone car splashes against shuttered doorways
a bundle stirs itself   goes back to stillness or sleep

■ ■ ■

A DREAM OF VALOR AND REBIRTH

My bed sways   swells to a moon
i wake wet from dull sheets
either this is dream   or the moon
counts out seconds
pushing them   reluctant   at me
its miser's nose snuffling over minutes
a myth wondering what more
can be risked from night's sack of hours
my life we're talking here
too scared to rise   i get up
immediately open and driven

now something formless   ancient
something urgent of blood calls me
to the streets of Barcelona
i cross against lonely lights at the Ramblas
stalls shuttered   cages open   trees
a blur deeper than night
the street nervous wavers   narrows
houses fluent rhythmical expand and pulse
breathless i am pushed and squeezed   thrust
towards the ocean   lights shimmer red/
green in rain streaked tarmac
overhead   moon glimmers white
before she settles in a nest of cloud
i follow a desolate nose through
dank courtyards   under occasional
arches dim sink holes of light
reveal aged eyes   savaged face
on a girl's still lissome body
before my eyes she bends into tender dark
shatters at my touch   fragments cling
here   where necessity hunts in pack
and each day   a tightrope walk over chasms
she has fashioned a parachute of lust
now here whisper expecting/suggesting disgust
crawls the air   a wind full
of salt sea   fish and oil   heavy with the wings
of gulls twitches in the trees
now i run driven
a cat between steep mossy walls
crouched in the darkest angle i wait
they rise: my mothers   clear pale
northern waters   my fathers   dark distant masked
forest fall   they rage in my veins
things rupture   bleed   separate
racked and purged
my tongue active in strange vowels

she steps out to gaze
sees slow swelling moon   tastes the flow
of blood and tides   knows centuries
knows nothing ever changes   in fact
there was never anything to change
in the end   rock and we turn through space to extinction
worms turn under the heart   and turn again
she sees me female reach for the hand
of god believing it must be there somewhere
in the curl of tongue or tide:
when i lay
when i lay me down
when i lay me down to sleep

and it is not

moon yawns a great raven   from its beak
a stream of heads gleam in street light
bounce silent on drowned pavement   flash
once   huge   before quivering to small grins
as at a joke too rich   too deep
for sharing   i move from them   pale
faces of whiskered albums   once
proudly displayed   i blunder
down the narrowing passage toward
something ancient
while brilliant fluorescent dragonflies
swirl and cloud
the walls pulse   contract to a crevice
i think *not here   not ready*   stones keen
slapped into grey-green air and dawn
how strange it is   how silent
in the mirrored sheen of cars   i see
a woman   rain lashed braids cling
to the dark face   long blue robe clutched
like a shield   stubby plain toes   she sways
in a puddle on the boulevard as if it were
a convent hall   her wide mouth nibbles

the edges of this night
cars rush past to wild red-eyed quiet
the pale moon wavers
it is raining silence   umbrellas
mushroom under trees   walk through her
a group of girls run past   toss silent giggles
their clear plastic too small to shelter
them all brushes against her heart
their dripping clothes catch on her ribs
an old man shifts his pace   tramps
in his shrinking gait   beyond them all
a great line of palms   and flag ships
riding at anchor like a litany
there the Nina/Pinta/Santa Maria

the blue robe sways on this bridge
rough-hewn wood and darkness take
her in   rope grey   sodden coils
around her   the boat rocking
she rocks   planks groan
her stranded face opens on a ladder
leading below deck   waves slap against
this slave ship rising
she swallows the wail   stench
of men shackled spoon shaped
a miasma of fear steams from all
their orifices   yet their faces
black with refusal of such circumstance
nevertheless smouldering eyes welcome her
and their god gone astray in flesh
their god drumming in her bones
takes her by the throat
her cramped legs burn at the ankles
he gathers her   his mouth a wound
howling into hers

afterwards   a rage to survive life
choirs of sea birds   this god

fluttering in all my veins   fluent
on my tongue
from the ship's deck i see
the abandoned country   the moon
slides out of clouds into the ocean
slim   generous as a girl with time

■ ■ ■

DEATH IN SUMMER

One known at home   our mail relays something of her
early summons   awash in the proverbial bed

its final currents strip her of luggage   she
nevertheless clings   I watch from this shore

four thousand miles away her desperate drowning motions
I try to decipher what works   what doesn't

how to save ourselves who no longer believe
in winged souls caged in flesh   nor yet

believe in shared rounds   in organic growth
and becoming   I shall drift through this city

alive to the possibility of this edge   if one
so vigorous . . . nothing   between me and the grave

I shall laugh   shall leave my stain here and there
dark energy of flawed creatures confused and clinging

to the bars   They say her face transparent under
the shock of black hair lifts with each morning's light

which she watches intently as if to be sure
she has seen

I know fading angels move through her as eagles
through the upper air

■ ■ ■

CONCEPTION OF WINTER

Sometimes in summer rain falls in great drops
heavy as loss   today
we see it black on ragged faces
on gypsy urchins crouched at the foot of columns
in this café   Not here spring's succulent promise
life like a peach
or even the thin stretched certitudes of winter
which we imagine as life   skin tight
drying on a frame nailed against a barn
in hot prairie summer
Only this rain stirring clichés   it dulls
the cold incurious eyes on bowed men sitting
under arches we have discovered
sailing behind the rundown façades
and unfashionable shops
searching a way east   it stains rusty mirrors
where our faces shift   and what is new and strange
quickens for a moment   We find a table settle parcels
guidebooks   order drinks   wait for the sun
But some gesture which haunts this place   something
in these women carrying trays of beer   and pregnant
with old age   reminds us of ourselves
We become sad   we walk apart in the wet aftergloom
of rain   know ourselves already seeded
And this is not the voluptuous sadness in great love
or even grief at our friend's dying
Just that here in this place   in our determined joy
we find ourselves fearing the birth of winter
We resolve to invent passion   imagine it as beyond
the circling of tongues   As the cold rage
which changes something

NO GOD WAITS ON INCENSE
for Rosemary

while babies bleed this is not the poem i wanted
it is the poem i could   though it is not that insistent
worm   it will not burrow through deaf ears
lay its eggs in your brain   yet it is all
for change
and it is not that beautiful weapon
it will not explode in the gut
despite your need   this poem is not that gift
it brings you nothing   you who insist on drinking
let your buckets into green and ruined wells   haul
in darkness   village women will lead you smiling
step back polite in the face of skulls
this poem will not catch you as you fall
not a net   no   it is nothing   this poem
not a key   not a charm   not chicken soup
and it is no use at all   at all
nothing at all
it won't beat a drum   it can't dance   it can't
even claim to be written in dust if this morning
the Bow sky-sheeted in light   the silver air is bright
with balloons   yet it talks from a dark bed
this poem   though no
woman can lie curled beneath its covers
can hide before boots
can hope to be taken for bundles of clothes   can hope
not to cry out when the knife probes
pray her blood not betray her   nor the tiny sigh
no   this poem   not even a place where anyone is safe
it can nothing   still nothing   still nothing at all
at all   in the night and disinterested air this poem
leaves no wound

■ ■ ■

from *Drawing Down A Daughter* **(1992)**

Gazing at piles of newspapers   she is wondering
why anyone bothers   when the voice comes
booming out of her past   "I'm saying this once
I don't care whether they're racist or not   you will
get all the education I can buy
ignorance is the luxury we can't afford"

she thinks of the *Sun   Globe and Mail*
ahistorical gropings in the *Lawyers' Weekly*
she smiles wishing she'd known then "ah   but it's
a luxury *they* cultivate"
and she laughs to think how he would have fumed
gathering to herself their furious
encounters   words whirling reckless around
their heads   bouncing off polished floors
ricocheting off walls to bruise innocent
bystanders   but they battened on the hail   dodging
weaving among Morris chairs they rode whims
ideas   never consenting to dust

Girlchild   i wish you something to be passionate
about   someone to be passionate with   a father for instance
natural opponent of any right thinking girl

and where the hell is yours

i'm telling you   Girl   you have to watch men
you leave the islands to come to Canada
you meet the man in Canada
he's born in Canada   his grandfather's born in Canada
you marry him in Canada
now he wants to live in the islands!

look my flight is called ... yes ... I know
we'll settle this when I get back
keep that kid where she is for a week or so   my lady!

some are born to murder   some have murder thrust upon them

she turns back to newspapers
litany of the world's woes
earth's destruction
celebration of its terrors
      we have become cheerleaders
she thinks of Daigle
                of Bush
tyranny
     greed   our game

O Girl   even the comics are cynical

she wonders   if she had refused this child   would he
O Baby   no! your father is an honourable man   well
most of the time anyhow

restless she stands   stretches   considers cleaning
the room   again   nesting syndrome   Girl we've read
all the right books   she strokes her belly
lifts the Great Mask to her shoulders   covers
her body with its bleached grass skirts
holding out her arms she sings from *Solomon*
"Yes   you are black! and radiant
the eyes of many suns have pierced your skin"

she goes back to cold news   the tea   the notebook

she writes:

Daughter   there is no language
i can offer you   no corner that is
yours   unsullied
you inherit the intransitive
case   Anglo-Saxon noun

she thinks of Africa

she should have insisted on Yoruba   not given in to the
angry gaze   the wanting to be rid of this North American
threatening to squeeze herself in to his ancient space

did he fear her lilt
that she would have taken over his
language   made it chip
to the beat of calypso

a woman without forest gods without red earth or sullen
rivers without shame or any tongue to exchange for his
harsh imperatives   the quick curd consonants

Child   all i have to give
is English which hates/fears your
black skin
         make it
           d
              a   c
                n   e
           s
              i   g

to sunlight on the Caribbean

she sighs   settles to papers that assume the North's
moral right to impose   here she votes   shares spoil

how sweet it is
          to shield
    even
        from ourselves
our own
     intimacy
with evil

she rustles through her notebooks   finds last year's poem
on this year's famine   too bored   too depressed to write
another

■

Daughter   to live is to dream the self
to make a fiction
this telling i begin
you stranded in landscape of your time
will redefine   shedding my tales
to grow your own
as i have lost our ancestors   your
daughters will lose me
remembering only a gesture   a few words
"what you don't want in your kitchen
will sit in your drawing room"
and a few recipes
history in a pinch of salt
a lower temperature   a turning
wrist   and Girlchild   as we move together
on this swell of water
this swimming and whirling
"the sea ain't got no backdoor"
and *"don't marry for colour   marry where*
colour is   else the race goin' lost in you"
            (snow no longer
                            falls
                            skies
            slate-grey
                            closed)

Girl   all of us in this family know how to make float   how
to make bakes   the real real thing   and acra   not even
your father's mother make so good   and pilau   and calla-
loo with crab & salt pork   barefoot rice   rich black cake
cassava pone (is true your Carib great aunt on your dad side
teach your mother that) but the coconut ice cream   and five-
fingers confetti   buljol   souse   those are our things

Child   this is the gospel on bakes

first   strain sunlight through avocado leaves

80   CLAIRE HARRIS

then pour into a dim country kitchen through bare
windows   on a wooden table freshly scrubbed
I'm warning you   a lazy person is a nasty
person   flurry of elbows
place a yellow oil cloth   on this   a bowl
a kneading board   a dull knife   spoons
then draw up an old chair   have a grand-father carve
birds flowers   the child likes to trace sweep of petals
curve of wings   to tease a finger along
edges softened by age   and numberless polishings
the initiate kneels on the seat
afterwards there will be a pattern of cane left
around her neck tie the huge blue apron
so that only her head   thin bare arms are visible
place a five pound milk can painted green
with yellow trim and full of flour
tall salt jar   salt clumping together
fresh grated nutmeg   sugar in a green can
butter in a clay cooler   red enameled
cup brimming with cold water
have someone say "be careful now
don't make a mess"
the child takes one handful of flour   makes a hill
outside a humming bird whirrs   sun gleams
on her hill   she adds another handful   another   another
she makes a careful mountain   lightly walks
her fingers to the top   flattens the crest   old
voice in her ear   *"don't you go making yourself out*
special   now"   she watches as flour sifts down
sides of her mountain   then scoops out a satisfactory
hollow   she can see humming birds at red
hibiscus   beyond   a small boy barefeet
on the plum tree his voice shrilling king
of the mountain threats   old voice eggs him on
into the hollow   Daughter   put a pinch of salt
a little sugar for each handful of flour
as much butter as can be held in a nutshell
"ready" she calls   waits
even if she looks straight ahead she still sees

from *Drawing Down A Daughter*   81

from the corner of her eye   lamps   their bowls full
gathering sunlight   the way girls should
waiting patiently for evening
behind her there is always some one preparing pastry
on a grey marble-topped table
the rolling pin presses dough   thinner
and thinner towards round edges
maker pushing pastry
to transparency   ices
the pin folds pastry over butter
begins again   finally that last stretching roll
till it seems skin must break into a ragged O
she is rigid with apprehension   this
is something to do with her
so she does not hear the voice over her shoulder say
"drizzle this baking powder all over"
handing her a spoon   until she is tapped lightly
starts to the chorus   "this child always dreaming yes
but what you going to do with her".
her mother saying ever so carefully "let her dream
while she can" she begins to knead
butter into flour   the mother sprinkles grated lemon
peel   and when she has crumbs she makes another hollow
adds water while someone clucks warnings
she begins to knead the whole together
not forgetting the recurring dream in which she climbs
through a forest of leaves she kneads   stepping
bravely from branch to branch   miles above ground
she kneads and kneads trying to make it smooth
she finds a bird that talks
but flies away just as she is beginning
to understand   she kneads   finally someone says
"that's good enough" she kneads just a little more
she is watching the bird   which is flying
straight into the sun
                        where it lives bravely
a rum bottle full of water is thrust into her hands
which she must wash again   then flour the bottle
to roll out her dough which she has made into a ball

outside the high-pitched yelling of small boys at cricket
she is better at cricket than at bakes
she will never be as good at bakes as her mother is
or her aunt   or her great aunt   or her grandmother
or even the kitchen maid who is smiling openly
because the child's bakes are not round
her mother says gently "I'll show you a trick"
she rolls the dough out for her again   takes a glass
cuts out perfect rounds of bakes
together they lay them out on a baking sheet
"we'll decorate yours with a fork   dad will be proud"
together they cover her bakes with a wet cloth
when the oven is ready her mother will test the heat
sprinkling water on a tin sheet

■

It is a matter of fact that the girl waits till the man from the capital begins to dress before she asks diffidently, "Where you leave your car?"

Burri buttons his shirt carefully before he replies, "It on the other side, near the big house. It park round the bend near the temple. Why you ask?"

"We could go for a drive."

"We could go for a drive!" He smiles. "Jocelyn, you ain't see how late it is? What your mother go say, girl?" His smile broadens, he strikes a pose and asks again, "You want she coming after me with a cutlass?"

"Well we have to talk."

"Eh, eh! I thought we was talking. What you have to say you can't say here?" He is laughing as he says this.

"It too late to stay here . . . I can't afford to catch cold!"

With a flourish, "Here, put on my jacket." Then seeing her seriousness, "You see how warm you get." His arm goes around her shoulders. He nibbles on her ear and chuckles.

"Look, I want to talk!"

"SO, talk!" He still nibbles, moving down the column of her neck, his fingers turn her face away from the river to face him.

"I ain't get my menses this month, again."

"What you saying . . . " he begins casually, then suddenly alert he sits

from *Drawing Down A Daughter*

up. "You ain't get . . . Look girl, what you trying on me?" His voice is rough. His movements abrupt.

"Nothing! Is true. I pregnant."

"Well, that's great! . . . So, you see a doctor? When?"

"I get the results Monday."

He stares at her, frowning.

"I want you to come and see my mother."

He has decided to be cool, "Me! What I want with your mother!" His eyes are wide. He is smiling. He puts his arm around her. "Is you I want." He pats her stomach. "I'll bet is a boy!"

"How we go marry if you ain't talk?"

"Marry!" He is amazed. "Look girl, I ask you to marry me? Is the man does ask!" He scowls, "I ain't ready to marry nobody."

"But ain't you say you love me? What you think my mother go say? Where I go go?"

He is contemptuous. "Is town you go to school? You never hear about tablet? If is mine, ask your grandmother to give you a tea to drink, because I ain't marrying nobody." He begins to gather his things together. He checks his car keys, his wallet. Draws his Seiko on over his wrist.

"But I can't . . . I ain't never . . . nobody . . . "

Now he is gentle again. He takes her hand and seems to think. "Girl, I sorry. Don't do anything yet. I go think of a way. Don't say nothing if you frighten."

"What you mean?"

"A way to fix everything. What? You think I just go leave you?" He smiles, bends to kiss her, straightens, looks around. "But look how late you keep me here! Is a good thing it have moon. How else to see to go through all that bush?"

"When you coming back?"

"Thursday."

The lie trips from his tongue as smooth as butter, and the girl hears it though she is desperate to believe. She stands on the ledge by the falls watching him bound down the hill towards the river. His jacket slung over one shoulder flaps in his lean surefooted grace. He does not look back until he comes to the clump of bamboo before the bend in the river and sets foot on the path. She knows he has turned, because she can see the trim white shirt tucked neatly back into his pants, and the gleaming silver buckle in his belt. He has come to her straight from his clean civil service job in the intimidating red pile of the Legislature. She does not return his wave. But waits to stop the tears that come of their own volition. When she is no longer shuddering, she wipes her face and begins to plan how to get to her room at the back of the house without coming face to face with her mother. Later she will claim a headache. This at least is true. She begins to climb up to the road to the village. Her fingers stray to the medallion dangling against her sore breasts.

Of all this: the river valley, the girl Jocelyn, the pregnancy, Burri as snake, the old storyteller will say nothing. She has no truck with this simple form, with its order and its inherent possibility of justice. Though she speaks the language, she knows the real world where men wander is full of unseen presences, of interruptions, of rupture. In such a world, men have only tricks and magic. When she makes her old voice growl, or rise and fall on the gutter and flare of candlelight, her tale is not only a small meeting: chance and the implacable at the crossroads, i.e. in the individual. Her tale is a celebration, and a binding of community. Her theme is survival in the current of riverlife. Her eyes scan the gathered children fiercely, "You can learn how to deal with life; you cannot avoid what nests in you." There is something of the ancestral, of Africa in this. The children hear. They are polite. They nod solemnly. But their eyes lust after the story.

She laughs in the disconcerting way of old women, lights the candles, orders the electric lights switched off. Now she is ready.

"*See-ah,*" she growls.

"*See-ah,*" the children growl back.

"*See-ah Burri See-ah.*"

"*See-ah Burri See-ah,*" the children sing hugging their knees and moving closer, almost huddling.

It have a man, Burri, he go see he girl by the river and he stay too late. They must have had talk or something because usually he leave while it light because he know about forest, riverbank, and La Diablesse. Well, this Burri, he hurry long through the tunnel form by the arching bamboo. All time he watching the forest, looking round and thing. He ain't really 'fraid, but he know in a few minutes darkness be King. Only moon for light. He ain't running, but he walking real fast. He feel he got to get to the car quick. It seem to him he walking and walking but he ain't getting nowhere. He think perhaps he miss the crossing stones. But he can't see how he do that because it ain't got no turn off. Well, this

from *Drawing Down A Daughter* 85

Burri, he decide to stop for a minute and light a cigarette. Well is who tell Burri do that?

"See-ah Burri See-ah
See-ah Burri Mammy oh.
See-ah Burri Mammy oh," respond the children.

"Crick-crack," says a small boy who wants to get on with the story.

First thing he know he can't find his lighter anywhere. He check breast pocket, breast pocket say, 'check shirt pocket.' He check shirt pocket, shirt pocket say, 'check pant pocket.' He check pant pocket, pant pocket say, 'check jacket pocket.' He check jacket pocket, and jacket pocket say, 'ain't my business if you drop it.'

Is now he in big trouble. Pitch black and no way to make a light. He begin to really hurry, and see heself looking straight into old eye of mappipi zanana. Snake straight and flat on the branch. Now he really begin to run. He run like he mad. Like snake chasing him. Branch catch at him, grass like it want to hold him back. A bird fly straight up out of the ground in front of him flapping and screaming. He running so hard that Burri half-way cross the clearing before he realize it.

He slow heself down. He bend over holding his knee like Olympic runner. When he heart return to he chest, he look back to the mouth of the bamboo grove. He ain't see nothing. He walk on now. He thinking how big and bright the moon. And is so it hanging low over the river. Well, is finally he come to the steppin stones and them. The water low in the river and he ain't think it go be slippery. And he standing there, shivering a little, because like is something cold trying to bind him, when he see a flash of something white. Like it moving in the trees on the other side of the river. Even before she come out in the moonlight he know is a woman. Is so some of those men does be. Anyhow she standing in the open looking frighten, and he see one time she pretty for so. Real pretty-pretty. And she got that high-boned face and full lips like the girl he just leave. Not that he thinking about she. What he thinking is how the moonlight so bright-bright, and how he clothes so mess up with all that running and thing. Instant he begin to fix up he shirt, and he jacket, he even take he tie out he pocket and put it back on.

And all the time he whistling. Like somebody give he something, and he real, real please . . .

"See-ah Burri See-ah
Burri cross de river oh
Burri itch he scratch-oh.

Burri itch he scratch-oh," sang the children happily.

"Crick-crack," says the small boy who knows his role.

The old woman turns to the small boy, "You is man, all you don't have no real sense. Is not only what you see that there." She pauses a moment, "And not all what smell sweet does taste sweet." Then she begins again.

Well, now that he tidy, Burri feel that he is who he is. He walk to the stones and all the whole time he smiling at the girl. He measure the first jump and he start crossing, jumping from stone to stone, and like he showing off a little for the girl. So he look up to see how she taking it, and he see her eyes. They like a lasso. They like a fishline, and Burri hook. He fall. He slip and he fall and feel heself struggling, the water close over he head, he thrash out and kick up, and he know the water ain't deep. But he head butt against sand, he eye open to the green wall of a pool. Current catch him, he toss like twig. His chest heavy and hurting, he see stars, and white light exploding, and red. Sudden he is boy again. This girl, Anita, skin like clay pot, that colour, her hair trailing in the water, her breast buds glistening, she floating on the surface of the river. Fragile and open as if she alone, as if none of the rest of them there. He swim over to her quiet, quiet, then he grab a bud in his mouth. How after the shock she scream and scream, and she grab his head and hold it down in the river bottom. How the thin wiry legs scissor and ride him. How the blood roar in he ears, and the darkness catch him. And then the weight lift and the light break through. How he jump and jerk and fight the line, the hooked finger. And how in the end he flop on the bank. How he lungs burn in the moonlight and water pour from eyes, nose, mouth. Meanwhile the woman just standing there under the cocoa. She ain't say nothing. He land on the riverbank at she feet where the skirt circle her in a frothing green frill.

Well, Burri fright leave as he see the woman kind of smiling, like she just too polite to laugh out loud. So now he start to feel stupid for so! But the girl bend down and give he a hand, and he stand up, and she say real nice, "You ain't careful, you catch cold!"

He just nod he head. Burri no fool, he figure he go let she do the talking and just nod and thing. He know if she start feeling sorry for him, he set. And right away he want to know she real, real well.

"You have far to go?" she voice have this sweet lilt.

Burri say, "It quite town I have to go!" He shiver a little bit then he say, "Is only my chest I 'fraid."

from *Drawing Down A Daughter*

"You could come by me and dry out. Is only my grandmother there." And she smiling real sweet, and her voice like she promising something.

Burri ain't stop to ask heself how come a girl standing out there in the moonlight by sheself. He ain't ask heself how come he feeling so happy all of a sudden. He feeling happy, he just feel happy. And the woman herself, she just looking prettier and prettier. The woman self, she too happy because normally she does have to beg, but this one he just coming with her easy-easy.

"See-ah Burri See-ah." The old woman is drumming on her knees.

"See-ah Burri See-ah." The boy has got a bottle an' spoon.

"See-ah Burri See-ah
Burri lock in a box oh
What lock he in, can't open oh."

Knees bent, turning slightly sideways, the old lady does a calypso shuffle, *"What lock he in, can't open oh."*

Arms waving, pelvis shifting, the children dance around the room.

"What lock he in, can't open oh
See-ah Burri See-ah."

The boy gets tired of the bottle an' spoon. He decides to assert control.

"Crick-crack," he says. And again, "Crick-crack!" The old lady sighs, sits. The children collapse at her feet. The old lady eyes the boy. "Your pee ain't froth, you can't be man," she says. The boy's eyes go round with surprise. The girls giggle. The old lady is talking rudeness! For a moment her voice crackles as she picks up the tale.

Well now, Burri, he going up the hill with the lady. And he noticing how sweet she smelling, like is flowers. And how she turn she head, and walk a little sideways. He thinking how lucky he is. And how he never realize Lopinot have so many pretty girls. His head so full a plans for the girl, he never notice she limping until they get to the car. Is when playing real gentleman he open the car door for she that he see the funny foot. Still his mind ain't tell him nothing. Is so when you talking love you don't see what you don't want to see. Burri get in the car, take out he car keys, and say to the girl, real formal, "So where do you live Miss . . . ?" and he kind of pause like he waiting for she to give he a name, but she ain't say no name. She just give him directions for a road near the ravine. The ravine about a mile and a half up the road. Burri thinking is so she want to play it? If she ain't give me a name, I ain't giving she one neither. He look at she sitting there beside him, and he thinking how smooth she skin, and he wondering what she grandmother going to say, and he hoping she real old. Perhaps is thinking of old that make he think of death. Anyway it suddenly hit him what the scent in the car remind him of. Is how the house smell when they bring all the wreaths for his mother funeral. Burri really love he mother now she dead. Just thinking about her could bring tears to his eye. The girl ain't saying nothing. She just sitting there smiling to sheself private like. Burri car have signal in the engine. But he begin to do show-off drive. He open the car window and begin to make pretty-pretty signal with his whole arm. Then he reach for he cigarettes. As soon as she see the cigarette, she begin to frown. She say "That does make me sick, yes?"

Burri forget all about he wet clothes, which practically dry by now. He thinking this woman bold, yes! She ask me for a lift. Now she telling me I can't smoke in my own car! Is right now to see who is boss.

He say, "The window open, you don't see?" But she smart too. Quick as crazy ants her hand move to the dashboard, and she grab the extra lighter he does keep there. All the time she laughing like is joke. Burri ain't think is joke, but he laugh like he think is joke.

He smiling and he smiling, but he mind working overtime. "God!" he say, "but you stubborn yes! And in my own car too?" Is because he was looking at her that he see she face slip a little when he say "God!" He think, "I ketch! Now is Lawd help me!" And he see she face. He see it slip. And she put she hand up to hide it, and he grab the lighter from she. The whole car filling up with the scent of dead flowers. And he light the cigarette.

"Ah, Burri!" the children exclaim.

"So what you think happen next?" the old lady asks. She is relaxed, at ease.

"You lucky, eh Burri, You lucky."

The children vie with each other in their banshee wailing,

"*I woulda break you neck fuh you*
de devil eat you, Burri."

They try to fill the room with wild laughter.

"Well, then she disappear," the old lady says, "*Is so Burri tell me and now I come here to tell you.*"

A small girl fingers her face. "Ah, Burri," she sighs, eyes busy with the horror of a face slipping. Is it possible to be a La Diablesse and not know it, she wonders, where would you go when they found you out?

from *Drawing Down A Daughter* 89

"But how she sitting here in the dark like that?"
"Girl, turn on the electricity and throw some light on things."

I'll try. But this isn't easy. For one thing, I doubt the ability of anyone to relate a series of facts accurately. For another, I doubt that it is possible to consider any event a fact except in the simplest use of that word. Take, for instance, the laughable, the incontrovertible idea that I am writing this. True, these are my hands that strike the keys. But I have so little control over what is being written that I know the story is writing me. I have been brooding over these events since I rediscovered them in 1983. Once I was determined to write a straightforward narrative. A soupçon of horror. A fiction. Yet this has become an autobiography. Of sorts. And this short paragraph a kick against that fate. For we do not know if any of this really happened. Yet I remember the story being told. I remember the old woman. And I am sure the story was told as I have written it because that is how the books say Afro-Caribbean tales are told. Your books, I mean. But this is not really about style. This is about plot. For, a few years later, seven years after the telling, to be precise, I met John Burian Armstrong.

He was dressed all in white except for a navy shirt. Close-cropped greying hair topped what I was later on to learn was called an ageless face. At the time I thought that in spite of the deep crevasses that ran down to the corner of his mouth, he was young. There I was curled up in my father's chair on the verandah, reading, I am sure, though I am not sure what I was reading. He stood there smiling at me, sucking at his lower lip as if I reminded him of food, and in spite of his cane, or perhaps because of it, managing to look Mr. Cool.

"You must be Mr. Williams's daughter!"

It crossed my mind suddenly to say coldly, "Not really, I'm a La Diablesse in waiting."

Well . . . Not really.

I'm trying for fact. A little artistic licence here, a little there, and the next thing you know I'm writing history.

A few minutes later I heard him say to my father, "I'm John Burian Armstrong. People around here say I should talk to you."

I was not very surprised by this opening. "Talking to my father" was something the villagers did regularly. He was the recipient of their dreams and their fears. As the only educated black man who came to the village regularly, he was frequently asked to help when anything 'official' or unusual came into their lives. Sometimes, perhaps often, the villagers simply needed someone to know what life, or 'they who does run everything' had done to them, again. So when Armstrong introduced himself, my father sat back in his dark mahogany easy chair with the cushioned slats and prepared to listen.

"Oh! So what is it you have to tell me, Mr. Armstrong?"

"Everyone calls me 'Burri'."

"Burri, then."

"Sir what I have to say is God's truth! People say I was drunk. But that time I didn't drink. A drink now and then, yes. But drink to get drunk, no! Not even till today."

It was the name, Burri, that did it. *"See-ah Burri See-ah."* I moved a Morris chair as close to the windows looking on the verandah as possible. Very quietly indeed I prepared to eavesdrop.

"Let me start from the beginning. Is true I get a girl pregnant. Is true I had no mind for marriage. We argue a bit and it get late. I leave her there and I start to walk along the river to get to the path what you cut there from the pool. Nothing so strange happen until I reach the steppin stones. Just before I cross to come to this side I see a girl standing on the bank, she just standing there on this side near the big cocoa tree where the steps begin."

"What time would that have been?"

"About what o'clock? About seven for the latest. I kind of wave to her and I start crossing. Half way I slip on the stones, fall into the water, and the current sweep me in to the little cave it have under the bank near the bend. I really thought I was gone. Every which way I turn I coming up water. Anyway the girl bend over and give me a hand."

"Did you see her do that yourself?"

"Well, Mr. Williams, there wasn't anybody else there! I figure it have to be her."

"Reasonable. But it's always better if you tell me exactly what you know for a fact. Not what you think it must have been."

"Well, when I get back my strength, I start talking and she offer to take me home with her to dry off my clothes. She tell me her mother gone to visit her sister in San Fernando, but the rest of the family, home. I ask her her name and she tell me 'Mera,' is short for 'Ramera.' I tell my name, Burri. Is true I never hear that name before, but they have lots of 'pagnol people living up here, so I ain't surprise."

"And she didn't look like anyone you know? Not even a little? You know how moonlight is tricky."

"To tell you the truth she look a lot like the girl I was seeing. I thought they might have been some relation. But she herself I never see before."

"Go on."

"We come to the top of the road, and as I crossing over to the car I see she limping. I figure is a stone or something and I walk over to the other side. I open the car door and I get in. She tell me where she live and I start driving. The car smelling musty so I roll down the car window. I don't want the girl thinking my car nasty. Mosquitos start coming in the car so I reach for a cigarette. She say smoke does bother her. I reach for my lighter and my hand touch the bible with the Christopher medal my mother put there when I first buy the car. As God is my witness, Mr. Williams, I light the cigarette. The next thing I know the car rushing into the bank and I can't do anything. Sametime I look over, put out my hand, and the woman ain't there. Before the car hit the bank I see the whole thing. The car door stay close but the woman gone!

"The car crumple like somebody fold it up. I wait there half an hour before anybody come. Then they couldn't get me out."

"You never saw her again?"

"I'll tell you. While I was waiting for the ambulance and the police, I tell the people there was a woman in the car. I describe her. They say perhaps she fall out. They look all night. Nobody see anything. Two days later the police come, question me. They say nobody reported missing. Nobody dead."

"You sure you didn't lose consciousness? Sometimes it's hard to tell."

"Well, I'll admit. My doctor tell me so too. So I come up here and I question everybody. Nobody ever hear of the family. Is that what convince me."

"You know you ought to write that down. One hears of these things, but no one ever has first-hand experience."

"But if a thing like that could happen what kind of world is this?" What kind of world indeed! For Mr. Armstrong claimed to have had his amazing experience three years earlier. Four years after the night we had danced wildly around the back verandah chanting:

"De devil eat you, Burri"

First you point out to your sceptical parents that you have never before or since heard the name Burri. Have they? No they haven't. Infected by Newton and the church, they insist on coincidence. You are invited to clean up your imagination, to attend daily Mass. But something lovely has been given to you. A world in which each fact like the legs of runners photographed at slow speeds is an amalgam of variations of itself. Myriad versions of event reaching out of time, out of space, individual to each observer.

It is March, 1954. Though he has friends among the villagers, we never see Mr. Armstrong again. My father, however, has discovered that his cane is merely a matter of fashion. "Just practising," he says, looking at me quizzically, "just practising."

The fiction persists that autobiography is non-fiction. A matter of fact. The question, of course, is what is fact: what is reality. Though the myth of La Diablesse sticks to convention, the stories themselves are specific to a particular event. Is it possible that that old lady bodying forth a world in that long ago August night gave it flesh?

Or was it Burri himself? The power of his experience/delusion stretching both backwards and forwards into time.

Or did the face of reality slip?

Here are the notes I made over thirty years ago for the last half of the story.
(i) In the darkness he slips and breaks his legs.
(ii) The villagers hear him calling in delirium but are convinced that a spirit calls them to doom.
(iii) He calls the girl by name: there is a dream sequence.
(iv) He is found four days later by a hunting pack. Barely alive.
(v) His leg never mends properly. (Serve him right!)

SEQUEL

He changes. Nice girl meets him and falls in love. He refuses to marry her and blight her life because of his leg. Somebody dies and leaves him a million dollars (US). The girl, who is poor, agrees to marry him because her little sister has nearly died from polio. The money helps them to buy better doctors. End on a kiss.

I could have been a romance novelist.

These I know to be facts: the 'Burri' tale; John Burian Armstrong; the Lopinot river; Jocelyn. By stopping here, I am being a purist. It is possible that the writing of this, this telling, began in 1983, when, on one of my rare trips to the island, I set out to visit the old lady, the storyteller of my childhood. I would have gone to see her anyway, but I also wanted to know if there had been an accident; more than that, I wanted to know where her story had come from. She was then 103 years old, this Great Aunt of mine, and she had the telegrams to prove it.

She looked at me cynically and observed, "All you so, ain't know what true from what ain't true!"

"You know. You tell me."

"You don't tell thing so to strangers."

"Come on! I am not a stranger!"

"Overseas water you blood! Don't know if you going or coming! Youself!"

She wouldn't sell me a plot of land either. She owned thirty acres, "All you had and you throw it away!"

But there had really been an accident. That much I had got from her. I discovered that a friend, Dr. Harry Wilson-Janes of UWI, could get me into the *Guardian* morgue. I wanted to find out if Mr. Armstrong's accident had been reported. It had been. Strong black lines to give it prominence. But I found it only by the merest fluke and in a paper dated *five* years after Mr. Armstrong's visit to my father:

> AROUCA – The police are interested in interviewing the woman who was riding with Mr. John B. Armstrong when his car crashed near the half mile post on the Lopinot Road at approximately 7:40 p.m. on Thursday, February 18, 1959. A witness saw a young woman get into the car about 7:36 p.m. You are asked to contact Inspector Jarvis at the Arouca police station. (J. Badsee)

After a few days of dithering, I called the Arouca police station. Inspector Jarvis had retired. But the desk sergeant cheerfully gave me his number at home. Because I didn't have the nerve to ask a retired Superintendent of Police whether he remembered a traffic accident which had taken place twenty-four years earlier, face to face, I decided to phone him. It took me several tries to contact him, but when I did, his voice was strong and clear.

Mine was hesitant. Did he remember the Armstrong accident? He did. He certainly did. Why was I asking? Armstrong had been a friend of mine ... I had been away ... some very funny stories going around. When had the accident taken place? February 1959. He was certain. Had there been another accident in 1954? 1955? No. He was sure of it. Armstrong had had only one accident. God knows he had made it his business to find out everything there was to know about that man. And he went to his funeral in 1980, yes, and made sure to check out the coffin. Did he ever find the woman? That was a funny, funny thing happened there. He remembered it still. Couldn't get it out of his head.

(Here he paused for several minutes to check out my genealogy: Which Williams? Oh, so soandso is your cousin! Which brother was grandfather? Oh, so you relate to soandso!

In some quarters it takes three generations to establish trust. Both sides of the family.)

His next question was direct and much to the point. Did I believe in the old-time things? Convince me. I don't know what I believe. Like everybody else. Silence. W ... ell, it was a long story, he would cut it short for me. When they got to the crash, Armstrong was conscious. Trapped. His legs twisted up. But his mind was clear. He said he picked up this woman and was taking her home when the car crashed. Asked him where the woman was. Funny look come over his face. Said he didn't know. To tell the truth, Jarvis thought it was going to be one of those gruesome cases. He and Sergeant Dick organized village search parties. Lanterns. Torchlight. Flambeaux. Ten groups of three spread out. Nothing. No woman. Next day, dogs and the police teams. Nothing. House to house; signals to every police station in the island. Signals to Tobago, Grenada. Nothing. He and Dick by themselves talked to every woman in the place. All the little tracks and hillhouses. Nothing.

By then the whole place started to panic. Country people. Taxi-drivers refused to drive after dark. Buses breaking down in the garage, come five-thirty. Visiting nurses sicken-off. Pressure! Pressure! He went to see Armstrong in the hospital, and Armstrong told him a strange, strange story. Went back to the accident reports. First thing, no skid marks. Yet that car, folded up like an accordion. De Silva, what own the plantation, he had called the station. Went back to see him. He wasn't there, he talked to his wife. The lady, English. At that time she was only here eight months. The lady didn't know anything about Trinidad. She swear she was sitting on her verandah having a drink after dinner. She, De Silva, and his brother. The car was parked under the hill, round the bend, after that is straight road. They saw the man come out the trees on the river track. They was watching for him. She know the girl young because she very slim, and though she had a limp she walk real queenly. Also she had on a very long skirt with a frill, like she was going to a ball. She thought it was funny to see that in the country, coming out of the bush. You know how those colonist type does think! She said it was bright moonlight.

Then the husband come in. He had hear all the rumours and he was kind of looking at Jarvis funny. Stressing that his wife English. He said they watch the couple get in the car. He stressed how modern they looked together. His wife laughed and said, "Like an advertisement." But then they get serious, and he said they watch the car drive real slow and kind of erratic as if the driver had only one hand on the wheel. Then the car head for the bank. De Silva gave him a queer look and said (he remembers his exact words), "The car head for the bank like it was going home. Quiet and peaceful. It hardly make any noise. The horn blare once and shut off." They stand on the verandah arguing about going down. His brother didn't believe the car crashed. They sent one of their men down to check and he came running back up the hill, shout up is a bad crash. De Silva said he didn't know why he asked him, but he ask his foreman, "How many people in the car?" The man said, "One."

There was a long silence. After a while I said, "Thank you. It's hard to get the truth of such a thing. The facts, I mean." Superintendent Jarvis wished me well. Then he said, "Nobody knows exactly what happen there that night. But is the kind of thing you think is story . . . You have to think is story."

[A version of this story, titled "A Matter of Fact," appeared in Imagining Women *(1988)]*

■ ■ ■

M. NOURBESE PHILIP

Marlene Nourbese Philip was born in Moriah, Tobago, in 1947. She took her first degree in Economics at the University of the West Indies, in 1968, then emigrated to Canada in that year. In 1970, she completed her MA in Political Science at the University of Western Ontario, and in 1973 she received her LLD, also from the University of Western Ontario. Between 1975 and 1982, she practised immigration and family law, but then she gave up the practice of law to devote more time to writing. She is the mother of three children.

Philip has been a contributing editor of the cultural journal *Fuse Magazine* since 1984, publishing there numerous articles on cultural and political subjects. In 1989, she was a member of the non-fiction jury of the Canada Council. From 1989 to the present, Philip has taught courses in creative fiction and women's writing at York University, the University of Toronto, and the Ontario College of Art.

Philip's fiction, poetry, essays, and book reviews have been included in literary magazines such as *Borderlines*, *A Room of One's Own*, and *Matrix*, and in journals such as *This Magazine* and *Brick* as well as in newspapers. Her poetry and stories have been published in a number of anthologies, including *Women and Words: The Anthology* (Harbour Publishing, 1984), *Other Voices: Writings by Blacks in Canada* (Williams-Wallace, 1986), *The Penguin Book of Caribbean Verse in English* (Penguin, 1986), *Imagining Women* (The Women's Press, 1988), *Poetry by Canadian Women* (Oxford University Press, 1989), and *Singularities* (Black Moss, 1990). Philip has given numerous in-person readings, talks, and workshops, participated in conferences, and broadcast on radio and television various interviews, readings, and discussions. She also made *Blood is for Bleeding: The Positive Values of the Menstrual Experience*, a seven-part audio tape completed with the assistance of the Canada Council Explorations Programme.

Philip's first book of poetry was *Thorns* (Williams-Wallace, 1980). Since then, she has published two more books of poems, *Salmon Courage* (Williams-Wallace, 1983), and *She Tries Her Tongue, Her Silence Softly Breaks* (Ragweed, 1989), which was awarded the prestigious Casa de las Americas prize for poetry in manuscript in 1988. A novel for young people, *Harriet's Daughter* (Heinemann, 1988), was a finalist for the Canadian Library Association Book of the Year Award for Children's Literature, the Max and Greta Ebel Memorial Award, and the City of Toronto Book Awards. In 1990-91, Philip received a Guggenheim Award for poetry, and she returned to Tobago to complete a novel. *Looking for Livingstone: An Odyssey of Silence* (Mercury, 1991) is a postmodernist narrative, *Frontiers: Essays and Writings on Racism and Culture* (Mercury, 1992) collects a number of her new and previously published prose work, and *Showing Grit* (Poui, 1993) analyses the presentation of *Show Boat* as a racist cultural phenomenon. Philip continues to write poetry and prose.

Philip names Audre Lorde and St. John Perse as poets who have influenced her own poetry. Prose influences include the work of Thomas Hardy, Sara Maitland, Angela Carter, Patrick White, Olive Senior, and Toni Morrison. She writes, "A strange grab bag, but I would say that Carter and Maitland are two writers whose melding of style/form/content ... particularly in the short story form ... most impresses me. Lastly, but perhaps most importantly, I would mention the Mighty Sparrow as symbolic of the best of the indigenous art forms of Trinidad – the calypso. I mention this because dialect, or the demotic language of Trinidad as I prefer to call it, keeps surfacing in virtually every genre I attempt – short story, prose, and poetry – and it is a continual challenge to keep its vitality on the page yet not lose the widest possible audience. So I must mention the street poets – the calypsonians – as influencing my work."

■ ■ ■

from *She Tries Her Tongue, Her Silence Softly Breaks* (1989)

THE ABSENCE OF WRITING OR HOW I ALMOST BECAME A SPY

I wasn't hard-backed but I definitely wasn't no spring chicken when I started to write – as a way of living my life I mean, although like a lot of women I had been doing it on the quiet quiet filling up all kinds of notebooks with poems, thinkings – deep and not so deep – curses and blessings.

The last thing I expected to end up doing was writing, and

when I upsed and left a safe and decent profession – second oldest in the world, they say – for writing, I was the most surprised person. Is in those growing up years as a child in Trinidad and Tobago that you will find the how, why and wherefore of this take-me-by-surprise change.

If someone had asked me when I was growing up to tell them what pictures came to mind when I heard the word "writer" I would have said nothing. What I wanted to be most of all was a spy, and after reading about spies in World War II, spying was much more real to me than writing. After all there was an Empire and we, its loyal subjects, had to defend it. Black and brown middle class people – my family, short on money but long on respectability, belonged to this class – wanted their children to get "good jobs" and, better yet, go into the professions. Massa day was done and dreams were running high high – my son the doctor! Education was open to everyone, girl and boy alike – my daughter the lawyer! And if your son or daughter didn't manage to get that far, there was always nursing, teaching or accounting. Failing that there was always the civil service.

Some people might say that this was normal since the writers we had heard about – all white – had usually starved and you couldn't say this about doctors or lawyers. Education was going to be the salvation of the black middle classes – so we believed – and a profession was the best proof that you had put servitude behind you, and were becoming more like the upper classes. Writing was no help in this at all.

In high school I was learning and learning about many things – English literature, French history, American history and finally in my fifth year, West Indian history – poor-ass cousin to English history and the name V.S. Naipaul was there somewhere. V.S. Naipaul, writer. It was a sister of his who taught me in high school who first mentioned him to us, her students. But V.S. Naipaul was Indian and, in the context of Trinidad at that time, in the eyes of the blacks, this was a strike against him. V.S. Naipaul the writer we didn't understand or care to understand. Maybe, without knowing it, we were already understanding how he was going to use us in his writing life.

Books for so! I wasn't no stranger to them – they were all around since my father was a headmaster and living in the city meant I could get to the library easily. Books for so! rows and rows of them at the library as greedy-belly I read my way through Dostoevsky, Moravia, Shakespeare, Dickens. Books for so! Other people were writing them. I was reading them.

I wasn't different from any of the twenty or so girls in my sixth-form class. None of them were looking to writing as a career, or even thinking the thought as a possibility. Profession, vocation, career – we all knew those words; we, the black and brown middle classes, scholarship girls whom our teachers were exhorting to be the cream of society, the white salt of the earth. Profession, vocation, career – anything but writer.

Some people are born writing, some achieve writing and some have writing thrust upon them. My belonging is to the last group, coming slowly to accept the blessing and yoke that is writing, and with so doing I have come upon an understanding of language – good-english-bad-english english, Queenglish and Kinglish – the anguish that is english in colonial societies. The remembering – the revolutionary language of "massa day done" – change fomenting not in the language of rulers, but in the language of the people.

Only when we understand language and its role in a colonial society can we understand the role of writing and the writer in such a society; only then, perhaps, can we understand why writing was not and still, to a large degree, is not recognized as a career, profession, or way of be-ing in the Caribbean and even among Caribbean people resident in Canada.

What follows is my attempt to analyse and understand the role of language and the word from the perspective of a writer resident in a society which is still very much colonial – Canada; a writer whose recent history is colonial and continues to cast very long shadows.

Fundamental to any art form is the image, whether it be the physical image as created by the dancer and choreographer, the musical image of the composer and musician, the visual image of the plastic artist or the verbal image, often metaphorical, of the writer and poet. (For the purposes of this essay I will be confining myself for the most part to the concept of image as it relates to the writer.) While, however, it may be quite easy to see the role of image as it relates to the visual artist, it may be less easy to do so with respect to the writer. The word "image" is being used here to convey what can only be described as the irreducible essence – the i-mage – of creative writing; it can be likened to the DNA molecules at the heart of all life. The process of giving tangible form to this i-mage may be called i-maging, or the i-magination. Use of unconventional orthography, "i-mage" in this instance, does not only represent the increasingly conventional deconstruction of certain words, but draws on the Rastafarian practice of privileging the "I" in many words.[1] "I-mage" rather than "image" is, in fact, a closer approximation of the concept under discussion in this essay. In her attempt to translate the i-mage into meaning and non-meaning, the writer has access to a variety of verbal techniques and methods – comparison, simile, metaphor, metonymy, symbol, rhyme, allegory, fable, myth – all of which aid her in this process. Whatever the name given to the technique or form, the function remains the same – that of enabling the artist to translate the i-mage into meaningful language for her audience.

The power and threat of the artist, poet or writer lies in this ability to create new i-mages, i-mages that speak to the essential being of the people among whom and for whom the artist creates. If allowed free expression, these i-mages succeed in altering the way a society perceives itself and, eventually, its collective consciousness. For this process to happen, however, a society needs the autonomous i-mage-maker for whom the i-mage and the language of any art form become what they should be – a well-balanced equation.

When, in the early 1900s, Picasso and his fellow artists entered their so-called "primitive stage" they employed what had traditionally been an African aesthetic of art and sculpture and succeeded in permanently altering the sensibilities of the West toward this aesthetic. In the wake of European colonial penetration of Africa and Oceania the entire art world was, in fact, revolutionized and the modernist art movement was born. These changes did not necessarily increase the understanding or tolerance of the West for Africans and Africa, but people began to perceive differently.

I-mages that comprised the African aesthetic had previously been thought to be primitive, naive, and ugly, and consequently had been dismissed not only by white Westerners, but by the Africans themselves living outside Africa – so far were Africans themselves removed from their power to create, control and even understand their own i-mages. The societies in which these New World Africans lived – North and South America, England, the Caribbean – lacked that needed matrix in which the autonomous i-mage-maker could flourish. The only exception to this is to be found in musical traditions, where despite the hostility of these predominantly white societies, the African i-mage-maker in musical art forms was successful in producing authentic art which has also permanently influenced Western music.

Caribbean society has been a colonial society for a much longer time than not, and the role of the i-mage, i-mage-making, and i-mage control are significant. The societies that comprise the Caribbean identity may be identified by:

(a) a significant lack of autonomy in the creation and dissemination of i-mages;

(b) opposition by the ruling classes both at home and abroad to the creation of i-mages that challenge their i-mage making powers and the status quo;

(c) restricting of indigenously created i-mages to marginal groups, e.g. reggae and calypso.

While changes like independence have improved some of these circumstances both within the Caribbean and within Caribbean societies in the large metropolitan centres overseas, these factors continue to affect the artist and particularly the writer. The tradition of writing for the Caribbean and Caribbean people is a brief one, and briefer still is the Afro-centric tradition in that writing.

■

It is, perhaps, ironic that New World Africans, descendants of cultures and societies where the word and the act of naming was the focal point and fulcrum of societal forces,[2] should find themselves in a situation where the word, their word and the power to name was denied them. Traditionally, for instance, in many West African societies, until named, a child did not even acquire a recognizable and discernible human identity. In the New World after the destruction of the native peoples, Africans would be renamed with the name of the stranger. If what the artist does is create in her own i-mage and *give name* to that i-mage, then what the African artist from the Caribbean and the New World must do is create in, while giving name to, her own i-mage – and in so doing eventually heal the word wounded by the dislocation and imbalance of the word/i-mage equation. This can only be done by consciously restructuring, reshaping and, if necessary, destroying the language. When that equation is balanced and unity of word and i-mage is once again present, then and only then will we have made the language our own.

■

In the accompanying journal I kept as I worked on *She Tries Her Tongue* I write as follows:

> *I am laying claim to two heritages – one very accessible, the other hidden. The apparent accessibility of European culture is dangerous and misleading especially what has been allowed to surface and become de rigeur. To get anything of value out of it, one has to mine very, very deeply and only after that does one begin to see the connections and linkages with other cultures. The other wisdoms – African wisdom needs hunches, gut feelings and a lot of flying by the seat of the pants, free falls only to be caught at the last minute. It calls for a lot more hunting out of the facts before one can even get to the essence, because in almost exact reversal with European culture not much has been allowed to surface – am almost tempted to say that one can for that reason trust that information more.*

I must add now that lack of information bears directly on one's ability to make i-mages.

The linguistic rape and subsequent forced marriage between African and English tongues has resulted in a language capable of great rhythms and musicality; one that is and is not English, and one which is among the most vital in the English-speaking world today. The continuing challenge for me as a writer/poet is to find some deeper patterning – a deep structure, as Chomsky puts it – of my language, the Caribbean demotic. The challenge is to find the literary form of the demotic language. As James Baldwin has written, "Negro speech is not a question of dropping s's or n's or g's but a question of the beat."[3] At present the greatest strength of the Caribbean demotic lies in its oratorical energies which do not necessarily translate to the page easily. Just as the language that English people write is not necessarily or often that which is spoken by them, so too what is spoken in the streets of Trinidad, or by some Caribbean people in Toronto, is not always going to be the best way of expressing it on the page. To keep the deep structure, the movement, the kinetic energy, the tone and pitch, the slides and glissandos of the demotic within a tradition that is primarily page-bound – that is the challenge.

■

While I continue to write in my father tongue, I continue the quest I identified in 1983 to discover my mother tongue, trying to engender by some alchemical practice a metamorphosis within the language from father tongue to mother tongue. Will I recognize this tongue when I find it, or is it rather a matter of developing it rather than finding it? Whatever metaphorical i-mages one uses – discovery or development – the issue of recognition is an important one, since implied within the word itself is the meaning, the i-mage of knowing again. . . .

1. Readers interested in exploring Rastafarian language further are referred to the works of Jamaican writer Valma Pollard.
2. Janheinz Jahn, *Muntu* (New York: Grove Press, 1961), p.125.
3. *Conversations with James Baldwin*, ed. Fred L. Standley and Louis H. Pratt (Jackson: University Press of Mississippi, 1989).

[This is an abridged version of the Introduction to She Tries Her Tongue, Her Silence Softly Breaks *(1989)]*

from *Thorns* (1980)

OLIVER TWIST

Oliver Twist can't do this
if so do so
touch your toe under we go
touch the ground and a merry go round,
and mother oh lady says to jump
mother oh grady says to cry
mother oh lady says be white
mother oh grady says be black,
      brown black
      yellow black
      black black
      black pickney stamped English
singing brown skin girl
stay home and mind baby,
growing up la di dah polite
pleasing and thank you ma'm, yet so savage
      union jacked in red
      in white
      in blue
and dyed in black to welcome Her
tiny hand moving slowly backward
slowly forward
painted smile on regal face
from the stately "buh look how shiny"
black limousine with air conditioned crawl,
and little children faint and drop
black flies in the heat singing
Britons never never never
shall be slaves and
all that land of hope and glory
that was not,
black flies in the heat singing
of Hector and Lysander
and such great names as these,
but of all the world's great heroes

there's none that can compare
with a tow row row row row row
of the British Grenadiers and
little black children
marching past stiffly white bloused
skirted blue
overalled and goin' to one big school
feelin we self look so proper —
a cut above our parents you know,
man we was black
an' we was proud
we had we independence
an' massa day done,
we goin' to wear dat uniform
perch dat hat
'pon we hot comb head
jus' like all dem school girls
roun' de empire
learning about odes to nightingales
forget hummingbirds,
a king that forgot
Harriet Tubman, Sojourner Truth
and burnt his cakes,
about princes shut in towers
not smelly holds of stinking ships
and pied piper to our blackest dreams
a bastard mother, from her weaned
on silent names of stranger lands.

■ ■ ■

FLUTTERING LIVES

    Fluttering lives
  among shuffled papers
  sunstained, sunstarved
  for the earth black blue

        and the poui
blazing on the hungered edge of pain
     yellowing with vengeance
         the frangipani
       scent-pinking the air
    and the earth black blue,

   bubbling larva brown laughter
      black throat eruptions
     brush with delicate green
         the coconut
  that gently palms the clouds
   and the earth black blue,
       fluttering lives
    among shuffled paper

    fierce fluttering lives.

■ ■ ■

JONGWE

Today was
the year of the cockerel
       the dondon weaves a rhythm
Jongwe
       the gongon replies
Now the statesman stalks savage
yesterdays
(the butcher of Salisbury)

today
       the dondon weaves the rhythm
Jongwe
Mugabe crows for yesterday
       the gongon replies
Tubman bleeds

bones gnawed white by truth

the dondon weaves
    we had one dream
a rhythm
    freedom would gift
the gongon
    it could not
replies

we had two dreams
    the dondon weaves the rhythm
yesterday
not one more shall die
    the gongon replies
many and one salted the Atlantic

the dondon weaves
    three dreams
a rhythm
    we had tomorrow
    we would return before
the gongon
replies before
    we sowed the new world
    with the seed of difference
    to harvest a strangeness
beyond
the dondon weaves
redemption

    to labour seven years
the gongon replies
    in the canefields of the soul

the dondon weaves the rhythm
    will you die
for freedom did you die
    for truth

the gongon replies
whose truth
whose freedom

Today
      the dondon weaves a rhythm
was the year of the cockerel
      the gongon replies
Jongwe!

■ ■ ■

BLACKMAN DEAD

The magnum pistol barked
its last command
broke his chest –
red words of silence erupt
silken ribbons of death
wreathe the sullen Sunday morning madness.

A magnum pistol broke the secret
Sunday morning pact,
red roads of silence
lead us
nowhere

but to bury him
bury him
in a plain pine coffin
and repeat after me
how bad he was because,
because he was
just another immigrant
I say repeat
after me
how he deserved to die

because he didn't learn our ways
the ways of death
repeat
after me blackman dead, blackman dead
blackman dead.

as we dress dong
in we tree piece suit
we disco dress
an' we fancy wheels –
dere is a magnum fe each one a we.

Listen me, listen me,
dey say every man palace is 'is 'ome
dat no man is
one hisland honto 'imself
dat if yuh mark one crass
pon yuh door
in blood
all we fus born is safe,

I say repeat
after me
how he deserved to die
because he didn't learn our ways
the ways of death
repeat
after me
blackman dead, blackman dead
blackman dead.

Toronto has no silk cotton trees
strong enough to bear
one blackman's neck
the only crosses that burn
are those upon our souls
and the lynch mobs meet
at Winstons. . . .

Blackman dead, blackman dead,
blood seeps beneath
the subterfuged lie
living as men
how can we die as niggers,
red roads of silence
lead us where
no birds sing
blackman dead
blackman dead
black roses for blackman dead.

■ ■ ■

THREE TIMES DENY

Three times deny their existence
a cock crows lazy,

flapping wings over sagging breasts
an overworked womb

nestling children lies
hatching a death of denials

never suckled
never fed

three times deny now
as then we sell them

then as now
we kill them

three times deny you
to leave
to birth

new lies to forget
the firsts as in
step, smile, laugh
and cry three times
to deny

to enter the maelstrom of lies
to forget that I lied and you
died

that I perfectly pierced each heart
beat through with love
to survive;

No sir, since you asked
I have no children.

■ ■ ■

E. PULCHERRIMA

I came awake –
swimming in a pool of blood
was the poinsetta
e. pulcherrima
Euphorbia Pulcherrima –
most beautiful Euphorbia
the poinsetta

the blood
the red
poinsetta

comes in to her passion
comes in to her own
passes her blood
normally

naturally in the tropic
days and nights of equal length
pools of blood
seeping slowly through
barking backyards
swiftly spreading
her menstrual stain
reddening finicky frontyards
hedges trying to hide
her touch
seducing children
their fingers sticky with her milk
old men
dagger eyes glazed with age
and lust weaned too soon
from her adhesive breasts
until she will be denied no more
before the cock crow breaks
the day into two impossible halves
she sashays into town
has to be forgiven seventy times seven
for that blood
that red
that poinsetta

e. pulcherrima
she bleeds
unseen
uncared for
unloved
untouched
understood and vice versa
"and if you cut her back
before her time of month
she bleeds even more –
just like a woman"

the blood
the red
poinsetta

e. pulcherrima
loosening her red
her blood
laughter over the sun stunned land
the suddenrains shocked into silence
her white sticky milk
gumming up the works
feeding and bleeding
bleeding and feeding

her blood
her red
poinsetta

e. pulcherrima
Euphorbia Pulcherrima
alias Mexican Flameleaf
alias Lobster Flower
alias Christmas Flower

description: a tall bright bush
identifying marks: flames
wanted possibly for imitating
the voice
the passion
the birth and death
the body, the blood of life
her dossier reads
"imitatio christi"
the north fears her
second coming prismed
in all of the above

"all that blood –
that red"

she hears the bloodcall
gives the response
– was the chance of a lifeline –
– to enter –
immediately she calls
into question
the bloodless snows
the shrieking silence
the hollow rings of emptiness
spotting with her blood
she refuses –
refuses to bleed
within
or without
her lover
will not be
unfaithful
will not die
will not bleed

the blood
the red
poinsetta

e. pulcherrima
insists on her rights
to privacy
to darkness
to silence
to blackness
(albeit makebelieve)
all of the above or none
insists on her right
not to bleed
not to feed
for fourteen out of every
twentyfour hours
not to feed or bleed

the blood
the red
poinsetta

e. pulcherrima came awake
in a pool of blood
birth blood
trickling down
thickening thighs
sticky
with her hot milky sap
spilling from broken limbs
milked white
forgot the sticky fingered children
(they were really only stick children)
where were the old men?
forgot her lover
(he came to her for twelve hours at a time)
was forced to bleed
the buds of blood
the blood of red
the blooded poinsetta
an immaculately forced conception
there was no anunciation

only a joyless mating
of light and darkness
in the ice wounded womb
she finally bled
e. pulcherrima

Euphorbia Pulcherrima
also known as
Mexican Flameleaf
Lobster Flower
Easter Flower
Christmas Flower
never as the Bleeding Flower

a tall bright bush
a flame
a woman
e. pulcherrima
she finally bled.

■ ■ ■

from *Salmon Courage* (1983)

ANONYMOUS

If no one listens and cries
is it still poetry
if no one sings the note between the silences
if the voice doesn't founder on the edge of the air
is it still music
if there is no one to hear
is it love
or does the sea always roar
in the shell at the ear?

■ ■ ■

SPRUNG RHYTHM

It was there I learnt to walk
in sprung rhythm,
talk in syncopated bursts of music,
moulding, kneading, distorting, enhancing
a foreign language.
There, family was the whole village, if not island,
and came in all shades of black;
there, I first heard the soporific roar
of the ocean, before I grew ears to hear.

Where fear was wind and wind was fear,
and terror had branches that moved,
swayed, cracked, moaned, hissed ... bent low with the trees
There, the swollen heavy bellied sky pressed
hard against a small hand clutching
a mother's skirt, before the rains came;
and the sun was always certain,
as we were of it.
Where every yellow March, the poui mocked
Sir Walter Raleigh's gesture to his queen,
and spread its coat of sunshine for me,
and the graceful ole time bouganvilla
stroked and brushed heads of boys and girls.
Colour like life was put on
thick with an artist's knife – not brush.
Red was hibiscus, cock's combs and pomeracs,
and Jacob's coat was a hedge of croton.
There, where neat days patiently dovetailed
each other, glued with rituals of purgings,
school, washing and braiding of hair,
Sunday mass and blackpudding breakfasts.
Was it there that I found the place
to know from,
to laugh and be from,
to return and weep from?
Was it there, or was it here?

■ ■ ■

A HABIT OF ANGELS

There is a presence here –
Is it God or
Woman that silently hums
Balanced as a spinning top
In this air?

In te deums of quiet hallways suspend
Around corners blue tails of habits
Vanish, leave an ocean of silence
That laps gently at this presence,
This Woman or is it God?

Along halls night lights glow
With the constancy of glow worms,
Spill comfort and light
Collects in small polished pools
Around this presence, be it God or Woman.

Patient with time, walnut tea wagons wait
With chairs and night tables on cabriolet legs,
All of a voice silently decry the label antique
Belonging to a time past yet extant,
Situate within context and this God
Or Woman presence.

Here reside no ordinary familiar,
Ring around the collar,
Mopping and glowing housewives
But the Brides of Christ;
Without collars, rings, housework or dirt.
Woman of the cloth, not rag, and this presence –
God or Woman.

In this hush harbour of women,
One black Jamaican cleaning lady
Plays Mary to their collective Martha;
As much the conjurer of this presence,
This Woman, this God.

This then is the House of Women,
Spore of a freeze dried religion
That waits in vain for the rains of fertility,
And flees the passionate presence of God
and Woman.

No, here there is no "getting down" to worship –
"Hmmmm Yes Lord Amen!"
But call it God, Woman,
Or merely the habit of angels in the house . . .
There is a Presence here.

■ ■ ■

SALMON COURAGE

Here at Woodlands, Moriah,
these thirty-five years later,
still I could smell her fear.
Then, the huddled hills would not have
calmed her, now as they do me.
Then, the view did not snatch
the panting breath, now, as it does
these thirty-five years later, to the day,
I relive the journey of my salmon mother.

This salmon woman of Woodlands, Moriah
took the sharp hook of death
in her mouth, broke free and beat
her way upstream, uphill; spurned
all but the challenge of gravity,
answered the silver call of the moon,
danced to the drag and pull of the
tides, fate a silver thorn in her side,
brought her back here to spawn with
the hunchbacked hills humping the horizon,
under a careless blue sky.

My salmon father now talks of how
he could walk over there, to those same hills,
and think and walk some more with his dreams,
then that he had,
now lost and replaced.

His father (was he salmon?)
weighted him with the mill stones of
a teacher's certificate, a plot of land
(believed them milestones to where he hadn't been),
that dragged him downstream to the ocean.

Now, he and his salmon daughter
face those same huddled, hunchedbacked hills.
She a millstoned lawyer, his milestone
to where he hadn't been.
He pulls her out, a blood rusted weapon,
to wield against his friends
"This, my daughter, the lawyer!"
She takes her pound of dreams neat,
no blood under that careless blue sky,
suggests he wear a sign around his neck,
"My Daughter IS a Lawyer,"
and drives the point home,
quod erat demonstrandum.

But I will be salmon.
Wasn't it for this he made the journey
downstream, my salmon father?
Why then do I insist on swimming
against the tide, upstream,
leaping, jumping, flying, floating,
hurling myself at under, over,
around all obstacles, backwards
in time to the spawning
grounds of knotted dreams?
My scales shed, I am Admiral red,
but he, my salmon father, will not
accept that I too am salmon,
whose fate it is to swim against the time,
whose loadstar is to be salmon.

This is called salmon courage my dear father,
salmon courage,
and when I am all spawned out

like the salmon, I too must die –
but this child will be born,
must be born salmon.

■ ■ ■

JULY AGAIN

July again, and every Italian house on the block
sports an earsplitting, earth spitting back hoe
that thrusts beneath skirted porches,
seeking cool dank basement secrets,
producing a fallout of cantinas.

July again, and old Queen Vic
raises her jowled head once more.
Fireworks day is what kids call it;
Spinning wheels, rockets, roman candles
fall swiftly charred,
brilliant for one brief moment . . .
like the Empire.

July again, and the hot heavy days
have won yet another war of independence
in the ceaseless struggle of
check – summer,
mate – winter,
in this bye bye lingual,
multied ethnic, mini-climacteric country.

Overnight front porches blossom,
from spinning wheel to begonia,
roman candles to petunias,
like the colonies.

All of a sudden flowers boom
with a hard hot defiance,

unlike this country where subtlety
is always fashionable.

July again,
the mornings, cool and clipped like BBC accents,
seem always to hesitate ...
caught between neither and nor
like Canada.

■ ■ ■

WHAT'S IN A NAME?

I always thought I was Negro
till I was Coloured,
West Indian, till I was told
that Columbus was wrong
in thinking he was west of India –
that made me Caribbean.
And throughout the '60s, '70s and '80s,
I was sure I was Black.
Now Black is passé,
African de rigeur,
and me, a chameleon of labels.

■ ■ ■

YOU CAN'T PUSH NOW

I understood
it knew me knowing it –
the pain that is.
We were on a first name basis
it and I was a woman
of forty and four weeks gestation,

well acquainted with it
snaking its way forbidden,
slithering up, around, between the legs.
It struck –
ONE, TWO, THREE and a quick jab
right between the eyes –
and she's out!
Isis stood to her left,
FOUR
Ta-urt stood to her right,
FIVE
pregnant as a sow.
SIX
Pain spilled to fill
SEVEN
the empty spaces,
EIGHT
grew hydra headed,
NINE
now here, now there,
TEN
And Isis laughed,
Ta-urt belched,
Mountains of muscle convulsed.

And in sorrow thou shalt bring forth children

Her body a foundry of furious energy,
forged stilettos of bright pain.
All things were possible:
it floundered, bunched, trembled,
shook itself,
flexed itself,
shuddered like an eighteen wheeler,
a mack truck of power, it spewed
molten pain fleeing head
long everywhere, anywhere;
stood suddenly still,
fell silent,

was urgently quiet,
grew prosaically dumb.
Isis stood to her left and laughed,
Ta-urt to her right said,
    "Now, for God's sake, push."

The woman in white arrived
(the nightingales were silent),
hawking her cold, liquid comfort.
It came in a tube, dangling
from nowhere
it dripped into nothing,
postponed the coming.
    "You can't push now
    Your doctor's not here
    your doctor
    Can't push
    Your doctor's not here
    Not here! not here! not here!"
Isis stood to her left and laughed,
Ta-urt to her right –
    "For God's sake
    For God's sake push!"
The oxytocin dripped,
the opened vein received it
hungry, greedily –

This is my body
This is my blood

    "But you can't push now
    For God's sake push
    You can't be that bold
    Put the revolution on hold
    You can't push
    Now
    Is not the time
    Starve a while longer
    For God's sake push!"

Laughing, Isis to her left,
Ta-urt to her right
told her why:
listen to the guns birth
hungry bullets seeking
warm flesh to nest
batteries of death.
See the Unknown Soldier known
to all of us. A woman cradles
his head with her tears –
the Unknown Mother, for whom
there have been no graves, no medals,
no cenotaphs, except those of her sons,
shows her bloodied face, bares her
teeth, aspirates the Word and makes it flesh.

But the boys in white were there,
the boys in white are always
there with the words
    "You can't push now
    Your doctor's not here
    You can't bleed now
    Your doctor's not here
    You can't be now
    Your doctor's not here
    You can't even die now.
    And there's always tomorrow
    Lenin
    You can't push now
    Try next week
    Mao
    You can't push now
    Fidel
    Don't yell
    You can't push now
    Mugabe
    How about yesterday?
    You can't push now
    Sweet Jesus! even you

    Can't push now
    Wait for a second coming."

Isis stood to her left
laughing in their faces –
the boys in white that is.
Ta-urt pregnant as a sow,
part crocodile,
part lion,
part hippo,
and all woman,
stood to her right and
belched her approval:
    "For the Goddess' sake push
    Now
    Give us all birth."

■ ■ ■

PLANNED OBSOLESCENCE

Once and for all
to cut
the umbilical cord to the body;
to cut, crush, sear, burn
the twin tubed conduits of life.

Not again the skin stretched taut,
urgent,
not again the waxing moon
belly,
not again to create world in microcosm
and be well pleased,
not again to feel future
in gut.

Words of violence –

cut, crush, sear and burn.
Inner mutilation for outward freedom –
that bodily balance of terror.

The horned womb will weep always
blood.

■ ■ ■

from She Tries Her Tongue, Her Silence Softly Breaks (1989)

AND OVER EVERY LAND AND SEA

Meanwhile Proserpine's mother Ceres, with panic in her heart, vainly sought her daughter over all lands and over all the sea.[*]

QUESTIONS! QUESTIONS!

Where she, where she, where she
be, where she gone?
Where high and low meet I search,
find can't, way down the islands' way
I gone – south:
day-time and night-time living with she,
down by the just-down-the-way sea
she friending fish and crab with alone,
in the bay-blue morning she does wake
with kiskeedee and crow-cock –
skin green like lime, hair indigo-blue,
eyes hot like sunshine-time;
grief gone mad with crazy – so them say.
Before the questions too late,
before I forget how they stay,
crazy or no crazy I must find she.

---

[*] Quotations are from Ovid, *The Metamorphoses*, translated by Mary M. Innes.

■

As for Cyane, she lamented the rape of the goddess... nursing silently in her heart a wound that none could heal...

ADOPTION BUREAU

Watch my talk-words stride,
like her smile the listening
breadth of my walk – on mine
her skin of lime casts a glow
of green, around my head indigo
of halo – tell me, do
I smell like her?
To the north comes the sometimes
blow of the North East trades –
skin   hair   heart   beat
and I recognize the salt
sea   the   yet   else   and ... something
again knows sweat   earth
the smell-like of I and she
the perhaps blood lost –

She whom they call mother, I seek.

■

It would take a long time to name the lands and seas over which the goddess wandered. She searched the whole world – in vain...

CLUES

She gone – gone to where and don't know
looking for me looking for she;
is pinch somebody pinch and tell me,
up where north marry cold I could find she –
Stateside, England, Canada – somewhere about,
"she still looking for you –
try the Black Bottom – Bathurst above Bloor,

Oakwood and Eglinton – even the suburbs them,
but don't look for indigo hair and
skin of lime at Ontario Place,
or even the reggae shops;
stop looking for don't see and can't –
you bind she up tight tight with hope,
she own and yours knot up in together;
although she tight with nowhere and gone
she going find you, if you keep looking."

∎

When kindly day had dimmed the stars, still she sought her daughter from the rising to the setting sun. She grew weary with her efforts and thirsty too...

THE SEARCH

Up in the humpback whereabouts-is-that hills,
someone tell me she living – up
there in the up-alone cocoa hills of Woodlands,
Moriah, with the sky, and self, and the bad bad of grieving;
all day long she dreaming about wide black nights,
how lose stay, what find look like.
A four-day night of walk bring me
to where never see she:
is "come child, come," and "welcome" I looking –
the how in lost between She
and I, call and response in tongue and
word that buck up in strange;
all that leave is seven dream-skin:
sea-shell, sea-lace, feather-skin and rainbow-flower,
afterbirth, foreskin and blood-cloth –
seven dream-skin and crazy find me.

∎

... the earth opened up a way for me and, after passing deep down through its lowest caverns, I lifted up my head again in these regions, and saw the stars which had grown strange to me.

DREAM-SKINS

Dream-skins dream the dream dreaming:
(in two languages)

Sea-shell

            low low over the hills
                  she flying
           up up from the green of sea
           she rise emerald
                 skin
                 fish belt
          weed of sea crown she

Feather-skin

           lizard-headed
             i suckle her
             suckling me
                 flat
           thin like the
                 host
           round and white
               she swells enormous with
           milk and child

Sea-lace

            in one hand the sun
           the moon in the other
            round and round
         she swing them from chains
           let fly till they come
             to the horizon
              of rest

Rainbow-flower

        six-limbed
     my body dances
              flight
from her giant promises
  she reaches down
               gently
    snaps my head
  a blooded hibiscus
    from its body
      crooning
she cradles the broken parts

Afterbirth

one breast
       white
the other black
      headless
in a womb-black night
a choosing –
      one breast
neither black
nor white

Foreskin

  a plant sprouts there –
   from the mouth
       mine
wise black and fat she laughs
 reaching in for the tree
  frees the butterfly
     in-lodged
  circles of iridescence
      silence

Blood-cloth

                  wide wide
                 i open my mouth
                          to call
           the blood-rush come up
                              finish
           write she name
           in the up-above sky
           with some clean white rag
           she band up my mouth
                  nice nice

Blood-cloths
(dream in a different language)

            sand
              silence
                 desert
                     sun
the wide of open mouth
    blood of rush
    hieroglyphs
    her red
    inscriptions
    her name
    up-above sky
                    sudden
  clean of white
              cloths
  wounded mouth
broad back
            hers
to tie
  carry
  bear

"the voice, the voice, the voice"
    she whispers
    she walks
    she whispers
        ceaselessly

Ceres knew it (Proserpine's girdle) well, and as soon as she recognized it, tore her dishevelled hair, as if she had only then learned of her loss: again and again she beat her breast.

SIGHTINGS

Nose to ground – on all fours – I did once
smell that smell,
on a day of once –
upon a time, tropic with blue
when the new, newer and newest of leaves compete,
in the season of suspicion she passed,
then and ago trailed the wet and lost of smell;
was it a trompe d'oeil –
the voice of her sound, or didn't I once
see her song, hear her image call
me by name – my name – another sound, a song,
the name of me we knew she named
the sound of song sung long past time,
as I cracked from her shell –
the surf of surge
the song of birth.

∎

For behold, the daughter I have sought so long has now at last been found – if you call it "finding" to be more certain that I have lost her, or if knowing where she is is finding her.

ADOPTION BUREAU REVISITED

blood-spoored
the trail follows
        me
following her
      north
           as far as not-known
          I trace it

              dream-skins dream
                     the loss
              ours and ancient
               unfelled tears
                   harden
           in the sun's attention
                  diamond
      the many-voiced one of one voice
                    ours
        betrayal and birth-blood
                unearthed

Something! Anything! of her.
She came, you say, from where
she went – to her loss:
"the need of your need"
in her groin

                 the oozing wound
              would only be healed
                on sacred ground
                  blood-spoored

     the trail . . .
            following
    she

            follows . . .

           ■ ■ ■

DISCOURSE ON THE LOGIC OF LANGUAGE

WHEN IT WAS BORN, THE MOTHER HELD HER NEWBORN CHILD CLOSE: SHE BEGAN THEN TO LICK IT ALL OVER. THE CHILD WHIMPERED A LITTLE, BUT AS THE MOTHER'S TONGUE MOVED FASTER AND STRONGER OVER ITS BODY, IT GREW SILENT – THE MOTHER TURNING IT THIS WAY AND THAT UNDER HER TONGUE, UNTIL SHE HAD TONGUED IT CLEAN OF THE CREAMY WHITE SUBSTANCE COVERING ITS BODY.

English
is my mother tongue.
A mother tongue is not
not a foreign lan lan lang
language
l/anguish
  anguish
– a foreign anguish.

English is
my father tongue.
A father tongue is
a foreign language,
therefore English is
a foreign language
not a mother tongue.

What is my mother
tongue
my mammy tongue
my mummy tongue
my momsy tongue
my modder tongue
my ma tongue?

I have no mother
tongue
no mother to tongue
no tongue to mother
to mother
tongue
me

I must therefore be tongue
dumb
dumb-tongued
dub-tongued
damn dumb
tongue

EDICT I

Every owner of slaves shall, wherever possible, ensure that his slaves belong to as many ethno-linguistic groups as possible. If they cannot speak to each other, they cannot then foment rebellion and revolution.

Those parts of the brain chiefly responsible for speech are named after two learned nineteenth century doctors, the eponymous Doctors Wernicke and Broca respectively.

Dr. Broca believed the size of the brain determined intelligence; he devoted much of his time to "proving" that white males of the Caucasian race had larger brains than, and were therefore superior to, women, Blacks and other peoples of colour.

Understanding and recognition of the spoken word takes place in Wernicke's area – the left temporal lobe, situated next to the auditory cortex; from there relevant information passes to Broca's area – situated in the left frontal cortex – which then forms the response and passes it on to the motor cortex. The motor cortex controls the muscles of speech.

■

THE MOTHER THEN PUT HER FINGERS INTO HER CHILD'S MOUTH – GENTLY FORCING IT OPEN; SHE TOUCHES HER TONGUE TO THE CHILD'S TONGUE, AND HOLDING THE TINY MOUTH OPEN, SHE BLOWS INTO IT – HARD. SHE WAS BLOWING WORDS – HER WORDS, HER MOTHER'S WORDS, THOSE OF HER MOTHER'S MOTHER, AND ALL THEIR MOTHERS BEFORE – INTO HER DAUGHTER'S MOUTH.

but I have
a dumb tongue
tongue dumb
father tongue
and english is
my mother tongue
is
my father tongue
is a foreign lan lan lang
language
l/anguish
  anguish
a foreign anguish
is english –
another tongue
my mother
    mammy
    mummy
    moder
    mater
    macer
    moder
tongue
mothertongue

tongue mother
tongue me
mothertongue me
mother me
touch me
with the tongue of your
lan lan lang
language
l/anguish
  anguish
english
is a foreign anguish

EDICT II

Every slave caught speaking his native language shall be severely punished. Where necessary, removal of the tongue is recommended. The offending organ, when removed, should be hung on high in a central place, so that all may see and tremble.

A tapering, blunt-tipped, muscular, soft and fleshy organ describes
(a) the penis.
(b) the tongue.
(c) neither of the above.
(d) both of the above.

In man the tongue is
(a) the principal organ of taste.
(b) the principal organ of articulate speech.
(c) the principal organ of oppression and exploitation.
(d) all of the above.

The tongue
(a) is an interwoven bundle of striated muscle running in three planes.
(b) is fixed to the jawbone.
(c) has an outer covering of a mucous membrane covered with papillae.
(d) contains ten thousand taste buds, none of which is sensitive to the taste of foreign words.

Air is forced out of the lungs up the throat to the larynx where it causes the vocal cords to vibrate and create sound. The metamorphosis from sound to intelligible word requires
(a) the lip, tongue and jaw all working together.
(b) the mother tongue.
(c) the overseer's whip.
(d) all of the above or none.

■ ■ ■

THE QUESTION OF LANGUAGE IS THE ANSWER TO POWER

LESSONS FOR THE VOICE (1)

Vowels are by nature either long or short. In the following list the long ones appear in capital letters. These vowels are all shaped predominantly by the lips, though the position and freedom of the blade of the tongue affects their quality.

When practising these words, it is helpful to use a bone prop.

OO   as in how did they "lose" their word?
oo   as in "look" at the spook.
OH   as in the slaves came by "boat" (dipthongal).
AW   as in the slaves were valued for their "brawn."
o   as in what am I offered for this "lot" of slaves?
OW   as in they faced the "shroud" of their future (dipthongal).
OI   as in they paid for their slaves with "coin" (dipthongal).

■

word it off
speech it off
word in my word
word in your word
I going word my word
              begin
the in of beginning   OO   as in how did they "lose" a language.
empires   oo   as in "look" at the spook.
       erect with new
"Make it new"
             he said
"Make it new"
floundering in the old

                but I fancy the new –
                        in everything
            insist upon it
            the evidence of newness
                is
            upon us
OH as in the slaves came   without nigger   slave   coolie
    by "boat."   the wog of taint
AW as in they were valued   the word
    for their "brawn."   that in the beginning was

                                                – not his
                    I decree it mine
                                    at centre
                    soft
                    plastic
                    pliable
                            doing my bid as in
                                                smash
                    the in-the-beginning word
                                                centre
                    it at open
                            clean-split

                    ■

FACTS TO REMEMBER

(1) Words collect emotional and physical responses.

(2) The larger the space, the more weight and friction is required on the consonant.

(3) Intention, sound and word together produce clarity.

(4) Anxiety to convey meaning often results in over emphasis and emphasis as a way of conveying meaning means that you are unconsciously holding on to meaning and limiting it.

(5) When you reach down for the sound, it is touched off like a drum; it releases itself and reaches as far as you wish. The sound is there to back the word.

                    ■

                            to reveal the heart
                                              pulse
                            that betrays as lover
                                                 as
                            weapon

jerk it
dove it
stew it
cook it
     down
run it down slow
run it down tender
  till it come to do the bid in
we
   this chattel language   o *as in what am I offered for this*
      babu english   *"lot" of slaves.*
      slave idiom   OW *as in they faced the "shroud" of*
      nigger vernacular   *their future.*
      coolie pidgin   OI *as in they paid for their slaves*
      wog pronunciation   *with coin.*

(I say old chap how goes it, what ho?)

this lingua franca
arrrrrrrrgot of a blasted soul

■

(HELPFUL QUESTIONS AND COMMENTARY)

(1) *Within the holds of the slave ship, how much weight and friction would be necessary to convey the meaning of life?*

(2) *Intention, sound and word of death would come together with astonishing clarity to banish anxiety – anxiety to convey the meaning of life.*

(3) *By holding on to the meaning of life, did the slaves unconsciously limit it – or merely the word?*

(4) *How far down would they have to reach for a sound that would banish the future, restore the past and back their word in the present?*

(5) *Do words collect historical responses?*

■

"The word, the word"
                             the Red Queen screamed

"Banish the word
Off with its head –
The word is dead
The word is risen
Long live the word!"

"Oh dear, oh dear," said Alice, "what will Tigger and Pooh and Eeyore and Mrs. Tiggy Winkle think of all this kerfuffle. She does carry on so – that Red Queen."

■ ■ ■

SHE TRIES HER TONGUE; HER SILENCE SOFTLY BREAKS

    All Things are alter'd, nothing is destroyed
           (Ovid, The Metamorphoses, trans. John Dryden).

the me and mine of parents
the we and us of brother and sister
the tribe of belongings small and separate,
when gone . . .
on these exact places of exacted grief
i placed mint-fresh grief coins

sealed the eyes with certain and final;
in such an equation of loss tears became
a quantity of minus.
with the fate of a slingshot stone
loosed from the catapult pronged double with history
and time on a trajectory of hurl and fling
to a state active with without and unknown
i came upon a future biblical with anticipation

■

It is important, when transplanting plants, that their roots not be exposed to the air longer than is necessary. Failure to observe this caution will result in the plant dying eventually, if not immediately. When transplanting, you may notice a gently ripping sound as the roots are torn away from the soil. This is to be expected: for the plant, transplanting is always a painful process.

The Practical Guide to Gardening

■

seek   search and   uproot
the forget and remember of root words
uncharged
          pathways electric with the exposed lie
circuits of dead
          currents of still
                words
synapses of unuse and gone
                words
wordless
       in the eden of first sin
               and
naked

■

1. *The limbic system along with the hypothalamus, hippocampus, amygdala, fornix and olfactory bulb rule the basic drives for food, sex and survival.*
2. *The limbic system or primitive cortex plays a significant role in emotions; it is indispensable in the formation of memory.*
3. *Human memory may be either immediate, short-term, or long-term.*
4. *The cerebral cortex is the storehouse of our memory – it makes us human.*
5. *What we choose to store in our long-term memory is closely linked to our emotions.*
6. *Memory is essential to human survival.*

                        Facts to Live By and Die

■

without the begin of word
grist in a grind and pound of together
in the absence of a past mortared with
                        apart
the harsh husk of a future-present begins

■

. . . and the big bad wolf came and said,
  "Little pig, little pig let me in."
  "No, no, not by the hair of my chinny chin chin."
  "Then I'll huff and I'll puff and I'll blow your house in."
  The wolf huffed and puffed and he huffed and puffed and couldn't blow the house down.

  The first pig built his house of straw; the second of wood. Did the third pig buy his bricks or was he given them, and why? Where did he get his money to buy his bricks with?
  Straw, wood or brick. The moral of this tale, is that the right choice of materials secures safety.

                  How to Build Your House Safe and Right

■

oath   moan   mutter   chant
         time grieves the dimension of other
babble   curse   chortle   sing
         turns on its axis of silence
praise-song   poem   ululation   utterance
         one song would bridge the finite in silence
syllable   vocable   vowel   consonant
         one word erect the infinite in memory

■

... the day of Pentecost was fully come ...
And suddenly there came a sound from heaven as of a rushing mighty wind, and it filled all the house where they were sitting.
And there appeared unto them cloven tongues like as of fire, and it sat upon each of them.
And they were filled with the Holy Ghost, and began to speak with other tongues ...
... every man heard them speak in his own language.

         The Acts of the Apostles *2:1, 2, 3, 4, 6.*

■

absencelosstears   laughter   grief
in any language
         the same
only larger
         for the silence
                 monstrosity
obscenity
tongueless wonder
blackened stump of a tongue
                 torn
out
     withered
     petrified
                 burnt

on the pyres of silence
a mother's child foreign
                            made
by a tongue that cursed
                     the absence
in loss
tears   laughtergrief
                  in the word

■

. . . and if a stranger were to touch her newborn child, the mother will have nothing to do with it. She can smell the stink of the stranger on her child and will refuse to suckle it, believing the spirit of her child to be taken by the stranger.

De Matribus et Advenis *(On Mothers and Strangers)*

■

I do not presume to come to this thy table
father forgive
most merciful father, trusting in my own righteousness
foreign father forgive
but in thy manifold and great mercies
forgive her   me   this foreignness
I am not worthy so much as to gather up the crumbs under thy table
forgive me this dumbness
but thou art the same Lord, whose property
this lack of tongue forgive
is always to have mercy
                      upon
                                      this
                          thisthisand this
                                   disfigurement this
                                                  dis
                        memberment
                                this
                                  verbal crippling
                                              this

        absence of voice
                        that
     wouldnotcould not

■

Kyrie eleison
Christos eleison
Kyrie eleison

Is it in the nature of God to forgive himself –
For his sin?

                  The Book of unCommon Prayer

■

Hold we to the centre of remembrance
that forgets the never that severs
word from source
and never forgets the witness
of broken utterances that passed
before   and now
breaks the culture of silence
in the ordeal of testimony;
in the history of circles
each point lies
along the circumference
diameter or radius
each word creates a centre
circumscribed by memory . . . and history
waits   at rest always

still at the centre

■

history, n – *L. historia, "narrative, story, narration, account," from Gk... "learning by inquiry, knowledge obtained by inquiry; account of one's inquiries; narration, historical narrative; history..."*
memory, n – *ME. memoire, fr OF. memorie (F. Memoire), fr. L. memoria, "memory," fr. memor, "mindful," which stands for *me-mor, and derives from I.-E. *mer-(s)mer-, reduplication of base *(s)mer-, "to care for, be anxious about, think, consider, remember..."*
Cp. memoir, commemorate, remember. Cp. also martyr, mourn, smriti.

Klein's Comprehensive Etymological
Dictionary of the English Language

Without memory can there be history?

■

That body should speak
When silence is,
Limbs dance
The grief sealed in memory;
That body might become tongue
Tempered to speech
And where the latter falters
Paper with its words
The crack of silence;
That skin become
Slur   slide   susurration
Polyphony and rhythm – the drum;
The emptied skull a gourd
                                      filled
With the potions of determine
That compel the split in bridge
Between speech and magic
Force and word;
The harp of accompaniment the ribcage
Strung with the taut in gut;
Flute or drumstick the bones.

> When silence is
> Abdication of word   tongue and lip
> Ashes of once in what was
> ...Silence
> Song   word   speech
> Might I...like Philomela...sing
>   continue
>   over
>   into
>
> ...pure utterance

■

...and on the day of the great salmon run, the first salmon caught is cooked and shared among the elders – men and women. The oldest woman of the tribe, accompanied by the youngest girl-child, then goes down to the waters and returns the skeleton whole to its watery home. This is the way the tribe ensures future gifts of winter food.
                                                       Of Women, Wisdom, Fishes and Men

■ ■ ■

from *Tessera* (1989)

WHOSE IDEA WAS IT ANYWAY?

From fireplace to desk – up and down – round and round – first the desk, next the room – back to the fireplace again he paces. The room is large, well appointed with furnishings that underscore and emphasize the owner's stability and comfort – his wealth even. Velvets; brocades; the gleam of polished wood; silver, even some gold, are all in abundance. Before the fireplace is the rug, in all likelihood Persian, but certainly of the Orient; the intensity and depth of its colours: red, sepia, burnt sienna, beige and black are held in perfect balance by its intricate patterning. It muffles his footsteps, provides further evidence, if any is needed, of wealth.

On the panelled walls hang paintings which further bespeak their owner's station in life. The fire's energy is caught and reflected in the occasional glint of gold leaf that frames the novelty and lustre of the still-new medium, oil. Portraiture: a group of plump women in diaphanous clothing; still life: a bottle of wine – the darkest of green – luminescent, a glass, some fruit with the sheen of freshness still upon them, pastries... all eternally ready to be consumed; landscape: a hayfield and in it a hayrick silhouetted against a red setting sun; classicism: Actaeon fleeing his hounds and the beautiful Artemis; biblical: a woman – Mary Magdalene – in deep meditation, her hand upon a skull; every genre is represented. There are, as yet, no Raphaels, Titians, or da Vincis; no Pisanellos or Caravaggios; those will undoubtedly come later. For the present these are the lesser works of lesser masters, and their illusion is better served by the firelight. Their purpose is to reflect back to him who paces, as nothing else does, his solidity, his wealth, his burgeoning power – his being.

The desk, fashioned from a dark wood – mahogany perhaps – and richly coloured, faces the fireplace; its polished surfaces gleam in the fire and lamp light. As befits the man who paces, it is a large desk; on it rests a globe – a Martin Behaim globe – a hymn book, a psalter, a book of arithmetic and Ptolemy's *Geographia*.

Every so often the man interrupts his pacing to stand before the globe, and, with the tip of his right index finger he sets it spinning – gently almost at first – only to increase its speed until its outlines are a mere blur. He laughs. Abruptly he uses the flat of his palm to stop the revolutions – the globe shudders and trembles under the impact of the sudden arrest.

Can we put an exact date to the man's pacing? A time? The fire and the light through the window suggest a dying day. Did he, that morning, leap out of bed with an exclamation, a shout as of surprise or discovery – of excitement? He might perhaps have echoed Archimedes – "εὕρηκα! Eureka! I have found it!" An idea the equal of Newton's discovery of the principle of universal gravitation; Galileo's discovery of the Milky Way; Copernicus' centring the motionless sun at the heart of our galaxy; the "*cogito ergo sum*" of Descartes. Such an idea, such a thought, such a plan that would – but as yet he had no idea of its enormous potential.

Who was he? A man, of course. Neither peasant nor serf – a nobleman perhaps – possibly a lord. Would a nobleman have sullied his thoughts with an idea so crass, yet so utterly brilliant? Spanish, Portuguese, English, French – was he any of these things? Does it matter? He was European – undoubtedly manifesting the European mind long before the word "European" would come into vogue. Some no doubt called him blessed – a genius; generations of mothers' sons and daughters would curse him, unknown that he was, into eternity. Too many and too few would die; too many and too few live out the diabolical plan that would change the world to come... and forever. Philosophy, medicine, jurisprudence, economics – no discipline would be left untouched; anthropology and craniology – new branches of knowledge would develop to manage the unmanageable.

Was it an idea that was solely his, or were there several like him, within his own nation and without, who would serendipitously conceive and nurture the same idea at the same time? An outburst – a veritable epidemic – of synchrony; a natural effervescence within national psyches that collectively manifested itself in these isolated instances of Promethean thought.

Were they all men who had risen with the morning sun from their beds of linen sheets, laundered by the many hands of their many female servants; men who had then washed themselves perhaps, dressed or were dressed – noblemen or good solid burghers; merchants with an eye for profit? Did they then shake their wives awake and, with a quietly controlled excitement, say in unison: "Listen my dear; écoute ma femme; oiga mi esposa; listen, listen, I have an idea," or perhaps, "I had a dream... last night... a dream, a cauchemar in which I saw one hundred thousand ships ... at anchor... under sail..."

They – these women – would have listened, as they had always listened to everything their husbands had to say – eyes widening under the import of what he told them – the brilliant simplicity of it all – seeing in their mind's eye larger houses, mansions perhaps, more servants, gold, jewels. Such an idea! And did he, did they then, wives and husbands all, embrace their children, flaxen or dark-haired, downy skin still damp and soft with sleep? Did he caress their youth, their innocence – their years not yet burdened with age, with doubt... with ideas, the infinity in their gaze turned toward history – not saying much, but transferring to them his excitement – his sin perhaps? Or was it merely business?

Did he not circle? no – that would come later, but did he not note the date, record it in his diary as he would have any event on his freehold estate, or at his business? On such and such a day, in the year of our Lord, I conceived – no – the idea came upon me – no – I saw clearly how – ... *On the sixth day of January, fifteen hundred and thirty-five, A.D.*, he might have written, or if he wished to reveal his learning, *anno domini*, or *le huitieme jour d'Aout, the fourteenth day of March, fifteen hundred and two, in the year of our Lord* – he could just as easily have written fifteen hundred and three, fifteen hundred and twelve or fifteen hundred and sixteen – *I sat at my desk*, he would continue, or, *walked in my garden admiring the roses of an evening; I sat drinking port after dinner on the evening of ... ; just before I rose from my bed ... ; while at prayers in the chapel ... as the reverend father ... during the Te Deum Laudamus, or was it the Nicene Creed ... a blinding flash of light, a sound as of rushing wings or water, a low murmur ... almost ... a susurration of voices ... a clap of thunder and there it was* – the idea. A brilliant insight it might have been called four centuries later – like Einstein's ... *mine eyes have seen ... the fusion of past, present, and future – change. ...*

It would have wanted for any competition – an idea such as this – had it been nurtured amid smoke, grime and filth, its brilliance and luminescence lighting up, between the picking and killing of fleas, ticks and other vermin, the hovel that wombed it. It demanded light, however, space, leisure ... it demanded wealth.

Wheresoever it happened to have been conceived, it deserved to have been conceived, it deserved to have been reported, recorded, annotated, copyrighted, data banked, chiselled in stone: on ___ the ___ day of ___, fifteen hundred and whatever, or maybe it was fourteen hundred (the Portuguese had a monopoly by 1450), but certainly no later than fifteen hundred and eighteen – we know the Spanish crown sanctioned the idea in that year – and most certainly in the year of our Lord.

Board rooms, flow charts, bottom lines – an advertising campaign to rival Coke's and Pepsi's; an idea of such magnitude – in today's world – would call for no less than these, its purveyors pin-striped, tailored – male and female both – blonde, blue-eyed and Christian, for that was the linch pin of the idea. The full and dark flowering of the messianic, crusading spirit of Christianity.

Idea: archetype, pattern, plan, standard of perfection; an idea the plan or design according to which something is created or constructed – 1581.

What was the idea? To prevent further genocide of the Indian (according to Bartholomew de las Casas)? To obtain a cheap source of labour? To convert from human to thing, pagan to Christian, the African?

Transubstantiation: the changing of one substance into another, bread and wine into body and blood... body and blood into thing, chattel, meuble, cosa.

    The bowels of each sailing ship designed for non-human cargo would entomb approximately three hundred Africans per voyage in their own stench and filth for however long it took to sail the Atlantic – Liverpool to the Gold Coast to the Caribbean and back to Liverpool. Equilateral triangle of trade and death. Some estimate as many as fifteen million Africans were brought across the Atlantic. And there are those who say one was too many.
    "Gentlemen, we estimate that on each voyage some of your cargo will be lost – this is unfortunate... and inevitable, but I believe, nay am confident that we can more than recover all of our expenses through our price per chattel at the auction block. I caution you, however, to be very careful when selecting Black ivory for the voyage – be very certain to choose the fittest and strongest – it is the only way to minimize your losses and maximize your profits. If you pack closely enough, each of our sailing ships could hold some four hundred pieces of the Indies, here, you can see for yourselves, I have sketched a picture of how they would lie for maximum use of your space." Black ivory; pieces of the Indies; the idea skulks and hides behind euphemisms.

"But be prepared for losses."

Cuffee	African man of some 30 years – jumped overboard
Quesaba	Negro woman of undetermined years – died this day of wasting illness
Quarshie	Negro man of some 30 years – passed away from dropsy
Abena	Very young woman – under 20 years – taken suddenly by fever
Jumpke	Husband to Abena – consumption, worms, and ague
Obafemi	Negro boy no more than seven years – ague
Ayo	Negro woman – very beautiful – departed this life suddenly
Bem	depted this life on account of convulsion and fits

Did the idea encompass minutiae such as these, or did its purveyor think in broader strokes? the repopulating of not one but two continents recently decimated of its indigenous populations; or of profits: hundredweights of sugar and tobacco, tons of slaves.

"You see, gentlemen," he strode up and down the room, "I have, without a doubt, ascertained that the Old World cannot populate the New – " He has all of their attention now, these well-fed, well-clothed gentlemen sitting around his table nursing their port as he nurses their captured attention. *"Simply put, there are not enough of us."* A low mutter of concern ripples around the table. *"Here on these spreadsheets you may see quite clearly what the population of the Old World is. Our computer projections confirm that there is not one but two continents for the taking, but we need people.* People! Bodies! *Unfortunately the indigenous populations have proven unequal to the task . . . succumbed to illnesses, indulged in useless warfare – "* A murmur of discontent and complaint eddies around him.

"The sine qua non of the development of these areas captured from the heathen and held in the name of our sovereign is the blackamoor, the African if you will. There is nothing which contributes more to the development of the colonies and the cultivation of their soil than the laborious toil of the Negroes – Negro slaves are the strength and sinews of our New World. About that I am certain." The murmur of approval swirls around the table. *"Now gentlemen,"* he got to his feet abruptly, *"a toast,*

I propose a toast," raising his glass and in so doing spilling some of its dark red contents onto the polished surface of the table.

"A toast! a toast!" The words echo around the table as the men get to their feet and hold up their glasses, the cut crystal refracting the lights from many lamps, the dark red liquid in each glass glowing preternaturally as the light is first trapped by it and then released.

"Magnum est saccarum et prevalebit! Great is sugar, and it will prevail!"

"Great is sugar," they all replied.

"To Black Ivory, Pieces of the Indies, and the Negro! To our profits!"

"Hear, hear!" There was laughter; the mood had lightened and was almost celebratory.

The black skin gleamed softly above him in the candle light, tiny globules of sweat beading her breasts. In the muted light it was as if she wore a necklace of crystals, as if she had been dusted all over with crystal droplets. Roughly he buried his fingers in the short cap of hair that curled and clung to her scalp.

"The idea, gentlemen, however, is to populate the continent with workers who have proved themselves able to withstand the work and the heat with minimal costs to their owners. Furthermore, these people are also savages, pagans who have no God. We can Christianize them at the same time as they produce our sugar, our tobacco and our cotton."

"Surely once they become Christians we can no longer enslave them – isn't that gainsaying the teachings of the Good Book?"

The man addressing them smiles. "We shall address that problem if *and* when *it does arise. Until such time our success is assured, gentlemen." They nodded in agreement.*

She had tormented him for months with her body – nothing but a servant – a maid to his wife . . . a savage really. The woman sat astride him, they both panted, she bit on her underlip drawing blood; he reached up and pulled her down so that she half lay, half sat on him his penis lodged deep within her. She washed, cleaned and served them, but oh how he wanted her! Like he had never wanted or desired his wife ... like he had never wanted anyone, or anything for that matter, before or since. And for that reason he hated her, could not reason her away: her smell, her touch. The taste of her! She made him do things he did not want to do and having done them he wished to repeat them again and again. Things that he had to do, made him no better than a rutting beast in the fields – like she was. Brought him to his knees before her, her beauty and ... their love. The word had risen unbidden to his thoughts and he felt himself flush ... with shame? embarrassment? He loved a savage!

"Gentlemen, I have worked out the figures here – our expenses will be increased because we need to erect and maintain forts to protect our enterprises but at one hundred cowrie shells per head – we may need to include weapons like the Birmingham gun – plus the cost of transportation, and allowing for some loss of cargo, we should be making a profit of one hundred dollars per piece of Black ivory. That is a conservative estimate gentlemen!" His audience smiles and nods in approval; general conversation has broken out around the table. He holds up his hand which commands silence: "Companies are essential to the protection and maintenance of our capital, gentlemen, and we must get to work immediately setting them up."

A plethora of companies: The English Guinea Company, The Senegal Company, The Royal African Company, The British West India Company, The Company of Royal Adventurers, The French West India Company, The Dutch West India Company, The Guinea Company. Each and every one devoted to the idea and ideal of treating human beings as chattels.

Transubstantiation: the changing of one substance into another. Bread and wine into body and blood, body and blood into thing, chattel, meuble, cosa, thing.

Was that where the idea started? To make her a thing – less than he? Less than human. So that he could control her ... and himself. Did that explain his fervour in getting this plan started? urging these ordinarily cautious, respectable men to get involved

– risk! invest! He always managed to control thoughts such as these. Except in his dreams where she comes holding her child – savage – his child – half-savage – their child . . . of their love, crying and begging his mercy and generosity . . . begging . . . as she should.

> *The Bishop strongly recommends that when cargoes of Negro slaves arrive in the harbour, priests should immediately be assigned to instruct them in the Christian faith and to teach them the doctrine of the Church in order to baptize them, and also to see to it that the Negroes hear Mass and go to confessions and communion.*[1]

Surely the progenitor and architect of this idea – if we could but identify him – should take his place alongside those who, like the Portuguese navigators, Cristobal Colon, or Adolf Hitler, have stood in the way of history and altered it.

> *It was a truly wonderful sight to see them all standing there, for some were fairly white and well-formed, some were as yellow as mulattoes, and some were as black as Ethiopians. . . . But who would have been so hard of heart as not to feel pity for them in their distress! Some lowered their tear-splashed faces, others bewailed themselves loudly and turned their eyes to the heavens, and still others struck themselves in the face and threw themselves to the ground. There were those who sang lamentations, and although we did not understand the words, the melodies told of their great sorrow. . . .*[2]

Maybe the idea was happenstance, developed by small accretions of practice – a few here, a few there – as gradual as a meandering river gracefully yet inexorably eroding a shoreline. An idea that was merely the result of the accumulation of capital needing to expand – to create new markets:

> . . . *it is no less than four months since traders took five hundred from Cape Verde to New Spain in one boat, and one hundred and twenty died in one night because they packed*

them like pigs or even worse, all below decks, where their very breath and excrement (which are sufficient to pollute any atmosphere and destroy them all) killed them. It was indeed a just punishment from God that these brutal men who were responsible for carrying them also died. The sad affair did not end there, for before they reached New Mexico almost three hundred died.[3]

A phenomenon of such gargantuan proportions and scale must have been deliberately conceived. By someone, somewhere, sometime: the man stands before the globe; his arms are folded, his head lowered as if in thought. Suddenly he throws his head back, exposing a smooth and cleanly shaven white throat, and laughs again and again. When he stops he sets the globe spinning again with his finger ... waits for the speed of its revolutions to lessen, and with a gentle motion – a caress almost – he brings the globe to a halt. Lightly, at first haltingly, he traces his right index finger down along the newly opened Indian ocean, around – the finger moves more surely now – Bartholomeu Dias' discoveries at the Cape of Good Hope, up ... along the west coast and across – now his finger is fully confident – the varnished ocean, painted blue ... to a new world not yet discovered, but which he would help to birth.

The fire is dying now; its light reddens the outline of his robe all along his right side, bleeds on to his right cheek painting his skin with a sanguinary glow as it embraces his head with its fiery corona. It is hard to tell in the dim light, but his eyes are blue, like the painted ocean, his hair is blonde, his skin fair, and he laughs again and again.

[1] Father Daimen Lopez de Haro, Bishop of San Juan, Report to a Diocesan Synod, San Juan, April 30 - May 6, 1645.
[2] Gomes Eannes de Azurara, Portuguese chronicler (1410 - 1474) *Cronica de Descobrimento e Conquista de Guine.*
[3] Fray Tomas Mercado, *Suma de Tratos y Contratos*, (Seville, 1587).

■ ■ ■

from *Looking for Livingstone* (1991)

THE FIRST AND LAST DAY OF THE MONTH OF NEW MOONS (OTHERWISE KNOWN AS THE LAST AND FIRST MONTH) IN THE FIRST YEAR OF OUR WORD

0300 HOURS

My own map was a primitive one, scratched on animal skin. Along the way, some people had given me some of theirs – no less primitive – little pieces of bark with crude pictures of where they thought I would find what I was searching for. I also had some bones and various pieces of wood with directions incised on them. And a mirror. Where was I going? I had forgotten where I had come from – knew I had to go on. "I will open a way to the interior or perish." Livingstone's own words – I took them now as my own – my motto. David Livingstone, Dr. David Livingstone, 1813-73 – Scottish, not English, and one of the first Europeans to cross the Kalahari – *with* the help of Bushmen; was shown the Zambezi by the indigenous African and "discovered" it; was shown the falls of Mosioatunya – the smoke that thunders – by the indigenous African, "discovered" it and renamed it. Victoria Falls. Then he set out to "discover" the source of the Nile and was himself "discovered" by Stanley – "Dr. Livingstone, I presume?" And History. Stanley and Livingstone – white fathers of the continent. Of silence.

Livingstone now lies buried at Westminster Abbey because he "discovered" and explored Africa, turning what had been "burning solitudes, bleak, and barren, heated by poisonous winds, infested by snakes and only roamed over by a few scattered tribes of untameable barbarians" into "a high country, full of fruit trees, abounding in shade, watered by a perfect network of rivers."

Perhaps he discovered something else – the same thing I search for –

■

THE HUNDREDTH DAY OF THE HUNDREDTH MONTH IN THE SEVEN BILLIONTH YEAR OF OUR WORD

4155 HOURS

NEECLIS – land of needlewomen and weavers. I had heard about their skill, barring none, with the needle and the loom, and for four hundred years lived with the anticipation of resting when I came to their land.

I was not disappointed – soft clothes, warm beds, woven blankets, linens and sheets. These would have been more than enough to seduce me into staying, but there was also the food – fresh fruit, succulent meats cooked in fragrant sauces, breads fresh from their clay ovens, and all in abundance – I hadn't tasted anything like it in centuries! The NEECLIS knew well how to feed and nourish the senses, *all* the senses; they had made an art of it, and willingly shared everything with me. With their excellent climate, and good location they could, unlike the LENSECI, afford to be generous.

More than anything else, I was glad of the talk, camaraderie and companionship – a welcome break in the isolation, the aloneness. Much as I loved it, the loneliness oppressed sometimes. What more could I ask for? good food to spare, excellent conversation, friendship, and love with Arwhal, the best needlewoman and weaver of the NEECLIS.

Two hundred years passed; I had begun to relax and take my surroundings for granted. There would be no challenge here – no skill testing questions, no circles or sweat-lodges – the NEECLIS were far too engaged with their weaving and needle work. They spent long hours discussing problems of aesthetics – debating designs and pattern, the weight of wool, the right colours of threads and yarns. From the smallest head band or woven bracelet to the largest wall covering, the NEECLIS brought the same concern and attention, and I too began to enter these discussions, observing how my eye for colour and shape and movement of lines had sharpened. All around were the fruits of these discussions: the outer walls of their houses with their red, yellow, and green geometric designs; hand-woven rugs and carpets covering the floors, as well as tapestries and embroidered cloths. I had come to take for granted that my every waking hour would be an encounter and engagement with beauty. In the calm, almost pastoral, surroundings of the NEECLIS compound, with its well-kept and colourful gardens, such craft seemed just and right.

I grew comfortable in my love of Arwhal and of the NEECLIS, although every so often I sensed the beginnings of a restlessness. The lush, opulent environment was beginning to stifle me, once again I felt the urge to move on, to look for Livingstone – but the surrounding comfort sapped all my energy to do so.

These were my thoughts as I lay one evening with my head in Arwhal's lap, while she reclined against a pile of cushions.

"I want to tell you a story." Her voice interrupted these inner reflections, bringing me back to the present. I smiled and settled myself more deeply into the cushions. Throughout my sojourn with the NEECLIS, Arwhal's stories had entertained and delighted me.

"There once was a girl who had six brothers." Her voice, low-timbred and musical, immediately banished any thoughts of my leaving her. "They were all younger than she was and she always did her best to protect them. One day these boys were playing in the forest and came upon a bush with beautiful red berries. 'Oh look,' said one of the brothers – 'berries. I'm so thirsty and hungry, let's eat some.' 'No,' said another, 'remember our sister has told us we're not to eat the red berries on the bushes in the forest.' 'But these aren't really red – they're sort of purple – and besides I'm hungry and she doesn't know what she's talking about.' 'She does,' another brother said. 'Remember, she warned us about going into a particular part of the forest and we didn't listen to her and fell into a hunter's trap.' 'Well, I'm going to have some of these berries,' the first brother said, and began eating them." I smiled to myself, wriggling my toes in their embroidered slippers, and thought, now here comes the good part.

"The others saw that nothing happened to him so they too began eating; soon they had eaten so much they all felt too full to move, so they all lay down and went to sleep." Arwhal's voice lulled me – I too felt as if I were going to fall asleep. She stroked my head and continued: "Several hours later, the boys awoke and found they had all been turned into roosters – six white roosters with bright red combs.

"When the girl saw what had become of her brothers she wept

for a long time, then she wiped her tears and went to visit an old, wise woman who lived in the forest. She wanted to learn how to help her brothers become human again." I now half-sat, half-lay, with my head in the crook of Arwhal's neck. With one hand she continued to stroke my hair, sometimes burying her fingers in it, sometimes gently turning and twisting the strands, her voice weaving a net that held us close. "The old woman told the girl she had to make six shirts for her brothers from the tiny African violets that grew in the forest. Each shirt, the old woman told her, would take her a year to make, and in the six years it took her to make the shirts, she was to be silent and not to utter a word. Six shirts and silence – that was her power – if she wanted to return her brothers to human form."

I sat up suddenly – Arwhal was telling me something important, but I wasn't sure I understood what it was. "She wasn't to say a word *and* she had to weave six shirts from flowers," I said. "That seems a hell of a price to pay for having six stupid brothers who wouldn't listen to her. If I were she, I would kill and roast the roosters over six years – " Arwhal looked at me and smiled; she knew I didn't mean what I said. I was suddenly afraid and anxious. Gently she placed a finger against my lips.

"Would you – kill them? Remember," she continued, "silence does not necessarily mean an absence of sound." I nodded as if I understood. I didn't.

"Come with me," she said, rising from where we lay. There was no preparation for it – "I want to show you something." There never is with betrayal – I followed her – especially when it comes in the shape and form of a friend. Just a walk – down a long corridor believing I was going to see a tapestry she was working on. The next thing I knew, we were in a huge room, ablaze with coloured fabric and yarn, and she was telling me I would have to stay there until I could "piece together the words of (my) silence."

"Bitch! Bitch! Bitch!" How long I yelled and screamed I don't know, and what I yelled I don't care to remember – but I traced her ancestors back to a mule and a jackass and threatened to kill her *and* hang her out to dry. Silence. That was the only response I got; it swirled around me and I remembered she had said that silence did not necessarily mean an absence of sound. I could picture her – straight, proud back, beautifully black face as profound as a midnight sky – walking away with the keys jangling at her waist – a smile on her pointed, pixie face.

How I loved her – the beautiful Arwhal – the bitch! And she had left me. I was alone; I looked around, saw the carpets on the floor, the tapestries on the wall – among all this beauty I was alone. Then I cried – because I was tired and frightened and alone and didn't want to be tested any more . . . and because . . . I couldn't bear to admit it, but had to – despite the betrayal, I still loved Arwhal, and she had left me. All alone. I sat and rocked, first howling then crooning my pain to myself, and I saw myself drinking from the calabash of tears the little girl had offered me in my dream in the sweat-lodge. I talked and babbled to myself in a delirium of pain and loss. "Livingstone!" I screamed, "if you have anything to compare with this . . . this . . ." I had to whisper the word, "betrayal – this perfidy – I will – " What would I do? "I'll pay you everything I have – *everything*! No – I'll even love you, Livingstone – I promise. Livingstone!" I screamed again, "do you hear me?" Silence.

"Piece together the words of your silence," she had said to me. "Or weave a tapestry." I had argued hard with her when she said this.

"But silence has no words," I countered, my heart racing at the certain knowledge that she was going to leave me. "So, there's nothing to do."

"Then do nothing," she replied, "but if you are wise, you will try and make a quilt – a spread perhaps, or weave a magic carpet that will . . . well, that is up to you. Weave us something," she had challenged, "as a thank-you for your stay here; weave yourself something – something new – never seen before – using what you have, what is yours," and she bent and kissed me on the lips. The fucking Judas! "Using what we all have," she had continued, "word *and* silence – neither word alone, nor silence alone, but word and silence – weave, patch, sew together and remember it is *your* silence – all yours, untouched and uncorrupted. The word does not belong to you – it was owned and whored by others long, long before you set out on your travels – whore words." Then she had laughed. "But to use your silence, you have to use the word."

"Whore words?" I asked.

"Yes, and there's the rub, my dear," she said, and gently drew me close and held me – "there's the rub – you need the word – whore words – to weave your silence."

There *was* the god-damned rub, and here *I* was robbed of my freedom once again. Oh, Arwhal, you could at least have warned me... memories of our time together – long walks across stubble-yellow fields; the quiet talk of long cool evenings before the fire; swimming, bathing – playing like children in sun-drenched pools and shaded water holes; reading to each other as we lay naked at the water's edge... watching the noon-day sun play hide-and-go-seek with water-damp bodies – first a flank then a nipple, challenging finger or tongue to follow – now a buttock, next the soft surround of navel, soon the long, swift curve of back, tufted, secret triangles of crinkly pleasure... braiding each other's hair, elaborately trying to outdo the other, how we laughed and talked our way into each other's silence... watching her weave her colours... the dying blaze of the autumn sun gilding the loom, setting fire to the deep reds and browns – the purple of her yarn, and gold-leafing the hem of her heavy, woven dress, her ringed fingers glinting in and out of the loom, her face half gold, half black – liquid – in the shifting evening light. We had shared time and space and bodies – our Silences – with each other – and how I loved her... and how little these memories did to dispel my anger.

I was getting fed right up to the teeth with all this imprisonment and challenge – she could have warned me – she could have *if* she wanted to. I had by now completely lost the trail of Livingstone, and to date the NEECLIS had been of no help in setting me back on course, except for letting me rest – until this most recent betrayal. I desperately wanted to find him – Livingstone – but I had to get out of here, and *there* was the rub.

I lost all sense of calendar time and could only track the moon through the windows at night. Between the moon and my blood, I figured it had to have been at least seven hundred years I remained in that room with my pieces of cloth, a loom and brightly coloured heaps of knotted yarn. As I worked at unravelling the yarn, or sorting the pieces of fabric, I remembered the story of the young girl weaving the six shirts from African violets for her brothers. I felt angry on her behalf – why did she have to do all the work for her brothers – they deserved to stay as roosters if they were so stupid. I was also angry at the NEECLIS and at Arwhal. (In all the time I was there, she never came once to see me.) I remained angry until I began to understand what she was trying to teach me – that there *were* two separate strands or threads – word *and* silence – each as important as the other. To weave anything I first had to make the separation, and before I could do that, I needed to find my own Silence.

I clung to my anger for a long time – it was very hard to let go of it – but when I began to give it up to the Silence around me, my fingers, as if of their own accord, began to weave. Like the girl in the story Arwhal had told me, in finding my own Silence I was finding my own power – of transformation. As I wove I talked and laughed and sang; I cursed *and* I swore. All to myself. And then I wove some more and came to understand how Silence could speak and be silent – how Silence could be filled with noise and also be still. And finally I understood what Arwhal meant – that Silence does not always mean the absence of sound, because in all that sound – of my own voice – I was able to find and hear my own Silence. And I was ashamed – of how much I had resisted the wisdoms Arwhal had offered me in presenting me with a chance to find my own Silence.

Earlier on in my travels, I had wondered and enquired of the ECNELIS what colour my silence was. Back then I hadn't known what I was looking for, and now here it was before me – any colour I wished – a riot – a carnival of colour – I had my choice. And how I loved the silence of purple – those purple silences – almost as much as I loved the absolute in the silence of black, or the distilled silence of white; the burnt sienna of silence – red, green, blue – colour greeting shape – pentagram, hexagon, octagon, circle – squares of silence – and as I worked, my anger left.

When they finally came to get me – when SHE finally arrived, I had woven a tapestry, and had pieced together a multicoloured quilt – of Silence – my many silences – held together by the most invisible of stitches – the invisible but necessary word. "Look," I said to Arwhal, "a quilt in all the colours of my Silence – to keep me warm on my travels." We looked at each other and smiled. We both knew I was now ready to move on.

I had forgiven her her "betrayal" although the pain of her abandonment had left its mark. We continued to love each other, sleeping together under the quilt of my Silence for another fifty years, until, thoroughly spoilt, I left her and the NEECLIS. They offered me pillows, sheets, cutlery and even recipes to help make my journey comfortable. I was tempted, but refused them all. They would only burden me and I needed to travel light. And so early one morning, as the sun came over the horizon, streaking the sky with red, and gilding the walls of the compound and houses, I held Arwhal in one long, last embrace. The sun had turned the tears in her eyes to little gold globules against her black skin. I turned swiftly walking towards the east and the rising sun, carrying only my quilt of Silence and a long wooden staff Arwhal had made for me. In pursuit once again of Livingstone. And my Silence.

    Single
    Solitary
    Unitary
Is it?
  this absence –
      of speech
Or legion
   wedged
In the between of words
A presence
   absent the touch
     the tarnish
In power
In conquest
   Silence
    Trappist
Celibate
  seeking
The absolute
   in Virgin
Whole

DIONNE BRAND

Dionne Brand was born in 1953 in Guayguayare, Trinidad. After graduating from Naparima Girls' High School in Trinidad in 1970, she moved to Toronto, where she has lived ever since. She graduated in 1975 from the University of Toronto with a BA in English and philosophy. She took an MA in the philosophy of education from the Ontario Institute for Studies in Education in 1989.

Since coming to Canada, Brand has worked with the black and feminist communities in many capacities. She has belonged to the Communist Party of Canada and remains committed to Marxist ideas, particularly to the principles of equal distribution of the world's wealth and ending the exploitation of the labour of the majority of the world's peoples. She was a founding member and editor of *Our Lives*, Canada's first black women's newspaper. She has edited, written, and done research for a number of alternative journals and papers, including *Spear, Fuse Magazine, Network, Our Lives,* the *Harriet Tubman Review, Fireweed, Poetry Canada Review, Canadian Woman Studies,* and *Resources for Feminist Research*. She guest-edited *Fireweed's* issues on Women of Colour (1983) and Canadian Women Poets (1986).

Brand has also done extensive community work and organizing. She has been a community worker for the Black Education Project, Toronto; a counsellor for the black-West Indian community at the Immigrant Women's Centre, Toronto; an Information Officer for the Agency for Rural Transformation, Grenada, and for the Caribbean Peoples' Development Agencies. She has chaired the Women's Issues Committee of the Ontario Coalition of Black Trade Unionists, of which she was a founding member; helped organize the Black and Native Women's Caucus of the International Women's Day Coalition; and served on the board of the Shirley Samaroo House, Toronto, a shelter for battered immigrant women.

Brand's poetry, essays, and films arise directly out of her political involvements. *'Fore Day Morning* (Khoisan, 1978) and *Earth Magic* (Kids Can Press, 1978), a book of poetry for children, were followed by two more politically engaged poetry volumes, *Primitive Offensive* (Williams-Wallace, 1982) and *Winter Epigrams and Epigrams to Ernesto Cardenal in Defense of Claudia* (Williams-Wallace, 1983). *Chronicles of the Hostile Sun* (Williams-Wallace, 1984) is a reaction in poetry to

Brand's experience of the US invasion, which occurred while she was working in Grenada. *No Language is Neutral* (Coach House, 1990), her most recent book of poetry, was nominated for the Governor General's Award. Major prose titles, which have also emerged from Brand's political work, include: *Rivers Have Sources, Trees Have Roots: Speaking of Racism,* with Krisantha Sri Bhaggiydatta (Cross Cultural Communication Centre, 1986); "Black Women and Work: The Impact of Racially Constructed Gender Roles on the Sexual Division of Labour" (*Fireweed* 1987 and 1988); and, with Lois de Shield, *No Burden to Carry: Narratives of Black Working Women in Ontario 1920s to 1950s* (Women's Press, 1991). Brand's National Film Board, Studio D, Documentaries are *Older Stronger Wiser* (1989), *Sisters in the Struggle* (1991), and *Long Time Comin'* (1993).

Brand's poetry and short stories have appeared in many anthologies, among them: *Other Voices, The Penguin Book of Caribbean Verse, Poetry by Canadian Women, Stories by Canadian Women, Her True-True Name: An Anthology of Women's Writing from the Caribbean,* and *Other Solitudes: Canadian Multicultural Fictions.* She has been writer-in-residence at the Halifax City Regional Library and taught poetry at the West Coast Women and Words Society Summer School and Retreat. In 1990-91, she was writer-in-residence at the University of Toronto. In 1991-92, she taught creative writing at the University of Guelph. She has now returned to writing on a full-time basis.

About influences on her writing, Brand has said: "What some white reviewers lack is a sense of what literature that is made by Black people and other people of colour is about. If you read my work, you have to read Toni Morrison, you have to read Derek Walcott, Rosa Guy, Jean Rhys, Paule Marshall, Michael Anthony, Eddie Brathwaite, and African writers and poets . . . Bessie Head. I don't consider myself on any margin, on the margin of Canadian literature. I'm sitting right in the middle of Black literature, because that's who I read, that's who I respond to." (*Books in Canada,* October 1990: 14). More recently, Brand has said that she counts as influences Pablo Neruda, Bertolt Brecht, Martin Carter, Roque Dalton, Taban Lo Liyong, Sonia Sanchez, Nikki Giovanni, Nicolas Guillen, and Aimé Césaire.

from *Language in Her Eye* (1990)

BREAD OUT OF STONE

I am writing this in Cuba. Playas del Este. It is January. The weather is humid. In Toronto I live in the semi-detached, old new immigrant houses, where Italians, Chinese, Blacks, Koreans, South Asians and Portuguese make a rough peace and the Hummingbird Grocery stands next to the Bargain Harold's, the Italian cheese shop, the Portuguese chicken place and the Eritrean fast food restaurant. There's a hit and run game of police and drug dealers in my part of the city, from Christie Pits, gaping wide and strewn with syringes, to Lansdowne and Bloor, where my cousin and so many young men and women walk, hustle, dry-eyed, haunted, hungry and busily, toward a fix. Here, the police carry out this country's legacy of racial violence in two killings of Black men and one shooting of a young Black woman in this city that calls its racism subtle, and the air stinks with the sanguine pronouncements of Canadian civility: "Oh no, we're not like the United States," be grateful for the not-as-bad racism here. I'm writing this just after the massacre of fourteen women in Montreal and the apologias of "madman," "aberration," in a country where most violent deaths of women are the result of male violence. Don't talk about the skeletons! Helen Betty Osborne dying in The Pas seventeen years ago, tortured and murdered by this country's fine young white men and denied justice by this country's white law and white law enforcers in this country with its pathological hate for Native people. What with all that, it ain't easy. So I began writing this essay weeks ago in Toronto but could not find the right way of starting. Somewhere in all of that there wasn't time. The real was more pressing than any rendering.

On the Playas del Este near Guanabo, I'm editing oral histories of older Black women in Ontario. It will become a film, but that's much later. I started this book two years ago, thinking that it would take one year. By now it's going on three years and is actually torture, and I ask myself why did I start this at all. Something about recovering history, history only important to me and women like me, so I couldn't just drop it, no matter how long it took. And then . . .

I remember a white woman asking me how do you decide which to be – Black or a woman – and when. As if she didn't have to decide which to be, white or woman, and when. As if there were a moment that I wasn't a woman and a moment that I wasn't Black, as if there were a moment that she wasn't white. She asks me this because she only sees my skin, my race and not my sex. She asks me this because she sees her sex and takes her race as normal. On the Playas del Este, near Guanabo, I bend closely to edit the oral histories of older Black women as I remember this encounter. I put the sun outside at the back of my head.

On the Playas del Este, from Marazul to Guanabo, men yell at me and my partner, "Aye que rica!," "Aye mamita, cosita!," "Que te la chupo!" They whistle without relief. In the first days, we yell back English obscenities, shake fists at them. But they are unrelenting. And women do not own enough obscenities to fill the air. Men own this language. We ignore the gantlet of sucking lips and stares. They do it so religiously, so instinctively, we realize it is a duty.

Outside the Brunswick Tavern on Bloor Street one night, a bunch of young white boys from the suburbs follow three of us. They say some words loudly, nothing understandable, but loudly, and at us. They hit their feet against the pavement, come close to us. We cross the road. All of us are older than these teenagers escaped from Mississauga but they make us cross the road. White and male, they own it.

A policeman tells a friend of mine, "Well, obviously the guy finds you attractive. You're an attractive woman, after all." This about the man living opposite who has hassled her since she moved into the neighbourhood. The whole neighbourhood knows he yells and screams alone in his apartment about "bitches" and "whores." They've heard him. But the policeman sees nothing amiss with the world here, nothing illegal, only an occasion for solidarity with the man living opposite who wants to kill a woman.

In my hotel on the Playas del Este, as I read about a Black woman's childhood on the Prairies, "... and because I was a girl I did everything...," I remember one noon in hilly St. Georges. I'm walking up that fatal hill in the hot sun. This is before those days when everything caved in. My legs hurt, I'm wondering what I'm doing here in Grenada with the sun so hot and the hill so hard to climb. Passing me going up and down are people going to lunch, kids yelling to each other, the dark cooler interiors of the shops and stores – the electricity has broken down. I decided to have a beer at Rudolph's. The customers, men alone or women accompanied by men, turn to look at me. I ignore this as I've been doing walking through town. I'm used to masculinity. It's more colourful on some street corners; in this bar it's less ostentatious but more powerful. A turn of the head is sufficient. I take a swig of my beer. I open my diary. I'm here because I've decided that writing is not enough. Black liberation needs more than that. How, I ask myself, can writing help in the revolution. You need your bare hands for this. I drink my beer over my open diary and face this dilemma. I wish I were a farmer. I could then at least grow food. I have a job as an information officer. I write reports, descriptions of farmers, so that they can get money, to produce food, from people in Europe and North America who read and love descriptions of farmers. I take the last swig of my beer, feeling its mixture with the noon heat make me cool. There's another difficulty, writer, information officer, or farmer, I will walk the streets, paved or unpaved, as a woman.

An interviewer on the CBC asks me: Isn't it a burden to have to write about being Black? What else would I write about? What would be more important? Since these things are inseparable, and since I do not wish to be separated from them, I own them and take on the responsibility of defending them. I have a choice in this.

Outside Wilson's, between Shaw and Ossington, before it closed down, Black men stare me down the street informing me silently that they can and want to control the terms under which I walk, appear, be, on the street, the sidewalk, the high wire, the string for Black women to trip on, even more vulnerable to white men and

Black men because Black women cannot, won't, throw Black men to white men. I stare the brothers back. They see my sex. My race is only a deed to their ownership. Their eyes do not move.

If some of this finds its way into some piece of fiction, a line of poetry, an image on a screen, no wonder. On the Playas del Este, I am editing an oral history of older Black women, furiously.

I'm working on a film. It is a film about women in my community. I've dreamt this film as a book, dreamt it as a face, dreamt it at a window. I am editing it on the Playas del Este; a woman's face, old and a little tired, deep brown and black, creased with everything that can be lived, and calm, a woman's face that will fade if I do not dream it, write it, put it in a film. I write it, try to make everyone else dream it, too; if they dream it, they will know something more, love this woman's face, this woman I will become, this woman they will become. I will sacrifice something for this dream: safety. To dream about a woman, even an old woman, is dangerous; to dream about a Black woman, even an old Black woman, is dangerous even in a Black dream, an old dream, a Black woman's dream, even a dream where you are the dreamer. Even in a Black dream, where I, too, am a dreamer, a lesbian is suspect; a woman is suspect even to other women, especially if she dreams of women.

I am working on a film. Another woman is working with me. She is a friend. I've known her for eighteen years. For four of those years, I've been a lesbian, and we've lost touch. She's told me nothing has changed, people still love me even though. . . . I tell her everything has changed. . . . She tells me I've changed since. . . . In secret, she says I hate men and children. That's why I only want to write about, to work around women. . . . She thinks my love for women must be predicated on a hatred of men, and, curiously, children.

We make a warm and respectful film. She hates it, thinking it is infected by my love for women. The night of the first showing, Black women's faces move toward us, smiling. They hug us, their eyes watery from that well, centuries-old but this time joyful, thanking us for making this film.

On the shoot, we are an all-woman crew. We are three Black women and three white. I am the only lesbian. I prepare my questions, sit next to the lens of the camera, look into these old women's eyes, try in ten-minute episodes to spin the thread between those eyes and mine, taut or liquid, to sew a patch of black, rich with moment and things never talked about in public: Black womanhood. We are all nervous; the Black women nervous at what they will hear; some part of us knows that in the moment of telling, we will be as betrayed as much as we will be free. I feel the other two behind me; they are nervous about me, too. Am I a sister? Will I be sister to their, our, silence? All three of us know that each question I ask must account for our race. I know that each question I ask must account for our sex. In the end I am abandoned to that question because women are taught to abandon each other to the suffering of their sex, most of all Black women who have the hard white world in front of us so much the tyranny of sex is a small price, or so we think. The white women are nervous, hidden under the technical functions they have to perform. They too may not be able to bear the sound of this truth woven between those old eyes and mine.

Each night I go to my room alone after the shoot. More and more I skip dinner as the talk around the table flickers as a fire on the edge of a blowing skirt. It's that talk of women suddenly finding themselves alone, with each other, inadvertently.

If men brag when they're together, women deny. They make sure that there is no sign of themselves, they assure each other of their love for men, they lie to each other, they tell stories about their erasure, they compete to erase themselves, they trap each other in weary repetitions, they stop each other from talking. The talk becomes thin, the language grinds down to brittle domesticity. To prove that they are good women the conversation singes the borders of lesbian hate (". . . well, why do they have to flaunt it?"), plays at the burned edges, firing each other to the one point of unity between Black and white women – fear, contempt for women who love women.

I rise and leave. One night I see the fire lighting and I speak. The next night I take dinner in my room. And the old women doing the telling, making the film—impatience crosses the other Black woman's face as they tell it. Perhaps she is not listening, perhaps she is thinking of her own life, perhaps she is going over in her mind a pained phone call to another city. But here, balancing on this thread, if she looks, is something that says we do not need to leave ourselves stranded, we can be whole and these old women need us to do something different, that is why they're telling us this story. This story is not an object of art, they did not live some huge mistake, they are not old and cute and useless, they're showing us the art of something, and it is not perfect, and they know it. They do not want us to repeat it.

I am working on a film. Another Black woman is working with me. We're making a film about women. Old women. All have lived for more than sixty years and there are five minutes in which to speak, feel those years. In a film, in a Black dream, will it be all right if five old women speak for five minutes? Black women are so familiar with erasure, it is so much the cloth against the skin, that this is a real question. In a Black dream, do women tell stories? If a Black woman tells the story in a Black dream, is it still a Black dream? The voices of old women never frighten me. I will pay for this fearlessness.

I listen to an old man's voice describing an old woman's life. The other woman is now the questioner; she has turned to the old man and asked the old man about the old woman's life. I suddenly ask the old woman from the back of the room where we are filming, "How was it for you?" I wanted to hear her voice. She was standing silently. We had come to film her. My voice breaks the room, her voice answers me, she comes alive, we rejoin the thread. The roll of film runs out. The assistant camera secures that self-doubt in the can marked "exposed film" and loads the camera again. The old woman speaks this time.

"How was it for you?" A simple question about a dream at a window. They say it is because I am a lesbian that I've asked, and that because I am a lesbian I am not a Black woman, and because I've asked I'm not Black, and because I do not erase myself I am not a Black woman, and because I do not think that Black women can wait for freedom either, I am not . . . and because I do not dream myself ten paces behind, and because I do not dream a male dream but a Black dream where a woman tells the story, they say I'm not. . . . How was it for you? In the Black gauze of our history, how was it for you? Your face might appear if I ask this. I would ask you this whatever the price. I am not afraid of your voice. How was it for you?

I've worked in my community for eighteen years, licking envelopes, postering lamp-posts, carrying placards, teaching children, counselling women, organizing meetings though I never cooked food, chanting on the megaphone though I never made a speech, calling down racists, calling down the state, writing about our lives so we'd have something more to read than the bullshit in the mainstream press. I've even run off to join a revolution. But I haven't bent my back to a Black man, and I have loved Black women.

In the cutting room of the film someone decides that my race should be cut from me for these last sins. For each frame of the film a year of my committed struggle is forfeited. My placard . . . my protest chant . . . my face on a demonstration . . . silenced . . . forgotten, my poems . . . I am losing my life just to hear old women talk. Someone decides that my sex should be cut into me. Not the first sex, not the second sex. The "third sex." Only the first two can be impartial, only the first two make no decision based on their sex. The third sex is all sex, no reason. In the cutting room, I reason, talk, persuade, cajole, finally insist away any erasure of these women. But erasure is their life. Yes, but it is not the truth.

In the oral histories and in the film, the women say this day I did this, this day I did that, this day I did "days work," this day I took care of things, and well, we got along all right you know.

The depression wasn't so bad for us, we were used to hard times. But I worked, just like a man, oh yes.

As the cutting ends, I feel the full rain of lesbian hate. It hits the ground, its natural place. It mixes with the soil ready with the hate of women, the contempt for women that women, too, eat. For me, it pushes up a hoary blossom sheltered in race. I will smell this blossom I know for many years to come.

And it will push up everywhere and sometimes it will smother me. I am a woman and Black and lesbian, the evidence of this is inescapable and interesting.

At a screening of the film about old Black women, a Black man first commends the film through barely open teeth, then he suggests more detail in future films, details about husbands, he says, details about children. He wants these details to set his picture right, he cannot see these women without himself. Even now as they are old he will not give them the right of the aged to speak about what they know; he must edit them with his presence, the presence of husbands to make them wives, children to make them mothers. His picture is incomplete without their subordination. The blossom between his teeth, as it bursts into words, is not just for me.

The night of the first showing, fifteen hundred people come to see the film. The theatre crackles with their joy; they recognize themselves.

You can see a hanging bridge through my hotel window on the Playas del Este. The Boca Ciega river running underneath to the ocean is shallow in the afternoon, deep in the evening. I only mention this because from my window on my street in Toronto the movement of the world is not as simple or perceptible, but more frightening.

Once, a Czech emigré writer, now very popular in the "free world," looked me dead in my Black eyes and explained the meaning of jazz to me.

The Atlantic yawning blue out of my window on the Playas del Este and beyond the bridge pulls my eyes away from the oral histories and into its own memory. I am a little girl growing beside the same ocean on another island some years before. I remember seeing women and men sitting quietly in the still midday heat of that town of my childhood, saying "Something must happen, something bound to come." They were waiting, after waiting for crop and pay, after waiting for cousin and auntie, after waiting for patience and grace, they were waiting for god.

Exasperated after hours of my crying for sweet water, opening her mouth wide, my mama would say to me, "Look inside! Aaah! you see anything in there? You want me to make bread out of stone?"

At a poetry reading on Spadina, another male writer tells me, "You write very well, but stay away from the politics." I look at this big white man from another planet and smile the dissembling and dangerous smile of my foremothers.

In my mama's mouth, I saw the struggle for small things.

Listen, I am a Black woman whose ancestors were brought to a new world lying tightly packed in ships. Fifteen million of them survived the voyage, five million of them women; millions among them died, were killed, committed suicide in the middle passage.

When I come back to Toronto from the Playas del Este, I will pass a flashing neon sign hanging over the Gardiner Expressway. "Lloyds Bank," it will say. Lloyds, as in Lloyds of London. They got their bullish start insuring slave cargo.

At an exhibition at the Royal Ontario Museum in June 1990, there is a display of the colonists' view of the plunder of Africa. "Superior" Europeans and "primitive" Africans abound, missionaries and marauders bring "civilization" "into the heart of Africa." "Into the Heart of Africa." The name of the ROM exhibition by itself is drenched in racism, the finest most skilful racism yet developed, the naming of things, the writing of history, the creation of cultural consent. Outside the museum, African-Canadians demonstrate against the exhibition every Saturday. Ten men and women have been beaten, strip-searched, and arrested by the Toronto police and bonded not to come within one thousand feet of the museum. An injunction by what the demonstrators call the "Racist Ontario Museum" prevents any demonstration within fifty yards of the building.

Pounding the pavement for the ground on which to stand, still after so long. All the Black people here have a memory whether they know it or not, whether they like it or not, whether they remember it or not, and, in that memory are words such as land, sea, whip, work, rap, coffle, sing, sweat, release, days ... without ... this ... pain ... coming ... We know ... have a sense ... hold a look in our eyes ... about it ... have to fight every day for our humanity ... redeem it every day.

And I live that memory as a woman. Coming home from the Playas del Este, hugging the edited oral histories, there is always something more to be written, something more important. You are always ahead of yourself. There is always something that must be remembered, something that cannot be forgotten, something that must be weighed. There is always, whether we say these things today or tomorrow, or whether silence is a better tactic.

There is never room, though there is always risk, but there is never the room that white writers have in never speaking for their whole race, yet speaking in the most secret and cowardly language of normalcy and affirmation, speaking for the whole race. There is only writing that is significant, honest, necessary – making bread out of stone – so that stone becomes pliant under the hands.

There is an unburdening, uncovering the most vulnerable parts of ourselves, uncovering beauty, possibility. Coming home from the Playas del Este ...

■ ■ ■

from *'Fore Day Morning* (1978)

SINCE YOU

Since you,
I passed some nights in hell,
thought of destroying myself,
then thought of destroying you.
Panicked, took an iron bird
on some dragon cloud,
and flew from summer to summer,
till tiring we landed
where demon shadows eat away at my sleep.
Since you,
I walked miles and miles with a close friend,
listened for hours to street cars passing by,
talked rivers and rivers to find myself,
climbed twenty hills to take one breath.
Since you,
I bought a painting,
wrote a verse,
devoured many books,
hung out with friends,
lived a whole year,
never once discovering
that you weren't there.

OLD I.

If I get old,
I want to sit near the water
in flour bag drawers.
My lumpy stretch marked legs
causing rivulets
where sand gives way to sea
bathing myself.
My naked flabby breasts,
my navel secreted in limp dead skin,
dipping sea water
with an enamel cup,
throwing it over my head
and cussing anyone who stares.

OLD II.

If I get old,
hell with them people,
they better not bother me anymore
'cause I'll do something old and crazy,
like spit through my gums in their faces,
they better not mess with me
'cause I've got some shabby secrets
like who I saw with his hand in my blood.
They better leave me alone then,
pretend I'm mad!
'cause I've got some rattling stories.

■ ■ ■

AFRO WEST INDIAN IMMIGRANT

I feel like a palm tree
at the corner of Bloor and Yonge
in a wild snow storm.
Scared, surprised,
trying desperately to appear unperplexed
put out, sun brown naked and a little embarrassed.

■ ■ ■

SHANTY TOWN

Perpetual motion,
yesterday's dust is today's dust
and tomorrow's debris.
Always wanting, never having,
sweeping dirt to find more dirt.
Perpetual needing,
hungry eyes, dry lips, slaked white
tongues and stinking mouths,
muddy toes spread to make sure
that poverty enters every pore.
Bare bottom boys pitch three hole.
Stone and giggle at dogs caught
in embarrassing heat,
and their manhood blows in the trades.
Perpetual dancing,
marking time, making time,
liming. . . . time.
As king corbeau circles
the caribbean,
sharpening his beak on
little boys' dreams.
And waits in the stench of the dying
and already dead.

from Primitive Offensive (1982)

CANTO I

ashes head to toes
juju belt
guinea eyes unfolded impossible
squint a sun since drenched
breasts beaded of raised skin
naked woman speaks
syllables come in dust's pace
dried, caked rim of desert mouth
naked woman speaks
run mouth, tell.
when the whites come they were dead men
we did not want to touch them
we did not want to interfere in their business
after the disappearances
many times there were dead men among us
and we cursed them
and we gave them food
when the whites came they were dead men
five men died in our great battles before
guns gave us more heads of our enemies
and those who disappeared were dead men
and the dead take care of their own
for things come and they leave
enemies were dead men and whites were dead men
and our city and our people flourished
and died also,
naked woman speak
syllables come in water's pace
long river mouth, tell.
for the skulls of our enemies
were the walls of our wealth
and we filled them with food
and palm wine for our ancestors
and everywhere there were skulls
white of beaten iron and guns and

white with the ancestors' praise and
white with the breath of the whites on our land
white as of eyes on sand on humid vastness
white as the tune of fingers, brisk on dry skin
not even pursed hungry lips were as white
and not even the sorghum was as white as this
not even the dust of the goat's grounded horn
and each night became different from the next
and we stood by our fires
and left the places outside our compound
to the skulls and the disappeared and the whites
and the skulls stood on their sticks
and no one was born on the nights after
and no one joined their age mates
the disappeared stayed away and did not
help us to kill our enemies
and we ground our breasts and our teeth to powder
belly roped in ashes as the sky falters on the rainbow
naked woman speaks
syllables come in palm wine's pace
run mouth, dry.

■ ■ ■

CANTO II

ancestor dirt
ancestor snake
ancestor lice
ancestor whip
ancestor fish
ancestor slime
ancestor sea
ancestor stick
ancestor iron
ancestor bush
ancestor ship

ancestor old woman, old bead
let me feel your skin
old muscle, old stick
where are my bells?
my rattles
my condiments
my things
to fill houses and minutes,
the fete is starting
where are my things?
my mixtures
my bones
my decorations
old bead! old tamerind switch!
will you bathe me in oils,
will you tie me in white cloth?
call me by my praise name
sing me Oshun song
against this clamor,
ancestor old woman
send my things after me
one moment old lady
more questions
what happened to the ocean in your leap
the boatswain, did he scan
the passage's terrible wet face
the navigator, did he blink or steer the ship
through your screaming night
the captain, did he lash two slaves to the rigging
for example?
lady, my things
water leaden
my maps, my compass
after all, what is the political
position of stars?
drop your crusted cough
where you want,
my hands make precious things
out of phlegm

ancestor wood
ancestor dog
ancestor knife
ancestor old man
dry stick
moustache
skin and cheekbone
why didn't you remember,
why didn't you remember
the name of our tribe
why didn't you tell me
before you died
old horse
you made the white man
ride you
you shot off your leg for him
old man
the name of our tribe is all i wanted
instead you went
to the swamps and bush
and rice paddies
for the Trading Company
and they buried you in water
crocodile tears!
it would have been better
to remember the name of our tribe
now mosquito dance a ballet
over your grave
the old woman buried with you
wants to leave.

■ ■ ■

CANTO VI

you, in the square,
you in the square of Koln
in the square before that huge destructive cathedral
what are you doing there
playing a drum
you, who pretend not to recognize me
you worshipper of insolubles
I know you slipped, tripped on your tie
the one given to you at the bazaar where
they auctioned off your beard
you lay in white sheets for some years
then fled
to the square
grabbing these colors, red, green, gold like some bright things
to tie your head and bind you to some place
grabbing this flute
this drum
this needle and syringe
this far from Lagos,
and you, the other day in Vlissengen,
I was so shocked to see you
in your bathing suit
on that white beach in Holland
what were you doing there
and again the other night
I saw you in Paris near St. Michel Metro
dressed like that
dressed as if you were lost,
Madagascar woman, hand full of pommes frittes
rushing to your mouth
looking at me
as if you did not know me
I was hurt
so hurt on pont neuf
so hurt to see us
so lost
Madagascar woman,

maybe rushing
off to some
dog work in Porte de Vincennes
or maybe to press hair
in that shop on Strasbourg-Saint-Denis
that shop, already out of place
the latest white sex symbol was in the window, in corn rows,
and me too, Madagascar woman
here in this mortuary
of ice,
my face
like a dull pick,
I wondered if
If I resembled you,
did you get my dead salutation
I sent it
dropped it as a dried
rose at your feet,
me too
on all fours
in this decayed wood
waiting
cloud of ice,
I must be
the gravedigger
or the dead,
but I stayed clear
of Bordeaux and Nantes,
no more trading me
for wine and dried turtles,
oh yes
I could feel their breath
on my neck,
the lords of trade and plantations.
not me
not Bordeaux
not Marseilles
not for sugar
not for indigo

not for cotton.
I went to Paris
to where shortarsed Napoleon said,
"get that nigger Toussaint"
Toussaint, who was too gentle,
He should have met Dessalines
I went there to start a war
for the wars we never started
to burn the Code Noir
on the Champs Elysees.
So hurt in Paris
Senegal man
trying to sell them
trinkets
miniatures of Africa
goat tail fly swatters
hand drums
flutes, toumpans,
you didn't see me,
there was a hum between us
refractory
light about us,
you sold a few things along the Seine that night,
I hoped you read Fanon
and this was just a scam
but I knew it was your life
because your dry face
was my dry face.
Senegal man
your eyes were
too quick
too easy to become lovers
too urgent
it would be minutes
before they would be in our room
in our bed
touching our skin
like silk for sale
palms

wanting more
trinkets, wooden
rhinoceroses
ivory
fertility gods
monkey tail
flyswatters
filling up our room
wanting
lion skins for mats
pricing our genitals
for tassels, victory regalia,
don't look at me, man
we need the business.

    I saw what you did
    gendarmes
    what you did to the
    old man on the train
    you took him to the middle of the car
    and searched him and squeezed him
    and laughed
    because he was afraid,
    he could have been my grandfather
    he tried to explain,
    his passport
    was in his luggage
    the man with the other uniform
    in Gare du Nord
    but, I don't understand
    but I am a . . .
    the man with whistle
    but I am a . . .
    but I have money . . .
    what . . . you're touching me
    look at my face
    I am a . . .
    corpse
    I have met another corpse,

he was going to his son
in Heidelberg
his son
had a scholarship
his son was studying
german linguistics for negritude
in Senegal
he tried to explain.
he could have been my grandfather
but you jabbed his ribs,
he did not want to stay in your country
he said he had a shop
in Dakar, reflection, rhinestone
of France.
he was astonished
I will not forget you, gendarmes.

■ ■ ■

CANTO VII

guajiro making flip-flops on the wing tip of the american airline
they decided,
hot,
carnival along the Malecon,
cerveza,
Jose, Miguel, Carlos,
I met them twenty years later,
Luis though, still dances for the turistas.
havana twinkles
defiant, frightening,
all the lights are on,
this decision they made
so clear, so bright,
with everything so much bigger.
the wing of the plane dips,

aren't they afraid?
it could be a bomber,
and they in the street!
Jorge Roberto Flores is sixteen,
he speaks english and russian.
Jorge Roberto Flores said,
that is the museum of the revolution,
there are many things in there
this thing I can't put my finger on
only now and then a quick look,
Gramma
and every chicken truck turned
tank and armed convoy.
guajiro turning cartwheels on the wing tip of my airplane
threatening havana with its powerful steel influence.
this thing they did!
a woman, she, black
and old said,
somos familia,
I could not understand,
it was spanish
so she touched my skin
todos, todos familia eh!
Yes, Si! I said
to be recognised!
she knew me!
and two others did too,
one night in the amphiteatro de la avenida de las puertas
and then in Parc Maceo
recognised me!
guajiro doing handstands on the nose of the airliner
with its uncertain purpose,
my friend thinks
socialists don't get drunk,
cerveza! triente cinco centavos
carnival along the Malecon
companeros, companeras
so certain

defiant, frightening,
all the lights in havana are on.
and when it was
Encomendero in Cuba
De Las Casas, the viceregent
drained
a continent of blood
to write the Common Book of Prayer
even as he walks
his quill drips
even his quill
is made of my tail feather
feather of balance
feather of gold
but this little pale viceregent
in his little pale robe
hail marys embroider his blue lips,
still he is not alone,
his acoloytes bear his accoutrements
lingeringly, kindly, even now
his sperm atonement on his dry hands,
lizards eat on the latrine floor,
that left, soaks into the oppressed
ground
and brings up dead
bodies from the bush.
terror's legate
scribes a hecatomb of this antillian
archipelago
scribes desert, bantustans to a continent
still plundered,
condemned to these antilles
fallen into the hell of them
De Las Casas
ecclesiastic nostrils
scent for gold
scent for sweat
scent delicate

keen
ecclesiastic nose hairs,
blood kisses
the cord around his vestments
the hem of his communion skirt
the edges of his communion slippers
the romanesque set of the stone in his communion ring
the light ric-rac braid of his
communion sash
the fawning glint of his communion chain
the host he consecrates in the eucharist
clot in his eucharistic wine cup,
hostia
victim
hostage in the vestry,
fingers of a counting house clerk
he counts me on his chaplet
for Ferdinand and Isabella
for Napoleon the little emperor
for virgin mother, child, and canon.
Toussaint, i loved you
as soon as i saw you
on that weevil eaten page
in 1961,
i learned to read for you
from that book with
no preface and no owner.
you waited for me
hundreds of years,
i learned to read for you
from that book with
no preface and no owner,
about how
a french courtesan
in Cap Haitien
threw
a black woman,
the cook,

into the hot oven because
the hens were not baked
to her liking;
about how
Dessalines was terrible
in war;
Toussaint, i loved you
as soon as i saw you
on that mice shit page
in '61.
that De Las Casas
counting me
on his chaplet
for Ferdinand
and Isabella
for Napoleon
the little emperor
for virgin mother, child, and canon.
the cataclysmic murmur of his breath,
"we adore you oh christ
and we bless you because
by your holy cross you have
redeemed the world"
describe 1492
describe 1498
describe 1502
describe 1590
describe 1650
describe, describe, describe
some one
describe,
lost words,instances
slave of adjectives
closer, closer
adjectives, nothing, what!
Dessalines you were right
I can hear that cry of yours
ripping through that night,

night of privateers
night of fat planters
leave nothing
leave nothing white behind you
Toussaint heard too late
when it was cold in Joux.

■ ■ ■

from *Winter Epigrams and Epigrams to Ernesto Cardenal in Defense of Claudia* (1983)

WINTER EPIGRAMS

4

they think it's pretty,
this falling of leaves.
something is dying!

9

I give you these epigrams, Toronto,
these winter fragments
these stark white papers
because you mothered me
because you held me with a distance that i expected,
here, my mittens,
here, my frozen body,
because you gave me nothing more
and i took nothing less,
i give you winter epigrams
because you are a liar,
there is no other season here.

11

winters should be answered
in curt, no-nonsense phrases,
don't encourage them to linger.

12

thank heavens
in the middle of it all
is "1348 St. Clair," "Hagerman Hall,"
Cutty's Hideaway, These Eyes
and El Borinquen,
where you get to dance fast
and someone embraces you.

15

it's too cold to go outside,
i hope there won't be a fire.

18

I've never been to the far north/cold,
just went as far as Sudbury,
all that was there was the skull of the earth.
a granite mask so terrible even
the wind passed hurriedly.
the skull of the earth I tell you,
stoney, sockets, people
hacked its dry copper flesh.
I've heard of bears and wolves
but that skull was all I saw.

it was all I saw I tell you,
it was enough.

22

here!
take these epigrams, Toronto,
I stole them from Ernesto Cardenal,
he deserves a better thief
but you deserve these epigrams.

28

one good day
if I lift the blinds
and the sun through the glass seems warm
and a woman passing wears a windbreaker,
I forgive you everything,
I forget the last hundred harsh white mornings.

34

comrade winter,
if you weren't there
and didn't hate me so much
I probably wouldn't write poems.

37

I've arranged my apartment
so it looks as if I'm not here
I've put up bamboo blinds

I've strung ever green hedera helix
across my kitchen window
I've bought three mexican blankets
to put on the walls
I've covered the floors in persian rugs
(or some reasonable facsimile)
hung pictures of Che and my childhood
bought a rattan-chair – peacock throne
and I've papered my book cases with latin american writers
I feel like I'm in Canton, Oaxaca, Bahrain and Cocale
now,
If only I could get York Borough to
pass a city ordinance authorizing
the planting of Palm trees along
Raglan Avenue –
my deception will be complete.

41

Dec. 18th – 20th, 1982

Just to sabotage my epigrams,
the snow fell,
these three days,
softly.
Throwing a silence on the streets
and the telephone wires,
whiffling against the north side of the trees.
Two days ago it began,
falling,
so slowly.
3 a.m., Sunday, driving along Bloor street,
Tony, Filo, Pat, Roberto and I
singing to Oklahoma, to a sailor in Valparaiso
and to Billie Holiday
with no wind to witness, to curse us
and this tender snow.

Walking down Greensides Avenue now,
I think someone sitting in a house this minute
and looking through a window at this silence,
cannot be a fascist,
Everyone is covered by this silence,
no one can be thinking of how to oppress anyone else
they will have to think of how silent it is
and how to shovel this quiet snow,
no one can make a telephone call
or press a button
or utter a racist slur in this gentleness
they will be struck by their own weakness
they will recognize this silence,
this sphinx of a snowfall
Just to sabotage my epigrams,
the snow fell,
these three days,
softly.

43

Oh yes, there it is
the kind that grows cruelty
there it is
what a wind!
the kind that gives a headache
that makes a christian,
that sculpts a grim mouth,
there it is
the one that blows on reservations
and Jarvis street.

45

– *winter suicide* –
shall I do it then,
now, here,
a riddle for februarys,
shall I,
here, under this mexican blanket
clutching my dictionary (Vol. II the shorter
Oxford Marl-Z),
Shall I do it before falling asleep
before the summer comes
before seeing the Chicago Art Ensemble again,
maybe if Betty Carter never sang,
or Roscoe Mitchell never touched a saxophone;
losing my life like that though,
mislaying the damn thing,
and right in the middle of winter,
me!
and it gone
flown
shall I chew the red berries
which I collected before the freeze.

47

coffin of a winter!

50

season of ambiguity
blinding sun, cold air
days imitating night
me, here.

53

Two things I will not buy
in this city,
mangoes and poinsettia;
exiled,
I must keep a little self respect.

54

comrade winter,
look what you've done,
I have written epigrams to you,
e'en poems,
can it be that . . . ?
no, no, I am not your lover,
perhaps . . . your enemy.

■ ■ ■

EPIGRAMS TO ERNESTO CARDENAL IN DEFENSE OF CLAUDIA

2

These verses are for you Ernesto,
not for all my lovers
whom I bad mouth in these lines,
poor things, they were smaller than these epigrams,
but a poet's ego needs entire pages.

3

If you were there when I came home
after that poetry reading on Spadina,
if you were there when I needed no talking
after that man told me that he liked my poems
but not my politics (as if they are different),
if you were there instead of that empty fellow
I slept with,
you would have held my head, kept me warm
and asked me for nothing else.

12

How do I know that this is love
and not legitimation of capitalist relations of production
in advanced patriarchy?

13

Often Ernesto,
women are quite desperate.
Often in your glance
we wish to be invisible.

14

so we spent hours and hours
learning Marx,
so we picketted embassies and stood
at rallies,
so it's been 13 years agitating
for the liberation of Africa,

so they still think, I should be in charge
of the refreshments.

27

Dear Ernesto,
I have terrible problems convincing
people that these are love poems.
Apparently I am not allowed to love
more than a single person at a time.
Can I not love anyone but you?
signed,
"Desperate."

30

Ars Hominis/the manly arts

Since you've left me no descriptions
having used them all to describe me
or someone else I hardly recognize
I have no way of telling you
how long and wonderful your legs were;
since you've covetously hoarded all the words
such as "slender" and "sensuous" and "like a
young gazelle"
I have no way of letting you know
that I loved how you stood and how you walked,
and forgive my indelicacy,
your copulatory symmetry, your pensile beauty;
since you've massacred every intimate phrase
in a bloodletting of paternal epithets
like "fuck" and "rape," "cock" and "cunt,"
I cannot write you this epigram.

32

Have you ever noticed
that when men write love poems
they're always about virgins or whores
or earth mothers?
How feint-hearted.

33

Ars Poetica

Yes, but what else was done
except the writing of calming lines
except sitting in artsy cafes
talking artsy talk.
what else except marrying three wives
beating them, flying into tantrums,
except tonal voices, bellicose sermons,
self-indulgent dulcimer expurgations
about fathers and women
what else was done, except
a disembodied anxiety, anger unable
to find a table to bang or a door to slam
what when the chance to speak is only taken
when it is not necessary, past,
what when the chance is lost,
what when only doodlings mark a great stone
visits to the asylum mark a great poet
and freedom is personal
yes what then was done except a poser
worse, a mole has infiltrated poems.

34

Ars Poetica (II)

cow's hide or drum
don't tell me it makes no difference
to my singing,
I do not think that histories are so plain,
so clumsy and so temporal;
griots take one hundred years
to know what they say
four hundred more to tell it;
I want to write as many poems as Pablo Neruda
to have "pared my fingers to the quick"
like his,
to duck and run like hell from numbing chants.
        – Pablo Neruda in "Ars Poetica (I)" for *Fin de Mundo*.

35

Ars Poetica (III)
"on being told that being Black is being bitter"

give up the bitterness
he told my young friend/poet
give it up and you will be beautiful.
after all these years and after all these words
it is not simply a part of us anymore
it is not something that you can take away
as if we held it for safekeeping,
it is not a treasure, not a sweet,
it is something hot in the hand, a piece of red coal,
it is an electric fence, touched,
we are repulsed, embraced and destroyed,
it is not separate, different,
it is all of us, mixed up in our skins,

welded to our bones
and it cannot be thrown away
not after all these years, after all these words
we don't have a hold on it
it has a hold on us,
to give it up means that someone dies,
you, or my young poet friend
so be careful when you say give up the
bitterness.
let him stand in the light for a moment
let him say his few words, let him breathe
and thank whoever you pray to
that he isn't standing on a dark street
with a brick,
waiting for you.

39

And take these too Ernesto
as I give them
once more with gratitude
I wish I was with you,
you let me look at "Managua in the evening sky,"
such a sky, memorious and red,
repels cruelties from the hondurean border.

40

Imitation of Cardenal

If Hitler waits at the corner of the Schmiedtor
and a girl is walking along the Landestrasse with her mother
and Hitler cannot dance
and everything is full of kisses
and Hitler cannot dance

so Hitler goose steps
and a girl dances with her mother and a cadet
and a girl walking now with her mother, with a cadet
is not to blame because Hitler has no rhythm
and a girl dances with her mother and a cadet
a girl bebops
and Hitler goose steps
and Hitler's finger snaps a war song
a girl is not to blame.

■

47

you say you want me to . . .
to what?
no I can't tap dance
at the International Women's Day rally.

■

54

Cardenal, the truth is that
even though you are not a country
or my grandmother
or coconut ice cream
or Marquez's Autumn of the Patriarch
or Sarah Vaughan
or cuban music
or brazillian movies
or Kurosawa
or C.L.R.'s *Black Jacobins*
or Angela
or Guayguayare
I love you for the same things.

■ ■ ■

from *Chronicles of the Hostile Sun* (1984)

AMELIA

I know that lying there in that bed
in that room
smelling of wet coconut fibres
and children's urine
bundled up in a mound
under the pink chenille and cold
sweating sheets
you wanted to escape,
run from that room
and children huddling against you
with the rain falling outside
and flies and mud
and a criminal for a son
and the scent of the sewer heightened
by the rain falling.
on those days
she tried to roll herself
into the tiniest of balls on the bed
on those days she did not succeed
except in turning the bed into a ship
and she, the stranded one
in that sea of a room
floating and dipping
into the waves, the swell
of a life anchored.
I think that she would have been better
by the sea
in guayguayare,
but in the town
hot with neighbours and want
she withered and swelled
and died and left me
after years of hiding
and finally her feet fearful and nervous
could not step on asphalt

or find a pair of shoes.
swimming in the brutish rain
at once she lost her voice
since all of its words contained her downfall.
she gargled instead the coarse water from her eyes
the incessant nights
the crickets call
and the drooping tree,
breathed, in gasps
what was left in the air
after husband and two generations of children.
lying in a hospital bed
you could not live by then
without the contradictions
of your own aggrieved room
with only me to describe the parking lot outside
and your promise, impossible,
to buy me a bicycle,
when they brought your body home
I smiled a child's smile of conspiracy
and kissed your face.

■ ■ ■

DIARY – THE GRENADA CRISIS

In the five a.m. dusk
grains of night's black drizzle, first stones
boulders of dark
sprinkle the open face
open eyes, incense of furtive moths
badluck's cricket brown to the ceiling
I am watching two people sleep.

in the morning smoke light
my chest and its arms cover my breasts,
the ground, wet, the night before,

soil scented,
the open vault of the morning,
scented as the beginning and end of everything
after a while, villainy fingers the eyes,
daubs the hills disenchant
and the mouth lies in its roof
like a cold snake.

coals lit
and contained in clay, glowing
a horizon like a morning coal pot,
still an old woman stooping – cold
churches coral their walls on the ridge,
I could exchange this caribbean
for a good night's sleep
or a street without young men.

the ghost of a thin woman
drifts against the rim of the street,
I thought nothing was passing,
in the grey light before the crying animals,
when I saw her dress and her pointed face,
I am climbing the steps to the garbage dump,
a woman frightens me.

In the pale air overlooking the town
in the anxious dock
where sweat and arms are lost
already,
the ship and the cement
drop against the metal skies,
a yankee paratrooper strangles in his sheet.

prayers for rain,
instead again this wonderful sky;
an evening of the war and those of us looking
with our mouths open
see beauty become appalling,

sunset, breaths of grey clouds streaked red,
we are watching a house burn.

All afternoon and all night,
each night we watch a different
fire burn,
Tuesday, Butler House
Wednesday, Radio Free Grenada
Thursday, The Police Station
A voice at the window looking
"the whole damn town should burn"
another "no too many of us will die."

eyes full of sleep lie awake
we have difficulty eating,
"what's that" to every new sound
of the war.

In the five a.m. cold light
something is missing,
some part of the body, some
area of the world, an island,
a place to think about,

I am walking on the rock of
a beach in Barbados
looking to where Grenada was
now, the flight of an american bomber
leaves the mark of a rapist in the room.

of every waking,
what must we do today,
be defiant or lie in the
corridor waiting for them,
fear keeps us awake
and makes us long for sleep.

In my chest,
a green-water well,

it is 5 a.m. and I
have slept with my glasses on
in case we must run.

the last evening,
the dock and the sky make one,
somewhere, it has disappeared,
the hard sky sends
military transports,
the darkness and my shoulders
meet at the neck,
no air comes up,
we have breathed the last of it.

In the Grand Etang
mist and damp
the road to Fedon
fern, sturdy,
hesitate
awaiting guerrillas.

■ ■ ■

OCTOBER 19TH, 1983

this poem cannot find words
this poem repeats itself
Maurice is dead
Jackie is dead
Uni is dead
Vincent is dead
dream is dead
lesser and greater
dream is dead in these antilles
windward, leeward
Maurice is dead, Jackie is dead
Uni is dead, Vincent is dead

dream is dead
i deny this poem
there isn't a hand large enough
to gesture this tragedy
let alone these words
dead insists itself on us
a glue of blood sticks the rest together
some are dead, the others will not mourn
most wait for the death announcements
Maurice is dead, Jackie is dead
Uni is dead, Vincent is dead
dream is dead
lesser and greater
dream is dead
in these antilles
windward, leeward
reality will die
i refuse to watch faces
back once again
betrayal again, ships again,
manacles again
some of us sold each other
bracelets, undecorative and unholy,
back to god!
i cannot believe the sound
of your voice any longer
blind folded and manacled
stripped
Bernard, Phyllis, Owusu, H.A.!
what now!
back to jails in these antilles!
back to shackles! back to slavery!
dream is dead
lesser and greater
drowned and buried
windward, leeward
a dirge sung for ever
and in flesh
three armoured personnel carriers

how did they feel
shot, shut
across Lucas street
this fracticide, this hot day
how did they feel
murdering the revolution
skulking back along the road
the people watchful,
the white flare
the shots
the shot, the people running,
jumping, flying,
the fort, fleeing
what, rumour, not true
please, rearrested not dead,
Maurice is dead
at 9:30 p.m. the radio
Jackie is dead ...
9:30 p.m. the radio
dream is dead
in these antilles
how do you write tears
it is not enough, too much
our mouths reduced,
informed by grief
windward, leeward
it is only october 19th, 1983
and dream is dead
in these antilles.

■ ■ ■

OCTOBER 25TH, 1983

The planes are circling,
the american paratroopers dropping,
later Radio Free Grenada stops for the last time

In the end they sang –
"ain't giving up no way,
no i ain't giving up no way"

The OECS riding like birds on a cow
led america to the green hills of St. George's
and waited at Point Salines
while it fed on the young of the land,
eating their flesh with bombs,
breaking their bellies with grenade launchers

america came to restore democracy,
what was restored was faith
in the fact that you cannot fight bombers
battleships, aircraft carriers, helicopter gunships,
surveillance planes, five thousand american soldiers
six caribbean stooges and the big american war machine,
you cannot fight this with a machete
you cannot fight it with a handful of dirt
you cannot fight it with a hectare of land free from bosses
you cannot fight it with farmers
you cannot fight it with 30 miles of feeder roads
you cannot fight it with free health care
you cannot fight it with free education
you cannot fight it with women's cooperatives
you cannot fight it with a pound of bananas or a handful of fish
which belongs to you

certainly you cannot fight it with dignity.

because you must run into the street
you must crawl into a ditch
and you must wait there and watch
your family,
your mother, your sister, your little brother,
your husband, your wife,
you must watch them
because they will become hungry,
and they will give you in to the americans,

and they will say that you belong to the militia,
or the health brigade,
or the civil service,
or the people's revolutionary army,
or the community work brigade,
or the New Jewel Movement –
they will say that you lived in the country,
they will say that you are Cuban,
they will say that you served cakes
at the Point Salines airport fundraising,
they will say that you are human,
they will say
that one day last month
you said that for four and a half years
you have been happy.
they will say all this because they want to eat.

And finally you can only fight it with the silence of your
dead body.

■ ■ ■

ON AMERICAN NUMERACY AND LITERACY IN THE WAR AGAINST GRENADA

Counting in american
you start with 600 cubans,
the next figure in that numeracy
is 1100 cubans,
trouble ascending, move to 2000 cubans,
P1 equals zero grenadians
which accounts for the resistance in the hills;
when deploying troops
or actually in most cases, thugs,
send 15,000
if 100 die it's friendly fire
and anyway that's less than if you
only send 500 (percentage wise you know)

when counting casualties in a war
the first is always american,
(for instance the first casualty in El Salvador
as reported in Newsweek was an american
army officer)
the 40,000 salvadoreans are just playing dead
and the grenadians lying face upward in the sun
at Beausejour are only catching flies.

The term "mass grave" does not apply
to those dug by marines or right wing death squads in Central
    America,
a "pre-emptive strike" or a "rescue mission"
is not a war,
except to the illiterate and the oppressed
who have no words for death,
therefore no real need for life.

■ ■ ■

P.P.S. GRENADA

I have never missed a place either
except now
there was a house
there was a harbour, some lights
on the water, a hammock
there was a road,
close to the cliffs'
frequent view of the sea
there was a woman
very young
her boy much older,
we planted corn and ochroes
and peas in the front garden
though the rats ate the corn
there was a boat,

I made friends
with its owner and he called
me on his way to work each morning
there was another road, the one to Goave,
all the way up looking back
the rainy season greened the hills
dry spells reddened the flambouyant
there was a river
at concord
seeing it the first time surprised me
big smooth stones, brown and ashen
and women standing in its water
with washing
there was a farm
on a hillside
as most are, forty acres with a
river deep inside, Jason and Brother-
man picked coconuts, the air,
the brief smell of cloves, Rusty
swam naked in the river's pond
after our descent, Jason's room
reminded me of a house when I was
a child, wooden windows, dated magazines
books and no indoor tap,
there was a wall of rock which sank into the street
in the trees and vine and lizards
it cooled the walk from town,
though town was hot and steep whenever I
got to the market it was worth the task,
there was a spot, in the centre of the women
and the produce, near to the blood pudding vendor
a place where every smell of earth and sweat
assailed the nostrils and the skin, I would
end up coming home, with the scrawniest provisions,
I don't know how, it was those women's eyes
and their hands, I'd pass by the best and
buy from the most poor,
there was a tree
at the head of the beach,

Grand Anse, not in a showy spot
but cool and almost always empty
of tourists
the ocean there was calmer, shallow,
more to Filo's liking
sea grapes, that was what the tree grew
sea grapes, not at all like grapes in north america
a tougher skin, a bigger seed
sweet and sour at once,
there was the carenage, street and harbour
dock and motorway
tied up to its sometimes "the sea shepherd"
"albatross" "Vietnam" "alistair"
the boats to Carriacou, banana boat, the "geest" and
the tourist boat – Cunard, envy and
hatred to these last two
"how many rooms in that boat, you think?"
this from Frederick, he's had to sleep in
one with his mother and her husband
and when they come down from country,
two more children.

■

there was a street
a few more really, perhaps
twenty or so would be accurate, inclined, terraced,
cobbled or mud
when I first saw them I remember blanching
at the labour and resolve required to climb them
I would give more than imagined to see them
as they were,
there was a night swimming in the dark
grande anse, morne rouge, la sagesse, with voices
after and brandy,
there was a woman thin and black like
a stick, though she mistrusted me, a foreigner,
I marvelled at her
there was a friend,

named for a greek,
storyteller like his namesake Homer
he would promise a favour this afternoon
and return five days later with a wild tale
about his car, his hands, the priorities
of the revolution and his personal safety
or a fight with his uncle.
the post office, its smell of yellowing paper,
stamps, its red iron mail box, wooden
posts, the custom's house, its stacks
of paper filled out by hand in quadruplicate,
its patience, its frustrated waiting lines
lunch hour, noon to one, everything is shut
the day's heat at its triumph,
there was a path
wet with grass, weedy
stones but people rarely walk there preferring
the high path overlooking the town,
another thing,
on woolwich road, the view on its left
incline, houses leaning down, lines of clothing
pots and flowering brush, the ever present
harbour framed through bits or wide angled
to point salines,
there was an hour actually many when
the electricity broke down,
my sister grew angry and I lit candles
and the lamps
looking forward to their secretness,
even when the electricity returned
and all around put on their flourescent lights
I left the candles burning.
there was a month when it rained
and I did not have an umbrella
or proper shoes,
more pot holes appeared in the streets
and pumpkin vines grew swiftly over Marlene's
doorstep,

that was when the sand in the ocean shifted
and levelled out the deep shelf,
that was when one day the beach was startlingly empty
that was when the sea became less
trustworthy,
after Dominica, St. Lucia, St. Vincent
I came back with such relief I
talked to the taxidriver from Grenville
all the way home,
Birch Grove, Beaulieu
after Vieux Fort and Marigot this was comfortable.

■

there was paul,
he was a farmer and very young,
in St. David he taught those young
still
to take care of the earth,
he prayed for rain and good students,
we went to a cricket game at Queen's Park
I slept through half of it,
it was a sunday and I shook his hand goodbye
deciding that I was not big enough for him,
sunday too when we drove up to Mt. Moritz
worried, a group of young men stopped talking
as we passed
then began again "they have no right,"
that was in the middle of the crisis
the fallen silk cotton tree lay across the pond
still growing
it was older than all of us put together,
jomo and damani showed us their passion
fruit tree and I took photographs of them
on the rise of Mt. Moritz and the sea in back.

■

there was a little rum and anxiety
about the coming week,
but hope, we did not want the newness
of this place to end
then everyone would lose their memory
as in Macondo
it was a new way of seeing everything
even though the sky was still oppressive
and the land smelled of hardship
there was a name for all of this, only
it was never said quite well
but had to do with a freeness which the body felt,
a joy even in the heat,
on bad days I went to the sea
after work, I sat with Chris, the bartender
at the Riviera,
I didn't like the proprieters
they only smiled for tourists but Chris
was good company,
he kept my money and an eye on my belongings
while I dove into the water;
just that was enough, so wide, so womanly
the gaze to the horizon
I would forget to fill my lungs
for hours, looking to this sea,
once I lay down on the edge
afraid to stand
past the cactus and the prickly shrub
at point salines' most eastern tip
the sharpened cliff, the dark blue water
the first meeting of the atlantic and the caribbean
gave me vertigo,
that was the last time I went there
before the war,
I suppose that now they've strung barbed wire
between the two

∎

there was a mass of insects, beetles
rain flies, nocturnal
moths, ants
they have a nest in the roof
when I think of getting rid of them
the thought that they are of greater number and stronger
holds me back, they liked dead mosquitos
I pity mosquitos
they die in atrocious ways
in hot candle wax, in pesticide fumes or
smashed against the walls,
I still have no idea what children talk about
even after eavesdropping on conversations of theirs
I have no memory myself, only
that the subjects were of some importance,
nor of traders,
two more months would have been sufficient time
to walk past the crates of fruits and provisions
these women, small and whip-like, broad and shrewd
slowly, listening for their constancy
there was that night
when carol took me to the "turtle back"
after the meeting of banana growers
and we talked about how this island
and the others
made us want and sad
that we could neither go nor stay,
looking at my hands, without a mark,
with self-indulgent palms to fondle paper,
I understood my ill-preparedness
for struggle.
when we left
I took my diaries, my passport and my Brecht
this is security too,
"so you're leaving,
how lucky for you, will you send for me?"

∎

Frederick would be alarmed
that I could not be there when the peas came
that some one else would live in the house,
I left that hat, the one the carib gave to me
the lamp shades, the mexican blankets, my
dictionaries, my roads, my evenings
that nuisance breadfruit tree, dominique promised
to cut it before the next flowering . . .
of course some little facts,
the sea in the night, that part which
the lights outside the Dome make clear,
is warm
warmer than the air, and the water
becomes something other than water, fog,
it rolls, rather, spreads toward the feet.

■ ■ ■

[UNTITLED]

four hours on a bus across alberta and saskatchewan
not in all the months standing over frozen river
antigonish at the wood stove should not come next to
right wing calgary which after all is self conscious and
naked oil and people gone apartment for rent only one
woman who gave her room and her boots signal of a heart
and poor amal says that she grows shorter there taking
what is fear to saskatoon to meet strangers plead innocence
explain why we had guns to defend against nuclear arms
do not remember the trip back edmonton crossed paths with
another third world supplicant before ignorance plead dead
edmonton at the huge warm room warm paths through blind
snow early morning sleeping through fog driving a young
man who likes to wake up early dark in saskatoon light in
edmonton gin in the union hall in winnipeg you wonder if
anyone sault ste marie lost luggage for three days swapo
visitors will lie in the same bed next night hurried through

library college public hall slide tapes conviction beg for
help to be left alone the sault just over the border american
television canadian will nuke 'em pugnacious boy in one
prairie town proverbial hope fled not seen in him sixties'
clarity sits only in the aged here in toronto the last
solidarity posters insert the newest names of the fallen
can't wait for construction sites to paste their latest position
on angola nicaragua grenada south africa as if people waited
there for pronouncements never struggle but know the correct
position either way taut cafes eager for montreal a woman
at mcgill back of the car from antigonish long road to sydney
an area of trees hiding the sign to monastary old as 1750
betrayed dropped off in a ship returning cargo of salted cod
nova scotia instead no remembered continent no black star
back in toronto eyes remaining on that area of trees to monastery
but miners in sydney understand death explosions strikes long
to sydney bridge cape breton john arthur's humour more familiar
to mirabeau farmers closer than far away toronto he said halifax
two days ago no sign of africville sent to preston by big money
a street in exchange for more of our grief yet above in a church
basement someone thanked us for our concern in our welfare but
america was great plead nothing say thanks leave for cherrybrook
digby truro bus knifing maritime winter short grass
fearing no return from coast comfort here it is possible
to go out jump off the land apologies to new brunswick
newfoundland someone on the phone asking for company
solidarity for loss lived in sauteurs one year do you
know what happened there is everyone alright hoarse voiced
don't know they have people in crates at the airport they
were bombing when you were there grenville too did you know
so and so you didn't hear sorrow is the hoarse voice then
the small expectant voice on the other end filling in stories
gaps time between this year and that village between renew
a friend never met before ringing of unfinished in the cold
hotel room 7 a.m. glad to go home only the wind and fog and
weepy sydney holds the plain to the edge of this continent.

■ ■ ■

from *Sans Souci and Other Stories* (1988)

BLOSSOM

Priestess of Oya, Goddess of winds, storms and waterfalls

Blossom's was jumping tonight. Oya and Shango and God and spirit and ordinary people was chanting and singing and jumping the place down. Blossom's was a obeah house and speakeasy on Vaughan Road. People didn't come for the cheap liquor Blossom sell, though as night wear on, on any given night, Blossom, in she waters, would tilt the bottle a little in your favour. No, it wasn't the cheap liquor, even if you could drink it all night long till morning. It was the feel of the place. The cheap light revolving over the bar, the red shag covering the wall against which Blossom always sit, a line of beer, along the window-sill behind, as long as she ample arms spread out over the back of a wooden bench. And, the candles glowing bright on the shrine of Oya, Blossom's mother Goddess.

This was Blossom's most successful endeavour since coming to Canada. Every once in a while, under she breath, she curse the day she come to Toronto from Oropuche, Trinidad. But nothing, not even snarky white people could keep Blossom under. When she first come it was to babysit some snot-nosed children on Oriole Parkway. She did meet a man, in a club on Henry Street in Port-of-Spain, who promise she to take care of she, if she ever was in Toronto. When Blossom reach, the man disappear and through the one other person she know in Toronto she get the work on Oriole.

Well Blossom decide long that she did never mean for this kinda work, steady cleaning up after white people, and that is when she decide to take a course in secretarial at night. Is there she meet Peg and Betty, who she did know from home, and Fancy Girl. And for two good years they all try to type; but their heart wasn't in it. So they switch to carpentry and upholstering. Fancy Girl swear that they could make a good business because she father was a joiner and white people was paying a lot of money for old-looking furniture. They all went along with this until Peg say she need to make some fast money because, where they was going to find white people who like old furniture, and who was going to buy old furniture from Black women anyway. That is when Fancy Girl come up with the pyramid scheme.

They was to put everybody name on a piece of paper, everybody was to find five people to put on the list and that five would find five and so on. Everybody on the list would send the first person one hundred dollars. In the end everybody was to get thousands of dollars in the mail and only invest one hundred, unless the pyramid break. Fancy Girl name was first and so the pyramid start. Lo and behold, Fancy Girl leave town saying she going to Montreal for a weekend and it was the last they ever see she. The pyramid bust up and they discover that Fancy Girl pick up ten thousand dollars clean. Blossom had to hide for months from people on the pyramid and she swear to Peg that, if she ever see Fancy Girl Munroe again, dog eat she supper.

Well now is five years since Blossom in Canada and nothing ain't breaking. She leave the people on Oriole for some others on Balmoral. The white man boss-man was a doctor. Since the day she reach, he eyeing she, eyeing she. Blossom just mark this down in she head and making sure she ain't in no room alone with he. Now one day, it so happen that she in the basement doing the washing and who come down there but he, playing like if he looking for something. She watching him from the corner of she eye and, sure as the day, he make a grab for she. Blossom know a few things, so she grab on to he little finger and start to squeeze it back till he face change all colour from white to black and he had to scream out. Blossom sheself start to scream like all hell, until the wife and children run downstairs too.

It ain't have cuss, Blossom ain't cuss that day. The wife face red and shame and then she start to watch Blossom cut eye. Well look at my cross nah Lord, Blossom think, here this dog trying to abuse me and she watching *me* cut eye! Me! a church-going woman! A craziness fly up in Blossom head and she start to go mad on them in the house. She flinging things left right and centre and cussing big word. Blossom fly right off the handle, until they send for the police for Blossom. She didn't care. They couldn't make she hush. It don't have no dignity in white man feeling you up! So she cuss out the police too, when they come, and tell them to serve and protect she, like they supposed to do and lock up the so-and-so. The doctor keep saying to the police, "Oh this is so embarrassing. She's crazy. She's crazy." And Blossom tell him, "You ain't see crazy yet." She run and dash all the people clothes in the swimming pool and shouting, "Make me a weapon in thine hand, oh Lord!" Blossom grab on to the doctor neck, dragging him, to drown him. It take two police to unlatch Blossom from the man red neck, yes. And how the police get Blossom to leave is a wonder; but she wouldn't leave without she pay, and in cash money too besides, she tell them. Anyhow, the police get Blossom to leave the house; and they must be 'fraid Blossom too, so they let she off down the street and tell she to go home.

The next day Blossom show up on Balmoral with a placard saying the Dr. So-and-So was a white rapist; and Peg and Betty bring a Black Power flag and the three of them parade in front of that man house whole day. Well is now this doctor know that he mess with the wrong woman, because when he reach home that evening, Blossom and Peg and Betty bang on the car, singing, "We Shall Not be Moved" and chanting, "Doctor So-and-So is a Rapist." They reach into the car and, well, rough up the doctor – grabbing he tie and threatening to cut off he balls. Not a soul ain't come outside, but you never see so much drapes and curtain moving and swaying up and down Balmoral. Police come again, but they tell Doctor So-and-So that the sidewalk is public property and as long as Blossom and them keep moving they wasn't committing no crime. Well, when they hear that, Blossom and them start to laugh and clap and sing "We Shall Overcome." That night, at Peg house, they laugh and they eat and they drink and dance and laugh more, remembering the doctor face when they was banging on he car. The next day Blossom hear from the Guyanese girl working next door that the whole family on Balmoral, Doctor, wife, children, cat and dog, gone to Florida.

After that, Blossom decide to do day work here and day work there, so that no white man would be over she and she was figuring on a way to save some money to do she own business.

Blossom start up with Victor one night in a dance. It ain't have no reason that she could say why she hook up with him except that in a dance one night, before Fancy Girl take off, when Peg and Betty and Fancy Girl was in they dance days, she suddenly look around and all three was jack up in a corner with some man.

They was grinding down the Trinidad Club and there was Blossom, alone at the table, playing she was groovin' to the music.

Alone. Well, keeping up sheself, working, working and keeping the spirits up in this cold place all the time.... Is not until all of a sudden one moment, you does see youself. Something tell she to stop and witness the scene. And then Blossom decide to get a man. All she girl pals had one, and Blossom decide to get one too. It sadden she a little to see she riding partners all off to the side so. After all, every weekend they used to fête and insult man when they come to ask them to dance. They would fête all night in the middle of the floor and get tight on southern comfort. Then they would hobble down the steps out of the club on Church or "Room at the Top," high heels squeezing and waist in pain, and hail a taxi home to one house or the other. By the time the taxi reach wherever they was going, shoes would be in hand and stockings off and a lot of groaning and description of foot pain would hit the door. And comparing notes on which man look so good and which man had a hard on, they would cook, bake and salt fish, in the morning and laugh about the night before. If is one thing with Blossom, Peg and Betty and Fancy Girl, they like to have a good time. The world didn't mean for sorrow; and suffering don't suit nobody face, Blossom say.

So when she see girl-days done and everybody else straighten up and get man, Blossom decide to get a man too. The first, first man that pass Blossom eyes after deciding was Victor and Blossom decide on him. It wasn't the first man Blossom had, but it was the first one she decide to keep. It ain't have no special reason either; is just when Victor appear, Blossom get a idea to fall in love. Well, then start a long line of misery the likes of which Blossom never see before and never intend to see again. The only reason that the misery last so long is because Blossom was a stubborn woman and when she decide something, she decide. It wasn't even that Blossom really like Victor because whenever she sit down to count his attributes, the man was really lacking in kindness and had a streak of meanness when it come to woman. But she figure like and love not the same thing. So Blossom married to Victor that same summer, in the Pentecostal Church. Victor wanted to live together, but Blossom say she wouldn't be able to go to church no more if she living in sin and if Victor want any honey from she, it have to be with God blessing.

The wedding night, Victor disappear. He show up in a dance, in he white wedding suit and Blossom ain't see him till Monday morning. So Blossom take a sign from this and start to watch Victor because she wasn't a hasty woman by nature. He come when he want, he go when he want and vex when she ain't there. He don't bring much money. Blossom still working day work and every night of the week Victor have friends over drinking Blossom liquor. But Blossom love Victor, so she put up with this type of behaviour for a good few years; because love supposed to be hard and if it ain't hard, it ain't sweet, they say. You have to bear with man, she mother used to say, and besides, Blossom couldn't grudge Victor he good time. Living wasn't just for slaving and it seem that in this society the harder you work, the less you have. Judge not lest ye be judged; this sermon Blossom would give to Peg and Betty anytime they contradict Victor. And anyway, Blossom have she desires and Victor have more than reputation between he legs.

So life go on as it supposed to go on, until Blossom decide not to go to work one day. That time, they was living on Vaughan Road and Blossom wake up feeling like a old woman. Just tired. Something tell she to stay home and figure out she life; because a thirty-six year old woman shouldn't feel so old and tired. She look at she face in the mirror and figure that she look like a old woman too. Ten years she here now, and nothing shaking, just getting older and older, watching white people live. She, sheself living underneath all the time. She didn't even feel like living with Victor anymore. All the sugar gone outa the thing. Victor had one scheme after another, poor thing. Everything gone a little sour.

She was looking out the window, toward the bus stop on Vaughan Road, thinking this. Looking at people going to work like they does do every morning. It make she even more tired to watch them. Today she was supposed to go to a house on Roselawn. Three bathrooms to clean, two living rooms, basement, laundry – God knows what else. Fifty dollars. She look at she short fingers, still water-laden from the day before, then look at the bus stop again. No, no. Not today. Not this woman. In the bedroom, she watch Victor lying in the bed, face peaceful as ever, young like a baby. Passing into the kitchen shaking she head, she think, "Victor you ain't ready for the Lord yet."

Blossom must be was sitting at the kitchen table for a hour or so when Victor get up. She hear him bathe, dress and come out to the kitchen. "Ah, ah, you still here? Is ten o'clock you know!" She didn't answer. "Girl, you ain't going to work today, or what?" She didn't answer. "You is a happy woman yes, Blossom. Anyway," as he put he coat on, "I have to meet a fella." Something just fly up in Blossom head and she reach for the bread knife on the table. "Victor, just go and don't come back, you hear me?" waving the knife. "Girl you crazy, or what?" Victor edged toward the door, "What happen to you this morning?"

Next thing Blossom know, she running Victor down Vaughan Road screaming and waving the bread knife. She hear somebody screaming loud, loud. At first she didn't know who it is, and is then she realize that the scream was coming from she and she couldn't stop it. She dress in she nightie alone and screaming in the middle of the road. So it went on and on and on until it turn into a cry and Blossom just cry and cry and cry and then she start to walk. That day Blossom walk. And walk and cry, until she was so exhausted that she find she way home and went to sleep.

She wake up the next morning, feeling shaky and something like spiritual. She was frightened, in case the crying come back again. The apartment was empty. She had the feeling that she was holding she body around she heart, holding sheself together, tight, tight. She get dressed and went to the Pentecostal Church where she get married and sit there till evening.

For two weeks this is all Blossom do. As soon as she feel the crying welling up inside she and turning to a scream, she get dressed and go to the Pentecost. After two weeks, another feeling come; one as if Blossom dip she whole head in water and come up gasping. She heart would pump fast as if she going to die and then the feeling, washed and gasping. During these weeks she could drink nothing but water. When she try to eat bread, something reach inside of she throat and spit it out. Two weeks more and Blossom hair turn white all over. Then she start to speak in tongues that she didn't ever learn, but she understand. At night, in Blossom cry dreams, she feel sheself flying round the earth and raging around the world and then, not just this earth, but earth deep in the blackness beyond sky. There, sky become further than sky and further than dream. She dream so much farther than she ever go in a dream, that she was awake. Blossom see volcano erupt and mountain fall down two feet away and she ain't get touch. She come to the place where legahoo and lajabless is not even dog and where soucouyant, the fireball, burn up in the bigger fire of the infinite sun, where none of the ordinary spirit Blossom know is nothing. She come to the place where pestilence mount good, good heart and good heart bust for joy. The place bright one minute and dark the next. The place big one minute, so big Blossom standing in a hole and the blackness rising up like long shafts above she and widening out into a yellow and red desert as far as she could see; the place small, next minute, as a pin head and only Blossom heart what shrink small, small, small, could fit in the world of it. Then she feel as if she don't have no hand, no foot and she don't need them. Sometimes, she crawling like mapeepee snake; sometimes she walking tall, tall, like a moco jumbie through desert and darkness, desert and darkness, upside down and sideways.

In the mornings, Blossom feel she body beating up and breaking up on a hard mud ground and she, weeping as if she mourning and as if somebody borning. And talking in tongues, the tongues saying the name, Oya. The name sound through Blossom into every layer of she skin, she flesh – like sugar and seasoning. Blossom body come hard like steel and supple like water, when she say Oya. Oya. This Oya was a big spirit Blossom know from home.

One night, Oya hold Blossom and bring she through the most terrifying dream in she life. In the dream, Oya make Blossom look at Black people suffering. The face of Black people suffering was so old and hoary that Blossom nearly dead. And is so she vomit. She skin wither under Suffering look; and she feel hungry and thirsty as nobody ever feel before. Pain dry out Blossom soul, until it turn to nothing. Blossom so 'fraid she dead that she take she last ball of spit, and stone Suffering. Suffering jump up so fast and grab the stone, Blossom shocked, because she did think Suffering was decrepit. Then Suffering head for Blossom with such a speed that Blossom fingernails and hairs fall out. Blossom start to dry away, and melt away, until it only had one grain of she left. And Suffering still descending. Blossom scream for Oya and Oya didn't come and Suffering keep coming. Blossom was never a woman to stop, even before she start to dream. So she roll and dance she grain-self into a hate so hard, she chisel sheself into a sharp hot prickle and fly in Suffering face. Suffering howl like a beast and back back. Blossom spin and chew on that nut of hate, right in Suffering eyeball. The more Blossom spin and dance, the more Suffering back back; the more Suffering back back, the bigger Blossom get, until Blossom was Oya with she warrior knife, advancing. In the cold light of Suffering, with Oya hot and advancing, Suffering slam a door and disappear. Blossom climb into Oya lovely womb of strength and fearlessness. Full of joy when Oya show she the warrior dance where heart and blood burst open. Freeness, Oya call that dance; and the colour of the dance was red and it was a dance to dance high up in the air. In this dance Oya had such a sweet laugh, it make she black skin shake and it full up Blossom and shake she too.

Each night Blossom grow more into Oya. Blossom singing, singing for Oya to come,

"Oya arriwo Oya, Oya arriwo Oya, Oya kauako arriwo, Arripiti O Oya."

Each night Blossom learn a new piece of Oya and finally, it come to she. She had the power to see and the power to fight; she had the power to feel pain and the power to heal. For life was nothing as it could be taken away any minute; what was earthly was fleeting; what could be done was joy and it have no beauty in suffering.

"Oya O Ologbo O de, Ma yak ba Ma Who! leh, Oya O Ologo O de, Ma yak ba Ma Who! leh, Oya Oh de arriwo, Oya Oh de cumale."

From that day, Blossom dress in yellow and red from head to foot, the colour of joy and the colour of war against suffering. She head wrap in a long yellow cloth; she body wrap in red. She become a obeah woman, spiritual mother and priestess of Oya, Yoruba Goddess-warrior of winds, storms and waterfalls. It was Oya who run Victor out and it was Oya who plague the gynaecologist and laugh and drink afterwards. It was Oya who well up the tears inside Blossom and who spit the bread out of Blossom mouth.

Quite here, Oya did search for Blossom. Quite here, she find she.

Black people on Vaughan Road recognized Blossom as gifted and powerful by she carriage and the fierce look in she eyes. She fill she rooms with compelling powder and reliance smoke, drink rum and spit it in the corners, for the spirits who would enter Blossom obeah house in the night. Little by little people begin to find out that Blossom was the priestess of Oya, the Goddess. Is through Oya, that Blossom reach prosperity.

"Oya arriwo Oya, Oya arriwo Oya, Oya kauako arriwo, Arripiti O Oya."

Each night Oya would enter Blossom, rumbling and violent like thunder and chant heroically and dance, slowly and majestically, she warrior dance against suffering. To see Oya dancing on one leg all night, a calabash holding a candle on she head, was to see beauty. She fierce warrior face frighten unbelievers. Then she would drink nothing but good liquor, blowing mouthfuls on the gathering, granting favours to the believers for an offering.

The offerings come fast and plentiful. Where people was desperate, Blossom, as Oya, received food as offering, boxes of candles and sweet oil. Blossom send to Trinidad for calabash gourds and herbs for healing, guided by Oya in the mixing and administering.

When Oya enter Blossom, she talk in old African tongues and she body was part water and part tree. Oya thrash about taking Blossom body up to the ceiling and right through the walls. Oya knife slash the gullets of white men and Oya pitch the world around itself. Some nights, she voice sound as if it was coming from a deep well; and some nights, only if you had the power to hear air, could you listen to Oya.

Blossom fame as a obeah woman spread all over, but only among those who had to know. Those who see the hoary face of Suffering and feel he vibrant slap could come to dance with Oya – Oya freeness dance.

"Oya O Ologbo O de, Ma yak ba Ma Who! leh, Oya O Ologo O de, Ma yak ba Ma Who! leh, Oya Oh de arriwo, Oya Oh de cumale."

Since Oya reach, Blossom live peaceful. Is so, Blossom start in the speakeasy business. In the day time, Blossom sleep, exhausted and full of Oya warrior dance and laughing. She would wake up in the afternoon to prepare the shrine for Oya entrance.

On the nights that Oya didn't come, Blossom sell liquor and
wait for she, sitting against the window.

■ ■ ■

from *No Language is Neutral* (1990)

JACKIE

Jackie, that first evening I met you, you thought I was
a child to be saved from Vincent's joke, I was a
stranger in the room that your eyes vined like a
school teacher's folding me in, child, to be taken care
of. An afternoon on that grand beach you threw your
little boy among the rest of children in the hissing
ocean surf, dreaming an extraordinary life, an idea
fanning La Sagesse and Carib's Leap then slabs of
volcanic clay in a reddened ocean, perhaps even
larger. Jackie, gently, that glint of yellow in your eyes,
end of a day, cigarette smoke masking your tiredness
and impatience with this gratuitous rain of foreign
clerks, then you talked patiently, the past burning at
the back of your head. That day on the last hill, bright
midday heat glistened on your hands you were in
yellow too, yellow like fire on a cornbird's back, fire at
your mouth the colour of lightning, then in the last
moment, bullets crisscrossed your temple and your
heart. They say someone was calling you, Yansa,
thundering for help.

For Jacqueline Creft
Minister of Education in the People's Revolutionary
Gov't of Grenada, killed on October 19th, 1983,
during a coup.

■ ■ ■

from NO LANGUAGE IS NEUTRAL

I walk Bathurst Street until it come like home
Pearl was near Dupont, upstairs a store one
christmas where we pretend as if nothing change we,
make rum punch and sing, with bottle and spoon,
song we weself never even sing but only hear when
we was children. Pearl, squeezing her big Point
Fortin self along the narrow hall singing *Drink a rum
and a* ... Pearl, working nights, cleaning, Pearl beating
books at her age, Pearl dying back home in a car
crash twenty years after everything was squeezed in,
a trip to Europe, a condominium, a man she suckled
like a baby. Pearl coaxing this living room with a
voice half lie and half memory, a voice no room
nowhere could believe was sincere. Pearl hoping this
room would catch fire above this frozen street. Our
singing parched, drying in the silence after the
chicken and ham and sweet bread effort to taste like
home, the slim red earnest sound of long ago with the
blinds drawn and the finally snow for christmas and
the mood that rum in a cold place takes. Well, even
our nostalgia was a lie, skittish as the truth these
bundle of years.

■

But wait, this must come out then. A hidden verb
takes inventory of those small years like a person
waiting at a corner, counting and growing thin
through life as cloth and as water, hush ... Look I
hated something, policemen, bankers, slavetraders,
shhh ... still do and even more these days. This city,
mourning the smell of flowers and dirt, cannot tell
me what to say even if it chokes me. Not a single
word drops from my lips for twenty years about living
here. Dumbfounded I walk as if these sidewalks are a
place I'm visiting. Like a holy ghost, I package the
smell of zinnias and lady of the night, I horde the taste

of star apples and granadilla. I return to that once
grammar struck in disbelief. Twenty years. Ignoring
my own money thrown on the counter, the race
conscious landlords and their jim crow flats, oh yes!
here! the work nobody else wants to do . . . it's good
work I'm not complaining! but they make it taste bad,
bitter like peas. You can't smile here, is a sin, you
can't play music, it too loud. There was a time I could
tell if rain was coming, it used to make me sad the
yearly fasting of trees here, I felt some pity for the
ground turned hot and cold. All that time taken up
with circling this city in a fever. I remember then, and
it's hard to remember waiting so long to live . . . anyway
it's fiction what I remember, only mornings took a long
time to come, I became more secretive, language
seemed to split in two, one branch fell silent, the other
argued hotly for going home.

■ ■ ■

from HARD AGAINST THE SOUL

X

Then it is this simple. I felt the unordinary romance of
women who love women for the first time. It burst in
my mouth. Someone said this is your first lover, you
will never want to leave her. I had it in mind that I
would be an old woman with you. But perhaps I
always had it in mind simply to be an old woman,
darkening, somewhere with another old woman,
then, I decided it was you when you found me in that
apartment drinking whisky for breakfast. When I came
back from Grenada and went crazy for two years, that
time when I could hear anything and my skin was
flaming like a nerve and the walls were like paper
and my eyes could not close. I suddenly sensed you

at the end of my room waiting. I saw your back arched against this city we inhabit like guerillas, I brushed my hand, conscious, against your soft belly, waking up.

■

I saw this woman once in another poem, sitting, throwing water over her head on the rind of a country beach as she turned toward her century. Seeing her no part of me was comfortable with itself. I envied her, so old and set aside, a certain habit washed from her eyes. I must have recognized her. I know I watched her along the rim of the surf promising myself, an old woman is free. In my nerves something there unravelling, and she was a place to go, believe me, against gales of masculinity but in that then, she was masculine, old woman, old bird squinting at the water's wing above her head, swearing under her breath. I had a mind that she would be graceful in me and she might have been if I had not heard you laughing in another tense and lifted my head from her dry charm.

■

You ripped the world open for me. Someone said this is your first lover you will never want to leave her. My lips cannot say old woman darkening anymore, she is the peace of another life that didn't happen and couldn't happen in my flesh and wasn't peace but flight into old woman, prayer, to the saints of my ancestry, the gourd and bucket carrying women who stroke their breasts into stone shedding offspring and smile. I know since that an old woman, darkening, cuts herself away limb from limb, sucks herself white, running, skin torn and raw like a ball of bright light, flying, into old woman. I only know now that my longing for this old woman was longing to leave the prisoned gaze of men.

■

It's true, you spend the years after thirty turning over
the suggestion that you have been an imbecile,
hearing finally all the words that passed you like air,
like so much fun, or all the words that must have
existed while you were listening to others. What
would I want with this sentence you say flinging it
aside . . . and then again sometimes you were duped,
poems placed deliberately in your way. At eleven, the
strophe of a yellow dress sat me crosslegged in my
sex. It was a boy's abrupt birthday party. A yellow
dress for a tomboy, the ritual stab of womanly gathers
at the waist. *She look like a boy in a dress*, my big
sister say, a lyric and feminine correction from a
watchful aunt, *don't say that, she look nice and pretty*.
Nice and pretty, laid out to splinter you, so that never,
until it is almost so late as not to matter do you grasp
some part, something missing like a wing, some
fragment of your real self.

■

Old woman, that was the fragment that I caught in
your eye, that was the look I fell in love with, the piece
of you that you kept, the piece of you left, the lesbian,
the inviolable, sitting on a beach in a time that did not
hear your name or else it would have thrown you into
the sea, or you, hear that name yourself and walked
willingly into the muting blue. Instead you sat and I
saw your look and pursued one eye until it came to
the end of itself and then I saw the other,
the blazing fragment.

■

Someone said this is your first lover, you will never
want to leave her. There are saints of this ancestry
too who laugh themselves like jamettes in the
pleasure of their legs and caress their sex in mirrors.

I have become myself. A woman who looks
at a woman and says, here, I have found you,
in this, I am blackening in my way. You ripped the
world raw. It was as if another life exploded in my
face, brightening, so easily the brow of a wing
touching the surf, so easily I saw my own body, that
is, my eyes followed me to myself, touched myself
as a place, another life, terra. They say this place
does not exist, then, my tongue is mythic. I was here
before.

■ ■ ■

from *The Malahat Review* (1992)

OUT THERE

In this country only nailed in the air with words, the
heart of darkness is these white roads, snow at our
throats, and at the windshield a thick white cop in a blue
steel windbreaker peering into our car suspiciously, even
in the blow and freeze of a snowstorm, or, perhaps not
suspicion, but as a man looking at aliens. Three Blacks in a car
on a road blowing eighty miles an hour in the wind between
a gas station and Chatham. We stumble on our antiquity.
The snow blue laser of a cop's eyes fixes us in this
unbearable archaeology.

How quickly the planet can take itself back. I saw this
once in the summer in daylight, corn dangling bronze, flat
farm land growing flatter, eaten up in highways, tonight,
big and rolling it is storming in its sleep. A cop is standing at its lip.

■

Coca-cola can light, the car shakes, trembles along as in a
gutter, a bellow of wind rushes into my face breathless
checking the snowbank, I might have seen something
out there, every two minutes the imagination conjures
an exact bridge, the mind insists on solidity, we lose
the light of the car ahead, in the jagged beam of the cop's
blistering eye we lose the names of things, the three of us,
two women who love women, one man with so many demons
already, his left foot is cold, still, making our way to Chatham,
Buxton, waiting as they once waited for Black travellers like us,
blanketed, tracked in this cold shimmering.

Out there I see nothing . . . not one thing out there
just the indifference of a cop. It takes us six hours
to travel three. I coil myself up into a nerve and quarrel
with the woman, lover, and the man for landing me in
this white hell.

■

We have been in this icy science only a short time. What
we are doing here is not immediately understandable
and no one is more aware of it than we, she from Uganda
via Kenya running from arranged marriages, he from Sri
Lanka via Colombo english style boarding school to make him
the minister of the interior, me hunting for slave castles with a
pencil for explosives, what did we know that our pan colonial
flights would end up among people who ask stupid questions
like, where are you from . . . and now here we are on their road,
in their snow, faced with their childishness.

How are we to say that these paths are involuntary and
the line of trees we are looking for will exist when we
find it, that this snow is just a cipher for our feverishness.

■

Only Sarah Vaughan thank god sings in this snow, Sarah
and her big band . . . gotta right to sing the blues . . . quick
I desert the others to her voice, fanning fire, then, even Sarah
cannot take me away but she moves the car and we live on
whatever she's given to this song, each dive of her voice,
each swoop, her vibrato holds us to the road, the outcome
of this white ride depends on Sarah's entries and exists from a
note. We cannot turn back, ahead Buxton must hear this so we can
arrive, up ahead Sarah singing she can see the midnight sun.

Only this much sound, only this much breath, only this much
grace, only how long, only how much road can take us away.

■

That cop's face has it. "They had been in this vast and dark
country only a short time."[*] Something there, written as
wilderness, wood, nickel, water, coal, rock, prairie, erased
as Athabasca, Algonquin, Salish, Inuit . . . hooded in Buxton
fugitive, Preston Black Loyalist, railroaded to gold mountain,
swimming in Komo Gata Maru. . . . Are we still moving. But
country was never anything but money, a few white guys with
ships and guns. . . . Are we still moving. . . . When will we arrive. In
a motel room later, we laugh, lie to ourselves that we were not so
afraid, we play poker and fall asleep, he on the floor with his
demons, she, thankfully, legs wrapped around me.

How can we say that when we sign our names in letters
home no one can read it, when we send photographs
they vanish. Blackheart, blackheart . . . can't take it tonight
across this old road . . . take me home some other way.

■ ■ ■

---

[*] from Joseph Conrad, "An Outpost of Progress."

RESOURCES FOR FURTHER RESEARCH

CLAIRE HARRIS
Primary Sources: Poetry

Harris, Claire. *Fables From the Women's Quarters*. Toronto: Williams-Wallace, 1984.

———. *Translation into Fiction*. Fredericton: Goose Lane, 1984.

———. *Travelling to Find a Remedy*. Fredericton: Goose Lane, 1986.

———. *The Conception of Winter*. Stratford: Williams-Wallace, 1989.

———. *Drawing Down a Daughter*. Fredericton: Goose Lane, 1992.

———. "O What Are You Thinking My Sisters." *Contemporary Verse II*. 15:4 (Spring 1993): 55-56.

Primary Sources: Prose

Harris, Claire. "Four From Fifty-one." *Camrose Review* 2 (1982): 27-29.

———. "Against the Poetry of Revenge." *Fireweed* 23 (Summer 1986): 15-24.

———. "Poets in Limbo." In *A Mazing Space*. Edited by Shirley Neuman and Smaro Kamboureli. Edmonton: NeWest, 1986: 115-125.

———. "A Matter of Fact." In *Imagining Women: Short Fiction*. Edited by the Second, Second Story Collective. Toronto: Women's Press, 1988: 101-112.

———. "Butterfly on a Pin." In *Frictions*. Edited by Rhea Tregebov. Second Story, 1989: 42-53.

———. "Working Without a Net." In *Cross/Cultures 2, Crisis and Creativity in the New Literatures in English: Canada*. Edited by Geoffrey Davis. Amsterdam: Rodopi, 1990: 71-75.

———. "Ole Talk: A Sketch." In *Language in Her Eye: Views on Writing and Gender by Canadian Women Writing in English*. Edited by L. Scheier, S. Sheard, and E. Wachtel. Toronto: Coach House, 1990: 131-141.

———. "Mirror, Mirror on the Wall." In *Caribbean Women Writers: Essays from the First International Conference*. Edited by Selwyn R. Cudjoe. Wellesley, MA: Calaloux, 1990: 306-309.

_____. "Why I Write." In *Jyan Aakaash ed Naganya Tamboo Chhe* (Gujarati translation of "Where the Sky is a Pitiful Tent"). Edited by Shirin Kudchedkar. Bombay: SNDT Women's University, 1991.

_____. "A Real Good Lemonade." In *Sudden Miracles: Eight Women Poets*. Edited by Rhea Tregebov. Toronto: Second Story, 1991: 87-89.

_____ and Edna Alford, eds. *Kitchen Talk: Contemporary Women's Prose and Poetry*. Red Deer: Red Deer College, 1992.

_____. "In Bold Face: Confronting Erasure ... The Final Testimony." *Contemporary Verse II* 15:4 (Spring 1993): 57-65.

_____. "And the Heart Pauses for Breath." In *Boundless Alberta*. Edited by Aritha Van Herk. Edmonton: NeWest, 1993: 46-62.

Selected Secondary Sources

Morrell, Carol. "Claire Harris." *Routledge Encyclopedia of Post-Colonial Literatures in English*. Forthcoming.

Reid, Monty. "Choosing Control: An Interview with Claire Harris." *Waves* 13:1 (Fall 1984): 36-41.

Salkey, Andrew. Review of *Drawing Down a Daughter*. *World Literature Today* 67:2 (Spring 1993): 435-436.

Tregebov, Rhea. Review of *Fables From the Women's Quarters*. *Fireweed* 24 (Winter 1987): 103-106.

_____. "Introduction." *Sudden Miracles: Eight Women Poets*. Toronto: Second Story, 1991: 17-20.

Williamson, Janice. Interview with Claire Harris. *Sounding Differences: Conversations with Seventeen Canadian Women Writers*. Toronto: University of Toronto, 1992: 115-130.

M. NOURBESE PHILIP
Primary Sources: Poetry

Philip, M. Nourbese. *Thorns*. Toronto: Williams-Wallace, 1980.

_____. *Salmon Courage*. Toronto: Williams-Wallace, 1983.

_____. *She Tries Her Tongue, Her Silence Softly Breaks*. Charlottetown: Ragweed, 1989.

Primary Sources: Prose Fiction

Philip. M. Nourbese. "The Tall Rains." *Women's Review* 12 (Oct. 1986): 29-32.

_____. *Harriet's Daughter*. Oxford: Heinemann International, 1988.

_____. "Burn Sugar." *Imagining Women: Short Fiction*. Edited by the Second, Second Story Collective. Toronto: Women's Press, 1988: 11-19.

_____. "Whose Idea Was It Anyway?" *Tessera* 7 (Fall 1989): 45-54.

_____. "Bad Words." *Border/Lines: Cultures Contexts Canadas* (Spring 1990): 30-33.

_____. "Just a Name." *Matrix* 31 (Spring-Summer 1990): 17-18.

_____. *Looking for Livingstone: An Odyssey of Silence*. Stratford: Mercury, 1991.

Primary Sources: Non-Fiction

Philip, M. Nourbese. "New World Voices: An Interview with Ann Wallace." *Fuse Magazine* 8:4 (Nov. 1984-Jan. 1985): 35-38.

_____. "Journal Entries Against Reaction." In *Work In Progress: Building Feminist Culture*. Edited by Rhea Tregebov. Toronto: Women's Press, 1987: 65-75.

_____. "Managing the Unmanageable." *City Arts Quarterly* 3:2 (Summer 1988): 26-27. Also in *Caribbean Women Writers: Essays from the First International Conference*. Edited by Selwyn R. Cudjoe. Wellesley, MA.: Calaloux, 1990: 295-300.

_____. "Who's Listening? Artists, Audiences, & Language." *Fuse Magazine* XII: 1-2 (September 1988): 15-24.

_____. "The Disappearing Debate: Racism and Censorship." In *Language in Her Eye: Views on Writing and Gender by Canadian Women Writing in English*. Edited by L. Scheier, S. Sheard, and E. Wachtel. Toronto: Coach House, 1990: 209-219.

_____. *Frontiers: Essays and Writings on Racism and Culture*. Stratford: Mercury, 1993.

_____. *Showing Grit: Showboating North of the 44th Parallel*. Toronto: Poui, 1993.

Selected Secondary Sources

Carey, Barbara. "Secrecy and Silence: Interview with Marlene Nourbese Philip." *Books in Canada* (September 1991): 17-21.

Carr, Brenda. "To 'Heal the Word Wounded': Agency and the Materiality of Language and Form in M. Nourbese Philip's *She Tries Her Tongue, Her Silence Softly Breaks*." *Studies in Canadian Literature* 19:1 (Summer 1994): 72-93.

Godard, Barbara. "Marlene Nourbese Philip's Hyphenated Tongue: or Writing the Caribbean Demotic between Africa and Arctic." In *Major Minorities: English Literatures in Transit*. Edited by R. Granqvist. Amsterdam: Editions Rodpoi, 1992: 151-175.

Hall, Phil. "The Continent of Silence." *Books in Canada* (Jan.-Feb. 1989): 1-2.

Morrell, Carol. Review of *Frontiers: Essays and Writings on Racism and Culture*. *University of Toronto Quarterly* 63:1 (Fall 1993): 154-56.

_____. "Contradicting the Work of M. Nourbese Philip." *CRNLE Reviews Journal* 1 (1994): 57-61.

Sanders, Leslie. "Marlene Nourbese Philip's 'Bad Words.'" *Tessera* 12 (Summer 1992): 81-89.

Vigier, Rachel. "Voiced Silence: The Poems of Marlene Philip." Review of *Salmon Courage*. *Fuse Magazine* 8:6 (Spring 1985): 41-42.

Williamson, Janice. Interview with Marlene Nourbese Philip. *Sounding Differences: Conversations with Seventeen Canadian Women Writers*. Toronto: University of Toronto, 1992: 226-244.

_____. "Blood on Our Hands: An Interview with Marlene Nourbese Philip." *paragraph* 14:1 (1992): 18-19.

DIONNE BRAND

Primary Sources: Poetry

Brand, Dionne. *'Fore Day Morning*. Toronto: Khoisan Artists, 1978.

_____. *Earth Magic*. Toronto: Kids Can, 1979.

_____. *Primitive Offensive*. Toronto: Williams-Wallace, 1982.

_____. *Winter Epigrams and Epigrams to Ernesto Cardenal in Defense of Claudia*. Toronto: Williams-Wallace, 1983.

_____. *Chronicles of the Hostile Sun*. Toronto: Williams-Wallace, 1984.

_____. *No Language is Neutral.* Toronto: Coach House, 1990.

Primary Sources: Prose

Brand, Dionne, Himani Bannerji and Prabha Khosla, eds. *Fireweed* 16 (Spring 1983). Women of Colour Issue.

_____. "'U.S. is Taking Charge': A First-Hand Account of the Grenadian Invasion." *This Magazine* 18:1 (April 1984): 4-9.

_____. "A Working Paper on Black Women in Toronto: Gender, Race and Class." *Fireweed* 19 (Summer-Fall 1984): 26-43.

_____. "The Caribbean." Poetry Column. *Poetry Canada Review* 6:1 (Fall 1984): 24; 6:2 (Winter 1984-85): 26; 6:3 (Spring 1985): 31.

_____ and Krisantha Sri Bhaggiyadatta. "The Production of Free Speech is the Production of Consent in the Management of Culture." *Issues of Censorship*. Toronto: A Space, 1985: 15-19.

_____. and Linda Carty. "Defining World Feminism: If This is Global Where the Hell are We?" Review of Robin Morgan, *Sisterhood is Global*. *Fuse Magazine* (Fall 1985): 42-44.

_____. "'Stripped to Skin and Sex.'" Review of Claire Harris, *Translation into Fiction* and *Fables From the Women's Quarters*. *Canadian Woman Studies/Les Cahiers de la Femme* 7 (Spring-Summer 1986): 222-224.

_____ and Krisantha Sri Bhaggiyadatta. *Rivers Have Sources, Trees Have Roots: Speaking of Racism*. Toronto: Cross Cultural Communication Centre, 1986.

_____ and Pamela Godfree, eds. *Fireweed* 23 (Summer 1986). Canadian Women Poets Issue.

_____. "Black Women and Work: The Impact of Racially Constructed Gender Roles on the Sexual Division of Labour." Parts I and II. *Fireweed* 25 (1987): 28-37; 26 (1988): 87-92.

_____. *Sans Souci and Other Stories*. Stratford: Williams-Wallace, 1988.

_____ and Linda Carty. "Visible Minority Women: A Creation of the Canadian State." *Resources for Feminist Research* 17:3 (September 1988): 39-42.

_____. "Bread Out of Stone." In *Language in Her Eye: Views on Writing and Gender by Canadian Women Writing in English*. Edited by L. Scheier, S. Sheard, and E. Wachtel. Toronto: Coach House, 1990: 45-53.

_____. and Lois De Shield, and the Immigrant Women's Job Placement Centre. *No Burden to Carry: Narratives of Black Working Women in Ontario, 1920s to 1950s*. Toronto: Women's Press, 1991.

———. "Who Can Speak for Whom?" *Brick* 46 (Summer 1993): 13-20.

Films

Brand, Dionne, researcher, writer, and associate director. *Older Stronger Wiser*. Directed by Claire Prieto. National Film Board Studio D Documentary, 1989.

——— and Ginny Stikeman, directors. *Sisters in the Struggle*. National Film Board Studio D Documentary, 1991.

———, director. *Long Time Comin'*. Music by Faith Nolan. National Film Board Studio D Documentary, 1993.

Selected Secondary Sources

Ball, John Clement. "White City, Black Ancestry: The Immigrant's Toronto in the Stories of Dionne Brand and Austin Clarke." *Open Letter* 8:8 (Winter 1994): 9-19.

Bannerji, Himani. "*Primitive Offensive* by Dionne Brand." *Fireweed* 16 (Spring 1983): 149-154.

———. "Dionne Brand." In *Fifty Caribbean Writers*. Edited by Daryl Cumber Dance. New York: Greenwood, 1986: 46-57.

Brathwaite, Edward. "Quick Radicle of Green: To See and Overstand the Voice." Review of *Winter Epigrams and Epigrams to Ernesto Cardenal in Defense of Claudia*. *Fuse Magazine* 7:4 (November-December 1983): 179-183.

Daurio, Beverley. "The Language of Resistance: Interview with Dionne Brand." *Books in Canada* (October 1990): 13-16.

McTair, Roger. "Introduction." *Winter Epigrams and Epigrams to Ernesto Cardenal in Defense of Claudia* by Dionne Brand. Toronto: Williams-Wallace, 1983.

Novak, Dagmar. "Interview with Dionne Brand." In *Other Solitudes: Canadian Multicultural Fictions*. Edited by Marion Richmond and Linda Hutcheon. Toronto: Oxford University Press, 1990: 271-77.

Sanders, Leslie. "'I Am Stateless Anyway': The Poetry of Dionne Brand." *Zora Neale Hurston Forum* 3:2 (Spring 1989): 19-29.

Thomas, H. Nigel. "A Commentary on the Poetry of Dionne Brand." *Kola* 1:1 (Winter 1987): 51-61.

Warren, Chris. "Dionne Brand's Writing is a 'clear project of freedom.'" Interview. *The Atkinsonian* (November 1985): 1, 9, 14.

GENERAL AND BACKGROUND

Allen, Lillian. "A Writing of Resistance: Black Women's Writing in Canada." In *In the Feminine: Women and Words*. Edited by Ann Dybikowski *et al*. Edmonton: Longspoon, 1983: 63-67.

Busby, Margaret, ed. *Daughters of Africa: An Anthology of Words and Writings by Women of African Descent from the Ancient Egyptian to the Present*. London: Jonathan Cape, 1992.

Burnett, Paula, ed. *The Penguin Book of Caribbean Verse in English*. Harmondsworth: Penguin, 1986.

Cromwell, Liz, ed. *One Out of Many*. Toronto: A WACACRO Production, 1975.

Cudjoe, Selwyn R., ed. *Caribbean Women Writers: Essays from the First International Conference*. Wellesley, MA: Calaloux, 1990.

Dabydeen, Cyril, ed. *A Shapely Fire: Changing the Literary Landscape*. Oakville: Mosaic, 1987.

Elliott, Lorris, ed. *Other Voices*. Toronto: Williams-Wallace, 1985.

_____, ed. *The Bibliography of Literary Writing by Blacks in Canada*. Toronto: Williams-Wallace, 1986.

Espinet, Ramabai, ed. *Creation Fire: A CAFRA Anthology of Caribbean Women's Poetry*. Toronto: Sister Vision, 1990.

Fireweed. Women of Colour Issue. 16 (Spring 1983).

Head, Harold, ed. *Canada in Us Now*. Toronto: NC Press, 1976.

Hunter, Lynette. "Writing, Literature and Ideology: Institutions and the Making of a Canadian Canon." In *Probing Canadian Culture*. Edited by P. Easingwood, K. Gross, and W. Kloss. Augsburg: AV-Verlag, 1991: 52-64.

_____. "After Modernism: Alternative Voices in the Writings of Dionne Brand, Claire Harris, and Marlene Philip." *University of Toronto Quarterly* 662:2 (Winter 1992-93): 256-281.

Mordecai, Pamela and Betty Wilson, eds. *Her True-True Name: An Anthology of Women's Writing from the Caribbean*. Oxford: Heinemann, 1989.

Petersen, Kirsten Holst and Anna Rutherford, eds. *Displaced Persons*. Aarhus: Dangaroo, 1988.

Smith, Charles C., ed. *Sad Dances in a Field of White*. Toronto: IS FIVE, 1985.

Telling It Book Collective, The, ed. *Telling It: Women and Language Across Cultures*. Vancouver: Press Gang, 1990.

Tregebov, Rhea, ed. *Sudden Miracles: Eight Women Poets*. Toronto: Second Story, 1991.

Wallace, Ann, ed. *Daughters of the Sun, Women of the Moon: Poetry by Black Canadian Women*. Trenton, N.J.: Africa World, 1992.

INDEX TO FIRST LINES AND TITLES

Absence of Writing or How I Almost Became a Spy, The 98
Afro West Indian Immigrant 183
All night the hibiscus tapped at our jalousies 40
Amelia 209
ancestor dirt 185
and   at this moment   the accidental world 67
And Over Every Land and Sea 128
And So... Home 66
And take these too Ernesto 208
Anonymous 117
ashes head to toes 184
August 60
Awakened 51
Black Reading, A 56
Blackman Dead 109
blood-spoored 134
Blossom 228
Bread Out of Stone 171
By thy senses set forth 51
Canto I 184
Canto II 185
Canto VI 188
Canto VII 192
Cardenal, the truth is that 209
coffin of a winter! 202
comrade winter, / if you weren't there 199
comrade winter, / look what you've done 203
Conception of Winter 75
Counting in american 218
cow's hide or drum 207
Daughter   to live is to dream... 80
Dear Ernesto 205
Death in Summer 74
Diary – The Grenada Crisis 211
Discourse on the Logic of Language 136
Dream of Valor and Rebirth, A 70
Dream-skins dream the dream dreaming 131
E. Pulcherrima 112
Each day at firstlight 56
English 136
Epigrams to Ernesto Cardenal... 203
First and Last Day of the Month..., The 160

Fleshed with Fire 61
Fluttering Lives 106
Fluttering lives 106
four hours on a bus across alberta and saskatchewan 226
Framed 65
Gazing at piles of newspapers 77
give up the bitterness 207
guajiro making flip-flops on the wing tip of the american airline 192
Habit of Angels, A 118
Hard Against the Soul 239
Have you ever noticed 206
Here at Woodlands, Moriah, 120
here! 199
How do I know that this is love 204
Hundredth Day..., The 161
I always thought I was Negro 123
I came awake 112
I cannot be sure 62
I do not know your name 55
I feel like a palm tree 183
I give you these epigrams, Toronto 197
I have never missed a place either 219
I know that lying there in that bed 210
I saw this woman once in another poem, sitting 240
I understood 123
I walk Bathurst Street until it come like home 238
I walk the raw paths through winds that crowd me 66
I've arranged my apartment 199
I've never been to the far north/cold 198
If Hitler waits at the corner of the Schmiedtor 208
If I get old 182
If no one listens and cries 117
If you were there when I came home 204
In the five a.m. dusk 211
In this country only nailed in the air with words, the 242
It is a matter of fact 83
It was there I learnt to walk 117
it's too cold to go outside 198
It's true, you spend the years after thirty turning over 241
Jackie 237
Jackie, that first evening I met you, you thought I was 237
Jongwe 107
July Again 122
July again, and every Italian house on the block 122
Just to sabotage my epigrams 200

My bed sways   swells to a moon 70
Mysteries 67
No God Waits on Incense 76
Nose to ground – on all fours – I did once 134
Nude on a Pale Staircase 34
October 19th, 1983 214
October 25th, 1983 216
Often Ernesto 204
Oh yes, there it is 201
Old I 182
Old II 182
Old woman, that was the fragment that I caught in 241
Oliver Twist 105
Oliver Twist can't do this 105
On American Numeracy and Literacy . . . 218
Once and for all 127
one good day 199
One known at home 74
Out There 242
P.P.S. Grenada 219
Perpetual motion 183
Planned Obsolescence 127
Policeman Cleared in Jaywalking Case 48
Question of Language Is the Answer to Power, The 139
Salmon Courage 120
season of ambiguity 202
Shanty Town 183
She awakes 34
She gone – gone to where and don't know 129
She is in your painting   the one you bought when the taxi 65
She Tries Her Tongue; Her Silence Softly Breaks 143
Since You 181
Since you 181
Since you've left me no descriptions 205
so we spent hours and hours 204
soft as the dark and strong 47
Someone said this is your first lover, you will never 241
Sometimes in summer rain falls in great drops 75
Sprung Rhythm 117
thank heavens 198
The city policeman who arrested . . . 48
The magnum pistol barked 109
the me and mine of parents 143
The planes are circling 216
Then it is this simple. I felt the unordinary romance 239

there are days when no shout 61
There is a presence here 118
These verses are for you Ernesto 203
they think it's pretty 197
this poem cannot find words 214
This Was the Child I Dreamt 47
Three bells calm the passing hour   a measured 69
Three Times Deny 111
Three times deny their existence 111
Today was 107
Towards the Color of Summer 69
Translation into Fiction 55
Travelling to Find a Remedy 62
Two things I will not buy 203
Up in the humpback whereabouts-is-that hills 130
Vowels are by nature either long or short 139
Watch my talk-words stride 129
What's in a Name? 123
Where she, where she, where she 128
Where the Sky is a Pitiful Tent 40
while babies bleed this is not the poem i wanted 76
Whose Idea Was It Anyway? 150
Why Do I Write? 26
Winter Epigrams 197
winter suicide 202
winters should be answered 198
Yes, but what else was done 206
You Can't Push Now 123
you, in the square 188
You ripped the world open for me. Someone said this 240
you say you want me to . . . 209